Need You for Mine

by marina adair

Need You for Mine

HEROES OF ST. HELENA SERIES

MARINA ADAIR

Montlake
Romance

Text copyright © 2016 Marina Adair
All rights reserved.

Published by Montlake Romance, Seattle

www.apub.com

Amazon, the Amazon logo, and Montlake Romance are trademarks of Amazon.com, Inc., or its affiliates.

ISBN-13: 9781503933200
ISBN-10: 1503933202

Cover design by Shasti O'Leary Soudant

Printed in the United States of America

To all of the first responders,
who put their lives on the line every day
to protect our families, our homes, and our communities.

chapter
one

There wasn't a person on the planet who Harper Owens couldn't friend. Problem was, there wasn't a single man in wine country who hadn't already sentenced her to a lifetime in the friend zone.

Until now, she thought giddily, staring up at her Mr. Tall, Dark, and—*ohmigod*—Mine.

It had taken her eighteen long months of casual conversations, lots of lash batting, three new shades of lipstick, and a well-orchestrated flash of cleavage, but Harper was about to get her kiss.

From Clay Walker. Respected pediatrician, a Doctors Without Borders frequent flyer, and, on top of being revered by every kid and parent in town, the guy Harper had been hot for since he moved to St. Helena with his son nearly two years ago.

"Thank you for walking me home," Harper said as they stopped in front of the yellow-and-white Victorian storefront on Main Street. She pointed to the upstairs window of her apartment. "Do you want to come up? I have some wine in the fridge."

Clay checked his watch. "I wish I could, but I promised the babysitter I'd be home by ten," he said, and didn't that warm her

heart. He was such a good dad. Devoted, involved, loving, and—
holy smokes—was Dr. Dreamy checking out her boobs?

She watched his eyes to see if they'd dart again, and they ended
up doing a mini-dip—not enough to be called an ogle, but enough
that she decided it was the bra, which took her from a moderate B
to a sexy C in one shimmy.

St. Helena rolled up its welcome mats at dusk, so there weren't
many people out. Just Harper and Dr. Dreamy, alone on the lamp-
lined sidewalk, the gentle summer breeze wrapping around them as
they stood under the twinkling lights of her grandmother's shop and
the million or so stars overhead. So she shimmied again and—*bingo*.

He was sizing up the goods. Which meant this was a premedi-
tated escort.

With the latest crime spree including senior citizens, barrel tip-
ping, and indecent exposure in the community fountain—all related
events—Clay hadn't offered to walk her home for her safety. She now
knew that he'd offered to walk her home so he could make his move.

And since her body hadn't been moved on in far too long, she
was ready.

"There's something I've been meaning to ask, but there was
never a time when Tommy wasn't around, and I didn't feel comfortable calling you at work," Clay said, that deep voice rolling over
her and lighting the anticipation that had been simmering since
he'd pulled up the barstool next to hers, offered to buy her a drink,
then started asking all the *right* questions. "So when I saw you at the
Spigot tonight, I figured it was perfect timing."

"Perfect," she repeated, stepping closer and looking up into his
deep brown eyes. It was perfect. The perfect place for their first kiss.
The perfect moment to take their relationship from *I teach your kid how
to paint* to *I know how to make you pant* in a single brush of the lips.

"I know this is last-minute, but I'm going to San Diego for a
medical conference next week."

"San Diego is beautiful in the summertime," Harper said, as if all of her knowledge about the coastal city hadn't come from the passenger seat of her mom's car when she was nine and her mother was racing toward the border for a starring role in a vacation-resort production of *Evita*.

"It is," he said. "It's a one-day conference, but I figured it's so close to the beach and Gaslamp district, maybe I'd stay the night. Go down Tuesday, come back Wednesday."

"I think it's great that you're starting to make time for yourself. All good parents need a break."

Clay let out a relieved sigh. "Thanks, I needed to hear that."

Which was why she'd said it. Clay was the most dedicated parent she knew, putting his son above everyone and everything else. Including himself. He deserved some time to be an adult, have some quiet R&R to reboot.

His eyes met hers, soft and warm, like melted chocolate. Harper loved chocolate. "Anyway, I was wondering if you were free."

"Me?" she asked, so excited she nearly choked on the word. "You want to know if I'm free? Next week?" Which was the worst possible time for Harper to get away. It was back-to-school inventory time at the Fashion Flower, the one-stop kids' shop in town for all things kiddie, crafty, and couture, and as manager she was the only person who could handle the delivery. But a night away? With Clay? Naked? "You bet."

"Really?" He put his hand on her shoulder and smiled.

At her.

It wasn't the same smile he gave her when picking Tommy up from class, or even the one he'd flashed when seeing her around town. This smile was different. He was looking at *her* different. As if she was special. As if she was—

"A lifesaver, Harper. That's what you are." Clay released a long, relieved breath. Funny, since she had stopped breathing altogether.

"My mom can take him Tuesday, but Wednesday is an early-release day from day camp and she can't pick him up in time. And his sitter is only fifteen, hence the reason I need to get her home tonight by ten, and can't pick him up until four, after her cheerleading practice. I didn't know who else to ask, and you are so good with him."

"You need me to babysit Tommy?" She had to ask because she'd had a drink or two, and her brain wasn't functioning on all cylinders, but she was pretty sure he'd just demoted her from *quirky but cute art teacher* to *back-up babysitter*. And her competition didn't have a driver's license.

"That would be great. He really adores you. You know?"

Oh, she knew. She knew this moment so well she wanted to cry. It was just like senior prom when Daniel McCree passed her a note saying he wanted to ask a special girl. Only after Harper had mentally picked out her dress, shoes, and the perfect place to lose her virginity had he explained that the "special girl" was Janie Copeland—captain of the dance team, and Harper's neighbor.

Harper had delivered Daniel's invite on her way home, then received a record eleven more invites to the prom that year. None of which were addressed to her.

"Tommy would probably be more comfortable at my place. You can hang out there, watch a movie in my room if that works for you," Clay offered, and Harper had to bite her lip to stop from laughing at the irony. Clay finally wanted to see her in his bed, only in the most chaste of scenarios. He couldn't manage to see her as more. It was a position she'd been placed in a million times in her life, yet never managed to master.

Clearing any trace of hurt from her expression, a trick she *had* mastered, she said, "I run the Sprouting Picasso class at the shop at three."

"I should be home before then." He looked at his watch again. "I'm late. Can we work out all the details later? Kendal's mom flips if I get her home after ten."

"That's the great thing about thirty-year-old women," she pointed out brightly, holding on to that smile even if her cheeks hurt from the weight. "No curfew."

"Something to keep in mind," he said with a wink. "Oh, and you have some kind of punch on your dress."

Harper looked down at her favorite daffodil-colored dress and saw the bright red splotch, right below her miniscule cleavage he'd been eyeing all night. And if *that* wasn't humiliating enough, he pulled her in for a hug. Not a dual-armed embrace, bodies touching kind of event. But a side-hug, pat-to-the-back combo that bros gave each other.

"Thanks, Harper. I owe you," he said and headed back toward the bar.

Unless he was offering up a tangled sheets kind of favor, Harper wasn't interested. At all. She didn't want a favor—she wanted passion, connection, adventure. She wanted to be wanted.

And speaking of wanted, she wanted cookies.

Not the kind with confetti sprinkles that her grandmother made, but the kind that only a strong, sexy man could provide. *And I want a baker's dozen,* she thought as she fished out her keys to open her grandma's shop.

The scent of rosewater and lavender greeted her as she stepped inside and felt as though she were transported back in time. The Boulder Holder was a lingerie shop owned by her grandma specializing in vintage seduction for the curvy woman. It also had a great stain remover in the storage closet.

Still at a complete loss, or maybe not so complete, since looking back the intimate questions Clay had asked earlier were all standard résumé info for applying nannies, Harper closed the door behind her and reached to disarm the alarm—which was already disarmed.

"Dang it, Baby," Harper mumbled, making a note to reprimand the closing manager for neglecting the alarm again. And, apparently, her job, since there was a vast collection of high-end merchandise hanging outside one of the changing-room doors.

The whole point behind hiring a closing manager was so that her grandma could work fewer hours, let someone else lift heavy boxes, and stock the store. Clovis needed to stay off her knee so it could heal from her most recent replacement surgery, but if Baby wasn't organizing the store at night, then her grandma would have to before opening. Which defeated the purpose.

Frustrated, Harper grabbed the stain cleaner and a rag from the closet and walked over to the large gilded mirror on the wall at the far end of the dressing rooms.

Normally being in her grandma's shop, surrounded by all of the bright fabrics and bold designs, could erase even the worst of days. The shop was every girl-next-door's haven—sexy with a touch of sophistication, and a brilliant kaleidoscope of intimates from time periods usually forgotten. A new adventure to be found on each hanger.

Not tonight, she thought, taking in the image staring back at her in the mirror.

Tonight, Harper felt like a big, stupid banana in a specialty candy store.

"Think of the bright side," she told herself, pulling her arm out of her dress and slipping it off so she could get at the stain easier. "At least he friended you before you showed him your panties."

The ability to see the bright side of even the worst situations was Harper's gift. It was how she'd made it through her eclectic childhood—and how she kept her smile genuine. And being thought of as a babysitter didn't even touch Harper's worst list.

"If you'd gone at him in those panties, I bet he'd have forgotten all about curfew," a distinctively male voice said from behind.

Harper spun around, the scream sticking in her throat as her heart lodged itself there first. Acting on reflex, she threw the only thing within reach at the tall, dark—emphasis on the dark—and dangerous-looking shadow. Only the shadow's reflexes were skillfully honed because he caught the flying object with one hand, leaving her nearly naked and him holding her favorite daffodil-colored dress.

"Whoa," the unexpected voice said from the dressing-room doorway. Harper spun around, her heart pounding with adrenaline at the sight of the big, built—and definitely unwelcome—male burglar looming behind her.

A cocky smirk and one *hey baby* wink was all it took for her brain to register the burglar in question, and for her fear to immediately turn to embarrassment. Because standing in her grandma's darkened shop, holding her dress and a slinky red robe, four hours after closing, was the only man in town who hadn't put Harper in the friend zone. Because he was the only man in town Harper hadn't bothered to friend. He was someone who, like her mother, was too busy soaking up that spotlight to make room for lasting connections.

St. Helena firefighter, bro of the year, and legendary ladies' man—Adam Baudouin.

"What are you doing here?" Harper demanded, looking up at him, and he could see the fire lighting her eyes.

It was a good question. One Adam had crafted a great answer to when she'd first turned around in that pink, teal, and gold embroidered number with the tiny matching thong, which looked as if she'd recently escaped from the Copacabana. Then she'd tossed her dress at him and things had gotten really interesting. Little Miss Sunshine wiggled a lecturing finger his way, which caused everything in silk and lace to do a little cha-cha of its own, and Adam's mind went to a bad place.

An incredibly good, bad place.

Oh, Harper was all sunshine and freckles up top. With her pert nose, twinkling blue eyes, and wild mass of waves piled on top of her head, she was cute, he decided. The crazy kind of cute. But she was a secret freaking bombshell below. High breasts, tiny waist, curvy hips, long lush legs that went on for miles. All that silky skin and willowy allure was intoxicating. Who knew she kept all that hidden under her Rainbow Brite attire?

Not the dildo with the kid who'd asked her to babysit, that was for sure. Because if he'd seen the view Adam was privy to, the guy would have taken her inside the shop—and right up against the wall.

"Apparently, I'm just in time for the show," he said, looking down into her face. If she'd been wearing heels instead of those granny flats, she would have nearly been eye-to-eye with him. "Nice panties. Need help?"

"They're called Parisian peek-a-boos, and there's no show," she said. "And no, the last thing I need is your help."

And wasn't that a damn shame. He was pretty sure he was the perfect man to help her with her problem, only she crossed her arms and snapped, "What are you staring at?"

"Apparently, Parisian peek-a-boos with a matching lace bra." He wiggled his brows. "A *see-through* lace bra."

"They're called boobs, Adam."

"Oh, trust me, I know, sunshine," he said, stepping closer and, being the expert on that subject, sizing her up in a single glance. Firm, perky—the perfect little handful who wished she were a C. That explained the creative clothing choices. "Just wasn't sure if you knew, with your outfit and all."

"What's wrong with my outfit?"

"You look like a yellow crayon who stepped in grape juice."

She looked at him in disbelief, then outrage. "I do not! That dress revealed more secrets than Victoria's new summer catalog."

He held up the dress and she grimaced. "Secrets or not, the only thing you're going to attract with this dress is honeybees, not a hookup."

"Yeah, well, I'm not looking for a hookup," she mumbled, snatching her dress back. And because he already knew the truth, just like he knew one more frustrated huff would have her popping right out of that bra, he let her take it. Even turned his back when she slipped it back on. Because getting a boner for Pollyanna wasn't a smart move.

"But if I were . . ." she said so quietly he turned back around to see if she'd even spoken. She was once again in the yellow jumper, zipped up to her sternum, and fiddling with the little silver heart charm dangling from her necklace. "Are you saying I have to change how I look to get a guy?"

"No." He actually liked the crazy cutie exactly like she was. Her blinding fashion sense was loud, quirky, and kind of adorable. Except, he remembered, those of the crazy cutie variety tended to want more than he was willing to give. So he checked himself, then gave a silent lecture that she wasn't asking about *his* preferences, but Dr. Dildo's. "However, if you want *that* guy with the kid, then yeah, you've got to up your game."

Her confusion apparent, he reached for the front zipper of her dress.

She smacked his hand away. "Hey."

"You asked for my help, so let me help. Here." He grabbed a red belt off the silk robe and tied it around her waist, cinching it in to showcase her flat stomach. With Harper no longer looking like a chewing-gum wrapper, Adam tugged the zipper south, far enough that the collar of her dress opened and slid down one arm. Her shoulder was now exposed, as well as a nice hint of her copacabanas. "Sexy is in the accessories. Oh, and you need new lipstick."

"My lipstick is not the problem. This is the third color I tried this month, and the saleslady at the drugstore guaranteed it is the perfect shade."

"The first problem with your statement was *drugstore*, since we both know that the saleslady in question is Mrs. Peters, who hasn't changed lip color since Carter left office." He undid her hair, which was secured by a chopstick. Not a decorative one, but a wooden one from the takeout joint down the street.

"I wouldn't do that. My curls are out of control," she said, her hands moving up in a defensive action that had him laughing.

He intercepted them, mid helmet pose, and set them back at her sides, squeezing her wrists so she knew to leave them there. And miracle of miracles, she actually listened.

"You have slept-in bed waves, not curls," he corrected. One pull and all of those soft brown waves came tumbling down to her mid-back. *Like walking sex,* he thought. "Back to the lipstick. Are you really wearing pink with glossy shine and glitter?"

She shifted on her feet. "So?"

"So, it's a problem." He handed her a tissue and waited while she wiped it off. Then he put his fingers in her hair and gave it a little shake, stepping back to study his work. "Better. But still missing something."

"Wow, you sure know how to sweet-talk a woman," she mumbled, and that's when he realized what it was. Sunshine was looking self-conscious, which he'd never seen before. She usually marched to her own beat and flashed those pearly whites at anyone who looked at her strangely—the good-girl version of flipping the bird. But right then, standing there looking bed rumpled and sexy as hell, she was uncomfortable.

So Adam did the only thing he knew would work. What he wanted to do wouldn't be appropriate, so instead, he slid his fingers deeper into her hair, and then he kissed her.

And *holy shit*, Harper Owens with her warm smile and rainbow dreams might have looked like the kind of girl one would bring home to Sunday dinner at the parents', but she kissed like she'd rock your world on the car ride over.

And back.

She made a soft little mewling sound that drove him crazy, because it was half surprised and wholly aroused. Without warning, she pulled his lower lip with her teeth, sucked on it for a good minute, and he manned up in the most embarrassing way. But then her hands were on him, threading through his hair, playing with the ends at the back of his neck, and he forgot what the problem was.

Forgot why crazy cuties were a bad idea.

Forgot every hard-learned lesson that had gotten him through fifteen years as a smokejumper for Cal Fire. Such as: the key to not getting burned was you had to get in, scratch some line, hook it, call it good, and cut out before catching too much heat. It was a technique that had saved his ass a dozen times over in wildfires—and with women. Only he was too busy enjoying the flame to notice it had gotten out of control. Until he heard his name being called.

"Adam?" she purred, and he started walking them backward into the dressing room when he realized Harper wasn't moving with him. She also wasn't kissing him anymore. In fact, she looked all prickly.

"Adam?" a sultry voice teased again. From the other room. "Where are you?"

Harper cleared her throat and took a step back. A big step back. "He's out here, Baby."

Four things hit Adam simultaneously. First, he'd come here tonight with the stacked blonde he'd met at the bar for a private lingerie show and a fun game of spin the spinner. Second, he'd almost had sex with a girl named Baby. Third, he'd just made out with the weird art teacher. And fourth, he'd liked it.

Hell, based on the tent in his pants and the way he was gasping for breath, he'd more than liked it. His lips still tasted like some kind of fruity umbrella drink, and he wanted another sip.

Which brought him to the biggest revelation of the night: Harper Owens was a closeted hottie. And if she'd disliked him before, which he could only assume since she'd never looked twice at him until tonight, then she'd hate him now.

Her hair was magically back up in its messy twist, her dress was zipped to the neck, and she was shooting glares frosty enough to cryogenically freeze his nuts for decades to come.

"Oh, hey, Harper," Baby said, stopping at the entry to the dressing room. She was in stripper heels, fishnets, and three leather straps that strategically crisscrossed her body. Her hair was ratted, her lips ruby red, and she should have had him revving to go. Only Adam was too busy watching Harper. "What are you doing here?"

"I was about to ask you the same thing," Harper said.

chapter
two

"Fired?"

Clovis Owens rested all her weight against the Fanny Wrappers display and patted her brow with the chartreuse cheeky boy-shorts she was folding. "Oh dear, that's not good. Not good at all."

"I know," Harper said, handing her grandma her cane, wondering just how betrayed the older woman felt. Clovis was the kind of person who gave her trust so freely, who wanted to see the good in everyone, and Harper hated to think of her being hurt by Baby's actions. "But she didn't take anything, no one got hurt, so it all worked out."

"I don't care if she took anything," Clovis said, her face going a little pale. She hobbled over to the counter, her cane clicking against the wood floor.

On cue, Jabba, the resident go-fetch king, came shuffling out from under the stool, a candy wrapper stuck to his muzzle. Shaped like an overstuffed sausage with kitten legs, Jabba was too short to sniff any higher than shin level, so he put a few wet doggie marks on Harper's ankle, then plopped down next to his master, eyes zeroing in on her cane, willing it to fall and roll across the room.

Clovis flipped through her phone book, a big round rolodex that was older than dirt and could rival Vera Wang's. "Do you think if I call her back, she'd give me a second chance?"

"Call her back?" Harper pulled up a stool and helped Clovis sit, then gave her a glass of water. She was more upset by the situation than Harper had guessed.

"The girl needs this job. I gave it to her as a favor," Clovis said, wringing the life out of the boy-shorts. "What am I going to tell her mom?"

"That she picks up strangers at bars and brings them back to her place of work." Clovis narrowed her gaze in warning. "Too soon? Okay, well she just graduated from college with a double degree," Harper said in a soothing voice, realizing Clovis was concerned over the girl's well-being. "She'll be fine."

Something Harper knew for a fact. She'd seen to it personally. Letting Baby go had been a no-brainer, and although Harper made a point to listen to her brain, she answered with her heart. And her heart had said Baby wasn't a bad person, just young and flighty. And after a lifetime of dealing with flighty women, Harper had formed a soft spot for them.

"Her degree is in microbrewing and dance"—Clovis reached for the phone—"and since she moved to *wine* country and the only gentlemen's club we have around here involves whacking weathered wooden balls and wearing regulation croquet knickers, she'll be homeless by the end of the week."

"Which is why," Harper said, putting the phone back on the hook, "I hooked her up with a job at the Barre and Tap. She'll be helping out with the evening dance classes since Sara is pregnant."

Sara DeLuca had moved to town a few years back with her son and opened the Barre and Tap, a kids' dance studio that also offered senior classes in the evening—including senior pole dancing. She's also fallen in love with one of her students, Trey DeLuca.

Sara and her reformed playboy were married within months and now expecting a child. It was incredibly romantic and gave Harper hope that love was everywhere—even in a town of six thousand.

She just had to keep her eyes open.

When Clovis still didn't look convinced, Harper took her hand. "You're not the bad guy here, Grandma. She was using the shop after hours to entertain her male friend. While wearing store merchandise."

Baby didn't end up entertaining Adam—at least not that Harper knew, since Baby and Fireman Frisky left separately—and Baby had paid for the merchandise before turning in her key. She'd also taken a handful of the Come Again Condoms Clovis passed out for swag.

"Have you seen that man's chest?" Clovis asked, placing a hand to her ample bosom, and Harper considered doing the same since her pulse was picking up pace at an alarming rate. Harper's eyes went to the Cuties with Booties calendar on the wall that was still opened to July—of last year. "I'd do the dressing-room dance with him, too," Clovis continued. "The month his photo came up in Shay's calendar, with him in only his helmet, suspenders, and turnout pants, my Fireman Saves the Day dildo sales went up three hundred percent. Can't say I blame the girl."

Unfortunately, neither could Harper, now that she knew first-hand just how incredible his abs were. And his lips? Confident, controlled, and so lethal under pressure she could still feel the effects two days later. She almost felt like a hypocrite when she said, "This time we were lucky. Baby was sweet-talked by the local playboy. Next time it could be by a playboy who wouldn't think twice about taking off her fishnets, then taking off with your cash."

"You're right," Clovis said, looking more concerned than comforted. "But now I'm short an assistant, and with National Underwear Day right around the corner, time is running out to order fall inventory."

"I can help you after I get off work until we hire someone new. Someone who is qualified to manage a retail store," she clarified.

Clovis shook her head, her gray bob bouncing. "No, you don't understand. I didn't hire Baby for her managerial skills—the girl can't even count change. She's my hired sex."

"Hired what?" Harper asked because surely she'd misunderstood. There was no way her grandma was a madam.

"I hired her for the sex."

Well, look at that. Harper suddenly felt light-headed. As if she needed a stool to hold up her weight. Because if Baby's credentials were that of sex for hire, then it meant—

"Adam was a, uh, customer?"

"He's one of my best customers," Clovis said and, *yup*, Harper was going to be sick. All over the Come Again Condoms basket. "But Baby was supposed to be my front person for when we meet with the rep next week. Be the sexy on my team."

Harper laughed—it was part hysterical and part relief, but it was a laugh—which was so much better than throwing up. "Since when do you need a team to meet with reps?"

Clovis had been handling buyers and reps since before Harper was born. In fact, she'd been in the sex business so long she predated Hugh Hefner. There wasn't a lingerie company or distributor Clovis hadn't worked with, or one she couldn't call.

"Since I lost my sexy," Clovis cried. "I went and got myself a man and suddenly I've become Ms. Missionary. Not in the bedroom, mind you, but in the boardroom and around town. One of my suppliers has pulled their terms for fall, leaving me with a pending order."

Harper ignored the bedroom part, because picturing the woman who practically raised her doing the dirty with Giles Rousseau gave her the shivers. "Small shops get pending orders all the time because of the quantities, you know that."

"Not my shop," Clovis said, and her eyes went misty. "Never my shop. A pending order with no expected ship date? That means I don't know what I'm going to be selling in the fall. I can't prep for the new season, can't update my website, or get my fall catalog ready."

"Didn't they give you an estimate?"

"They were too busy sending in a secret shopper who reported back that the Boulder Holder has"—she took a shuddery breath—"'lost its sexual edge, catering to the senior demographic,' which we all know means granny panties. I am not a granny panty pusher!"

"That's one manufacturer," Harper said, putting her arms around Clovis's meaty shoulders.

"But it's the only one that counts," she whispered, and Harper's chest pinched at the defeat and humiliation she heard in her grandma's voice. "And if they pull my shop from their list of retailers, I don't know what will happen."

"Oh, Grandma." Harper knew that the businesses on this side of town had been struggling financially, but she'd thought sales had picked up. Thought her grandma had put herself in the right position. "How bad is it?"

Clovis looked around her shop, disappointment welling up in her eyes. "It's Lulu Allure."

"Lulu Allure?" That same panic that had overtaken Clovis at the mention of firing Baby filled Harper's chest. "You've been with them since they started."

Clovis sniffed and Jabba scooted closer, rolling his sausage of a body onto Clovis's foot, offering support. "I was their flagship store on the West Coast." She was also their exclusive retailer in wine country, which was why their merchandise was prominently displayed throughout the shop.

Over the years, Clovis had taken chances on smaller lines, start-ups that no one else would sacrifice shelf space for. She had an eye for design and a heart for underdogs, which was how the

Boulder Holder had managed to break out some of the biggest up-and-comers in the industry and give them their starts.

Just like she'd given Harper a fresh start at having a real home years ago. "I thought you were one of their biggest sellers," Harper said.

"I am. I'm also losing my edge." Clovis rubbed the crystal handle of her cane, something she did to calm her nerves. Jabba, on the other hand, gently gnawed on the foot of it.

"You're not losing your edge," Harper assured her. "You don't even know why they're coming out."

"When I called to see what the holdup was, they told me they were sending someone to discuss the 'exclusive territory rights' in my contract. When they did that to Gertie down in La Jolla, they gave her territory to some sexed-up honey who doesn't know the difference between a chemise and a camisole." Clovis shook her head, her silver halo moving with every heartbreaking motion. "If I lose Lulu Allure's business, I lose a third of my fall merchandise. Maybe even my shop."

Harper handed Clovis a tissue. The older woman bowed her head to dab her eyes.

"Your grandfather and I worked so hard to open this shop. If I lost it now . . ." Clovis broke off and looked up, and the expression she wore was like an arrow straight through Harper's chest. It was the same broken look her grandmother had worn when her husband passed, and when she'd had to tell Harper that her mom wasn't coming for her weekend visit.

Something Harper had come to accept throughout her lifetime, since Gloria Owens was a slave to the stage, and a resident of nowhere in particular. In fact, last Harper had heard, she was headlining at the Sunnyhills Senior Community Theater in Plano, Texas.

"We won't lose the shop, Grandma. I promise."

Clovis offered up a watery smile. "When you talk like that, so confident about the good in the world, you sound just like your grandpa."

Chester Owens saw potential and possibility where others only saw problems. He was small in stature but big at heart, making everyone around him feel welcomed and treasured. Especially when it came to the love of his life.

Even two decades after his passing, the dreamy look that he inspired in her grandmother whenever she talked about him made Harper's heart ache with longing. What would it be like to have a love affair like that? To be cherished so thoroughly that even in death she couldn't be forgotten?

Harper looked around the shop, with its Victorian charm and sensual landscape, and realized that it wasn't just losing the shop for Clovis—it would be losing her identity.

"I promised him I'd look after you. And this shop is as much a part of you as your heart." For Harper, it represented a safe escape from her fractured childhood. It was an important piece of her past that inspired warm memories and had helped her to become the woman she was today.

"You're my heart." Clovis reached up to cup Harper's cheek, the feel of her plump hand as comforting as it had been when Harper was a scared little girl. "And my favorite grandchild."

"I'm your only grandchild."

"Why mess with perfection?" Clovis said, and Harper felt a burst of determination. Not just to save the shop, but to be the kind of granddaughter she'd promised Chester she could be. The kind who took a problem and made it into a possibility.

Clovis was bold, yet loved frills. She was soft where it counted but firm in her support of others. She had a beautiful way of helping women find their inner seductress, claim their femininity, and take pride in the power of being a woman.

Harper was bold and supportive, but unlike the other Owens women who had come before her, she'd missed out on the feminine seductress gene.

Or had she, she wondered, remembering that kiss. She knew Adam was trying to prove a point, but when he pressed his lips to hers, ran his hands over her body as though he liked what he found, she had felt that power simmer from deep within. And it was intoxicating.

Then she remembered he'd been on a secret tryst with another woman and happened to stumble and fall into Harper's mouth.

"You don't need Baby to impress that rep," Harper said, just like she didn't need to change to impress some guy. She straightened to her full five feet eleven inches and squared her shoulders. "You're Clovis Owens, respected panty pusher and living lingerie legend. And I'm Harper Owens, summa cum laude graduate from San Francisco School of the Arts. Between your boardroom skills and my design and merchandizing genius, we'll have Lulu Allure begging you to carry their fall line."

Clovis chuckled, but Harper held her ground, because what was there to laugh about?

The shop had a wonderful history, a loyal customer base, and great bones. Some of the customers may have been born in the wrong century, and some of the bones were in the wrong spot, but so what? It wasn't about changing the heart of the Boulder Holder— it was about how it was staged. By moving some of the sexier things forward and downplaying the less appealing items by placing them in the back, such as body-shapers, girdles, and banana-hammocks, they could make this shop that exclusive, sensual, high-end environment that manufacturers like Lulu Allure were dying to place their products in.

Not to mention, Harper wasn't just a graduate from one of the top art design schools on the West Coast—she had graduated top of her class. Sure, her fine arts degree was in set design, which meant

she could dress an amazing window, but she'd taken several art edi-
torial classes, excelled in market research, and even interned for a
famous men's magazine.

Her first job had been for a food network, dressing sets for cooking shows. Then she'd moved into kids' television. Not that knowing
which colors promoted deeper learning would help here, but looking around the shop, Harper knew that all it needed was a facelift—
a little updating to the already strong foundation.

It would be fun even. She loved her job managing the Fashion
Flower, but she missed the creative freedom of setting a scene that
told the right story.

"Oh dear," Clovis said in a hushed voice. "You want to help."
It wasn't a question, nor was it a compliment. It was a statement.

"Why not? I'm the demographic they're targeting, I know more
about merchandising and staging than anyone in town, and I have
to admit, I dress a mean window."

"That you do."

"I could re-dress the window to be more boudoir chic and stage
the shop to feel like a trunk show, draped in lace and silk and full of
secret fantasies and firsts. Not in a raunchy way, but more of a summery breeze meets Nicholas Sparks film way. Fun, flirty, hot, sexy."
Harper snapped her fingers. "Summer of Seduction."

"It sounds lovely, dear, and I appreciate the enthusiasm," Clovis
said, patting Harper's head and making her feel like she was twelve
all over again. Harper hated twelve. She'd grown five inches that summer—and not a single cup size. "But who's going to bring the sexy?"

It was well past the lunching hour by the time Adam dragged himself through the doors of Stan's Soup and Service Station. He was
supposed to meet his brothers there for a bowl of chili at one, but

after pulling another all-night shift, which included corralling a few of the smart-assed seasonal hires into doing their jobs, he'd slept through his alarm.

He'd kept on dreaming a crazy dream about him and a Playboy bunny in a game of pin the tail—only when the ears came off, it was Harper standing there in that fiesta-inspired bra and thong. Her lips were shiny from his kiss, her legs wrapped around his waist, and she was suddenly holding a ruler, having morphed into the role of naughty schoolteacher.

"Jesus." He ran a hand down his face, wondering what was wrong with him, then decided he'd been too long without sex. Yup, that was his problem—he was in a sex drought.

Not surprising, since he'd spent the past thirty days with a bunch of dudes in the heart of a summer fire that was raging south of Tahoe, digging ditches and sharing the occasional fart jokes when things got squirrely, and it had taken its toll. Then he'd blown his first chance at getting laid by kissing Little Miss Sunshine.

Sure, Harper was one hell of a kisser. And she had boobs, so what? Of course there was expected standard equipment on a grown woman—and she was a woman, no question. He just wasn't sure he'd noticed before.

They'd grown up in the same town, but they'd lived in very different worlds. Harper was the sweet, sunny girl-next-door who paraded around town befriending everyone and their mother.

Everyone except him. Which never bothered him. Until now. Now he couldn't help but feel bothered—and in all the right kinds of ways.

As unexpected as that reaction was, so were those long, lush legs. Miles of them, it seemed. Tanned, toned, to her neck, and a total turn-on. Only she was looking for Mr. Right, when he was the reigning Mr. One Night.

And now there he was, going on day thirty-five of what was becoming a serious sex drought, getting all menstrual over some kiss. Which was piss-poor timing because Harper might be the cute girl-next-door with the surprising cleavage, but in a few months she would be a regular at family events, since Adam's youngest brother was marrying Harper's best friend.

Adam took a deep breath, checked his man card to see if it was still valid, and strode through the open door of Stan's. The sun was high and the warm summer air stirred the daisies in the window-box planters.

Stan's was a soup kitchen meets auto body shop with a counter made from an old tailgate and cooking utensils and engine tools hanging from the ceiling. It was the only place in the county, probably the state, where one could get a smog inspection and a bowl of chilled tomatillo avocado soup with cilantro-infused oil.

It was a cash only, service questionable kind of place where the chili was award winning, the beer was on tap, and his baby brother was, on occasion, the line cook. Not by trade, but by necessity. It seemed chopping vegetables helped keep Dax's demons at bay—and Adam's brother had more than his fair share.

"Nice apron," Adam said, taking a seat at the counter.

Dax smiled, goofy and stupid. "Emerson bought it for me."

Emerson Blake was mouthy and stubborn, and she had his large military-grade brother wrapped around her itty bitty finger. Which explained why the apron was a little bit leather, a little bit lethal, and had a picture of an apple below the words BITE ME.

When Adam smirked, Dax got serious. Real serious.

"You have a problem with it?" Dax looked at the butcher knife, then at Adam, and lifted a questioning brow. Yeah, Adam might be a few years older, but Dax had at least two inches and thirty pounds on him. Plus fifteen years of Army Ranger bad-assery under his belt.

"Nope, just noticed that the metal rivets on the ties really bring out your eyes." Adam looked around for the other brother. "Where's Jonah?"

"We had lunch plans, not dinner," Dax informed him as though the concept of meal times were too difficult for Adam to grasp. "He got tired of waiting. I'm only still here because Emi has the food truck parked up the valley at some summer craft fair."

"We ran three calls last night, all after 1:00 a.m., the last one being a fire on a hillside vineyard that kept us going well into the morning. I didn't get to sleep until after sunup."

Dax looked at the sun streaming in the windows. "It's nearly four fifteen, so what's your point?"

Adam looked at his watch. Four fifteen exactly. "How do you do that?"

"It's a gift." Dax grinned, then went back to making short order of the pile of potatoes he was butchering.

A fresh breeze blew through the open door and stirred up the spicy garlic, roasting chilies, and baking bread. Adam's stomach growled. "I'll have a bowl of the chili and two orders of garlic bread."

"First, I'm not a damn waitress, and second, you're too late. I can't give you any chili."

Adam looked at the pot of chili on the stovetop behind the counter. "It's full. I can see it from where I'm sitting."

"Then move so you don't have to look at it." Dax waved the knife toward a booth in the far corner. "I'm under strict orders not to give you any chili. Or garlic bread. In fact, if I serve you anything at all, other than a fist to the throat, I'll be sleeping on the couch with my hand and lotion for company."

"What does my lunch have to do with your sex life?"

"Don't know, don't care," Dax said. "All I know is Emi laid out the rules, and I just want to get laid. Sorry, but I know you get it."

No. He didn't. He didn't get it at all.

He didn't get what he'd done this time to tick off his future sister-in-law. Or how sometime over the last year both of his brothers, who had exactly zero game with women, had hooked up with two of the biggest hotties in town. His oldest brother, Jonah, had married one, Dax was two breaths away from saying *I do* to the other, and Adam, the fucking life of every party, was suddenly the odd man out. Fine with him since it also meant he wasn't saddled down with a relationship.

He was free to do what—and who—he wanted. Anytime, anywhere. No one to answer to—or disappoint. Adam had no limits on his life, a situation he'd worked hard to create.

One that worked for him just fine.

"Oh, and I wouldn't cross her path for a few days," Dax said. "She was sharpening her chef's knives when she was telling me to steer clear of you, and I'm not sure whether those knives were for work or for the next time she saw you."

"Great," Adam said, wondering if he could skip Emi's food cart for a few days and bring his own lunch.

His phone rang.

"Baudouin," he answered.

"Yeah, um, hey Adam, it's Seth." Seth was a summer hire who was hoping to be brought on full time at the end of the season. He was crafty, well trained, determined, and as the house's FNG—I.e., Fucking New Guy—a colossal pain in Adam's ass.

"This had better be good," Adam said. "Because if you'd taken the time to check the schedule before calling, you'd have seen I'm enjoying my day off."

"Cap doesn't come on until tomorrow. And, uh . . ." Adam could practically hear him crying through the phone. "I kind of have a problem."

"Define problem," Adam said, and FNG's sheepish silence had Adam resting his head on the counter. Hard.

The kid had a major talent for screwing the pooch with the best of intentions. The last time he'd called Adam, he'd taken one of Adam's pranks too far—an April Fool's petition Adam had circulated to have a condom vending machine installed for "safety" reasons—and replaced all the candy in the machines with tropical-flavored condoms. It was also the day they'd had a scheduled visit from St. Vincent's Academy. Sister Margaret was not happy when her students spent all their lunch money on Tropical Temptations.

"I kind of dinged the engine."

Adam sat up. "Which engine?"

"The new one."

Adam closed his eyes as the thoughts—all having to do with damage control—pinged around his head: *Who's gonna get pissed at who? How will this affect the FNG? Will it only be a letter in his file? Or a five percent dock in pay?*

It was a ping, ping, ping that landed right back on him.

As an equipment apparatus engineer, it was Adam's job to ensure all of the department's equipment was in pristine condition. Especially the rigs. But their new rig? His battalion chief would rupture a nut if he heard it was dented.

Adam released a breath. "I'm on my way."

chapter
three

Praying for a miracle, Adam headed toward the fire station. It was only six doors down from Stan's, a two-minute walk, tops. He'd figure out the problem, implement a solution, and get back to business as usual.

He wasn't sure what that was yet, but he hoped it involved a hot meal and an even hotter woman.

However, as his luck would have it, the only woman in sight was wearing bright orange shorts, sunglasses from *I Love Lucy*, and a denim smock tied at the waist with a dozen or more strips of tape stuck to the front. Unfortunately, it was not the getup Harper wore last night in his dreams, but weirdly it had its own appeal. The smock hid any kind of cleavage she might have going on under there, but those shorts were soft, snug, and showing off her assets.

And what a spectacular asset she had. That he hadn't dreamed up.

Harper was fighting to hang a sign in the library window and the sign was winning. In her defense, it was pretty big. More like a banner and a two-person job. But since Little Miss Sunshine had made it clear the other night that she didn't welcome his help, and

Adam always listened when a lady spoke her mind, he leaned against a lamppost and watched for a good minute or so, enjoying the view.

A little amusing, a little odd, and fully entertaining.

Then the wind picked up, catching a corner of the banner, which smacked Harper in the forehead. Adam suppressed a laugh, barely, as she struggled to right it. Only it slowly folded over her until all that was visible were those bare legs.

"Need help?" Adam finally asked, and the struggling stopped. He was pretty sure her breathing stopped too. But her frustration— that seemed to grow thick in the air.

"I can't afford your help," she said from beneath the sign, which he could now see advertised the upcoming Beat the Heat Festival.

"Helping out with Beat the Heat, huh?" He crossed his arms and grinned. "Does that make you a fire bunny?"

Beat the Heat was an annual festival held at the start of every summer that brought in visitors from all around wine country and beyond. Locals came for the food and the fanfare, and tourists came to experience the beauty of the valley when covered with wild mustard and blooming vines. A fire bunny—well, those were ladies who offered up their services during the event in hopes of servicing one of the single St. Helena Fire Department firefighters.

"I'm not a fire bunny. I offered to help Stephanie Daugherty with the banners since she's due anytime now and the smell of paint makes her sick," she clarified. "And I'm fine, thank you for asking."

As if to prove her wrong, the banner got the upper hand and swallowed her whole, toppling over and taking her down with it. Arms and legs flailed to find purchase, but the sign was too much for her.

"Stupid sign."

"Now what did that sign ever do to you?"

Ignoring her protests, Adam lifted the banner up and off her with one hand. The other wrapped around her waist and hauled her to a stand. After all, Beat the Heat was an SHFD sponsored event, and as a firefighter, it was his civic duty to step in and help a citizen in need. It was his lucky day the citizen turned out to be Harper.

"It snuck up on me," she said, flicking a few stray strands of hair out of her face. Strands which, he noticed, were straight and slicked back into that on-the-go messy bun look that took twenty minutes, a flat iron, and a gallon of product to secure. A valley favorite for PTA members and soccer moms, but weird for Harper since she was neither, yet she'd definitely spent quite a bit of time on her hair to make it look carefully casual. "Not a smart move."

"I don't know about that." Adam pressed the sign securely to the window with one hand, then peeled off a band of tape—the one right above that cleavage she was hiding—and attached it to the corner. "I snuck up on you last week and it worked out pretty well for me."

He reached for another piece of tape, and she smacked his hand. "I said I was fine, and we aren't going to talk about it."

She secured the other upper corner and then one of the lower ones.

"*It* as in the stupid sign and how I saved you?" He stepped closer and leaned in. "Or *it*, as in the kiss?"

"None of it," she said, and if her blush was any indication, she might not want to talk about it, but she was thinking about it.

Interesting.

"You're right," he said, snatching another piece of tape, which had stuck to her assets in the spill. "This is more of a conversation to have over drinks."

She snatched the tape back. "No drinks. No talking. No funny business." She crossed her arms and then leveled him with a glare as if he were one of her students.

"Says the woman wrestling with a sign."

Her face heated again. "It's a big sign, and I have three more to hang up before my next class starts, so this is where I say thank you, then you go back to your world and I go back to mine."

"If that's what you want," he said, as if that weren't exactly what he'd decided to do a few minutes ago. So then why did the thought of coexisting in the same town with no interaction start a tingling of unease?

Because riling up the town's biggest optimist was fun. It was like pissing off the tooth fairy.

"It's what we *both* want," she said, but her eyes were working double time not to look at his mouth.

So he winked. "Then you and that sign have a good day, sunshine." With that Adam headed toward the firehouse. Three doors down he half turned and said, "And you might not want to watch my ass when I walk off. Wouldn't want our two worlds to collide."

"You're so annoying," she hollered.

"You're so watching."

He heard a gasp, then some fancy shuffling and what sounded like a huff, seconds before the banner hit the sidewalk and a frustrated "You wish" echoed down Main Street.

With a smile, he kept walking. Right past the flower shop and the party supply store and the urge to go back, until he reached the open bay of St. Helena Fire Station #1.

Built in 1912 and crafted from brick and hand-carved stone, the station was large enough to house two engines, an ambulance, a grass wagon, two support trucks, and a seven-man crew. Out back were spots for several search-and-rescue ATVs and the fire captain's truck—which was empty.

Presently there was no captain on duty. Not an uncommon occurrence, since their captain worked four on and three off. Lucky for Seth, Captain Roman Brady was off today. Unlucky for Adam, the FNG had called him to fix the situation.

Adam shouldn't complain—he'd been asking for more responsibility around the station. He'd committed the first few years of his career as a seasonal smokejumper, spending his summers fighting wildfires, and the rest of the year fluctuating between snowboarding in Tahoe and surfing in Mexico. Eight years back, he was hired on as a full-time firefighter, and he'd quickly moved up to an equipment apparatus engineer. Now Adam was ready again to move up the ranks.

The fastest way to lieutenant was to take on training rookie smokejumpers in no-man's land. Check. Take additional courses and ace the lieutenant's exam. Check and check. Handle things in the captain's absence and prove he was ready for a promotion.

Adam was on it.

He strolled toward the kitchen, stopping right outside the doorway. Two guys were standing at the counter making dinner, while the other three sat on the couch watching the Giants game on the plasma. Seth sat in the armchair in the corner of the room.

"It's at least a double D–sized ding," Will McGuire said as Adam entered the kitchen—a place he frequented more than his own. "Which means whoever distracted you was way out of your league, freshman."

McGuire was all lean muscle, young ego, and, until Seth had come on a few months ago, the station's resident FNG. Coincidentally, up until a few months ago Adam had been the station's resident smart-ass—excelling in ribbing, pranks, and making a party out of twist ties, tinfoil, and downtime. But that was before Cap had told him he was up for review in a few months, before Adam learned that if he played his cards right, a promotion was a possibility.

Even with his colorful past.

"Then explain how I got her digits," Seth said, waving a piece of binder paper like it was the Holy Grail.

"Dude, you humped bumpers with the Cal State cheerleading team's car and you only got one girl's digits?" McGuire asked, dumping enough spaghetti noodles into the colander to feed a small country. "What kind of victory lap is that?"

"It was the dance team," Seth argued as if *that* made it all okay. "And it wasn't a victory lap. Besides, you were the one who sent me out in the first place to get bananas."

"Is that what she wrote her number on? Your banana?"

The other guys laughed, and Adam could tell that Seth was two verbal jabs away from a swift smack to Will's head.

Adopting his best *don't mess with me* face, Adam strolled all the way into the kitchen.

"McGuire," Adam said, and all the men looked up. He looked back, cool and assessing. "Remember the call we took where you came across that eight-foot python?"

The smug look cleared from his face, McGuire nodded. "The one in that attic?"

"That's the one." Adam's smile said it was also the one where McGuire had pissed himself, and instead of making a big deal out of it, Adam had kept his mouth shut, because he knew this job was hard. Scary as shit. And sometimes they were bound to act human and screw up. Seth had screwed up dinging the engine, severely enough that his job might be on the line, and McGuire shoving it in his face was bad form.

"Yeah, I remember it."

"So do I," Adam said in his best lieutenant voice. "We done here?"

That was all it took. The men straightened, McGuire zipped it and went back to making dinner, while Seth pretended to watch the game.

Adam patted FNG on the shoulder and beckoned him toward the garage. They walked to the truck in question. Not a word was said as Adam circled the engine. Not a breath was taken when he studied the bigger-than-double-Ds dent in the back fender.

"That ding is more than a damn bumper, so spill." Adam locked gazes. "And I mean everything."

"Everything?" Seth's eyes went big and his ears went pink, telling Adam this was going to be a whole lot more complicated than a little fender bender with a pretty girl.

"If I wanted the crib notes I would've listened to them over a bowl of chili at Stan's, not here with a bunch of giggling ladies."

"Right." Seth swallowed. "But I'd first like to express just how sorry I am for calling you in on your—"

"The dent, freshman."

"McGuire sent me on a banana run. He said it was for some dessert he was making, but I know it was his way of reminding me I'm the fucking new guy. So I went, got the bananas, let it roll off my back, then I met this girl in line. A spinner with tits. Real tens too, not the purchased kind," Seth said, as if retelling his account of coming face-to-face with the chupacabra of women. "She looked at my uniform, started chatting me up, paid for her things, then slipped me her number and left. I got in the truck and was pulling out, when she appeared in my side window and stood out the top of her friend's sunroof."

Adam looked at the ceiling because he knew, *knew*, where this was going.

"Then she lifted her top—no bra and definitely all real—and I don't know what happened. My foot slipped off the brake. I was in reverse and boom."

Adam ran a hand down his face. "Please tell me you didn't hit another car."

"Worse," Seth said, sounding defeated. "I hit a crate of tampons."

"Tampons? Are you shitting me?"

Seth shook his head. "The delivery guy had just taken them off the truck and was going to roll them into the back bay of Picker's Market."

Adam wanted to strangle the kid, but he understood that this kind of attention came with the uniform. It was also the kind of attention that took some getting used to. And for a fresh-out-of-school, freckle-faced new guy, it would have been distracting.

"Aw, man," Seth said. "When the guys find out I hit a crate of tampons and not the girls' car, I will be the butt of every single joke until I retire."

At this point, Adam was more concerned about the kid having a career with the department to retire from. Seth was good at his job, feared the right things and nothing else, was a team player, and knew how to take an order. Problem was, when he wasn't geared up and beating back a flame, Seth could be persuaded into doing just about anything. And when Roman found out what had transpired from his latest screwup, he was going to hit the roof.

Only Adam could talk his way through this with Roman. Explain it in a way that Roman, who was also one of his closest friends, could write off. Because it wasn't Roman who Adam was worried about pissing off—it was Roman's boss, Chief Lowen.

The battalion chief had a reputation for scaring off FNGs, which was why the station was short staffed.

Adam had dedicated too many of his personal hours transforming Seth from a death-defying frat boy into the beginnings of an incredible firefighter. He couldn't lose him to a crate of tampons. Plus, Adam had been that same fearless troublemaker at one time too, getting distracted by a flash of cleavage and making shit decisions that nearly cost him his entire career—and worse. If it hadn't been for his former captain seeing the potential in Adam and giving him a second chance, he wouldn't be a fireman, living his dream.

"Here's how this is going to play out," Adam said. "I'll call Roman, tell him I was driving the truck and—"

"No way," Seth said. "I can't let you take the fall."

"As opposed to you getting passed on for the job?" When the kid still looked ready to argue, Adam added, "And McGuire getting written up for giving you the keys to go on a banana run? Not to mention, whoever else knew what was going on and didn't step in?"

Seth thought about that long and hard, until Adam could see the frown split his brow. And okay, the situation wasn't quite as dire as Adam was making it out for the other guys, but Seth didn't need to know that. Once word got out of exactly why Seth had hit the tampon crate, Chief Lowen would rain down on him like Hurricane Katrina.

"So we go with my plan," Adam said when he heard a car idling out front.

"I don't like it," Seth finally said, "but I'll go with it."

Adam didn't like it either. In fact, the second he saw the polished red truck pull into the drive, he was rethinking the plan. The plan sucked. And he needed a new one. A-SAP. One that didn't involve him, on his day off, dealing with this BS.

Because this hurricane had just turned into a Category 5. It wasn't Roman behind the wheel of the department vehicle, but Battalion Chief Lowen. A notorious hard-ass who'd spent too many years behind a desk to remember what it was like to be in the field. He upheld the letter of the law, rather than the person's intent, and based all decisions on potential media coverage.

Adam was so screwed. There was no way even a guy like Lowen could positively spin a fender bender involving a new engine, a tampon crate, and a banana run. Not with the implications about wasting taxpayer dollars on engine repairs when they were already suffering from budget cuts.

To make matters worse, Lowen also had an extreme dislike for Adam.

Partly because Adam lived to walk the line, but mostly because when Adam had been an FNG he'd taken the chief's goddaughter on the grand tour of the station—ending with a ride around town in the engine—where she'd rung his bell.

"Baudouin. Why am I not surprised?" Lowen barked, negotiating his spare tire around the steering wheel to get out of the truck and inspect the dent. Then he inspected Adam, who was about to take the blame for a collision he hadn't caused—while wearing nothing but flip-flops, shorts, and a PLAY HARD tee.

"Chief," Adam said, smiling. "How's the family?"

"Still off-limits."

chapter
four

Mondays had always been Harper's favorite. There was something about the start of a fresh week, the unlimited possibilities the next seven days held, and the sounds and smells associated with Main Street coming alive. Monday had a rhythm, an ebb and flow of the unexpected and the familiar that brought her comfort.

Residual effects of the unconventional childhood she'd shared with an unconventional mother.

Today was the perfect Monday. The sun was out, the sky was clear, and the zinnias and morning glories filling the wine-barrel planters that lined downtown were in full bloom, painting Main Street with all the colors of summer. Even better, Harper had channeled her inner sexy to try to help her grandmother.

Maybe *channeled* was too strong a word, but she'd definitely acquired enough intel to fake it.

Harper pulled the "Fast Track to Seduction" article she'd discovered online out of her purse and looked at the first rule. According to the twelve-step article, sexy was a state of mind. So, contrary to popular belief, there was nothing wrong with faking it.

Harper gave herself a stern nod, then put the article back. If she wanted to save her grandma's shop, then she needed to stop thinking like Suzie Sunshine and fake herself right into the role of a bedroom bombshell. At least until she got through this meeting with Lulu Allure.

And maybe got herself some adult cookies to go with a tall glass of yummy man.

Which was why, instead of wearing one of her go-to farm dresses with floral-patterned tights and Mary Janes, Harper had come to the shop early to dress for sex-cess.

Embracing rules number five, less is always more, and seven, the profound power of red, she'd purchased a body-hugging scarlet number that was sleek, sophisticated, and posed more questions than answers. Then, since sexy was in the accessories, or so she'd heard, she'd slipped on the naughtiest pair of panties in the shop, mile-high heels, and applied just enough makeup to appear flushed.

With one last look in the mirror, she fluffed her hair and hoped it looked more like bed-rumpled waves than corkscrew curls, then strutted out of the dressing room and into the shop. Where she nearly tripped over her feet.

The Boulder Holder, where she'd spent countless hours after work giving it a fresh, new, youthful look—a transformation, really—was packed full of customers. Women of all shapes and sizes—curvy, petite, willowy, and buxom—had turned out in a show of support. The problem was, they were all retired.

There wasn't an arthritis-free or girdle-less gal among the group. Except for one—the runway-ready thirty-something with shiny black hair and perfect allure who stood at the entryway of the shop, a red journal in hand, frantically taking notes as someone asked where the banana-hammock display had been moved.

"Grandma," Harper whispered, dashing over to the register, her head pounding each time she watched a customer rifle through the racks like it was the yearly bloomers blowout and not the most important day for the shop. "Why are all these people here? We have the Lulu Allure meeting today."

"That's why I called in backup. I figured if the rep saw how packed the store was she'd change her mind. All it took was me mentioning a free banana-hammock with every purchase of twenty dollars or more before noon, and the knitting club cleared out and the girls started lining up." Clovis took in the crowded store and smiled, big and proud.

Harper took in Clovis with her blue eye shadow, coral lips, and emerald lace bustier she was wearing as a top and groaned.

"We wanted to prove we have a youthful edge. Flirty summer romance, boudoir sexy—that was the plan, remember?" It was a good plan. One that ten minutes ago Harper had been certain would sway the rep's opinion of the shop.

"Oh, I remember all right. That's why I told the girls no dentures or orthopedic shoes allowed." Which explained why Mrs. Sharp was moving her lips like she was a ventriloquist.

"These aren't girls, they're grandmas," Harper pointed out. "And call me crazy, but when I think of Summer of Seduction, saggy breasts and Bengay don't really come to mind."

"We might be up there in age, but we are all widow's peak women," Clovis chided, clearly offended.

"Widow's peak women?" Harper asked.

"Women in their seventies who are embracing their sexuality. In fact, WPWs are enjoying the best sex of their lives, and enjoying it three times more often than you and your youngster crowd. Just ask Giles."

Harper gagged a little. "I'll take your word for it."

Giles Rousseau was weathered, pushing eighty, and Clovis's gentleman friend. They had both stubbornly circled each other for two decades, then last year Giles finally made his move, taking them from foes to frisky in a single night, and now they cohabitated in a quaint cottage off Main Street and co-parented their dog, Jabba.

"Good sex or not—"

"*Great* sex, dear. There's a difference."

It had been so long, Harper wouldn't know.

"The point is, how am I supposed to present our ideas to the rep when your widow's peak women are rifling through the merchandise and picking apart the store we worked all last night finishing up?"

Clovis took in the store once again, the swarm of biddies, the picked-over displays, and leaned heavier on her cane, letting loose a deflating sigh. "Oh my, I really blew it, didn't I?"

Clovis didn't understand the concept of moderation. Everything she did, she did with gusto—including love. Which was why Harper pulled the older woman into her arms and whispered the same comforting phrase her grandmother had told her a hundred times as a kid: "Anything done from the heart can't be wrong." With a final squeeze, she pulled back. And then because she didn't want to let down the woman who had sacrificed so much to be both a grandmother and a mother, Harper added, "Now you find a way to clear some of the customers out and I'll go do what I do best."

Making friends wasn't Harper's only superpower. She could also tell a story and captivate an audience through images. Today she was doing both.

Pretending the shop was in tip-top shape, Harper headed toward the window display—and the woman who held the fate of her grandmother's shop in her hands. Determination pushed her shoulders back, even though nerves had her heart pounding.

"I'm Harper Owens, senior merchandising manager." Harper stuck out her hand. "You must be from Lulu Allure."

The woman studied her for a long moment, taking in every inch of Harper's attire—especially the shoes. She didn't appear overly impressed, but she also didn't appear as if she were going to ask for tips on papier-mâché crafts for kids. Harper considered it a win.

"Chantel," she said, offering Harper a glossy black-and-gray business card that read, CHANTEL LARUE, VP OF SALES AND MARKETING, LULU ALLURE.

Harper swallowed. They hadn't sent a low-hanging sales rep— they'd sent in the big guns—which had Harper wondering just how bad these *contractual changes* were going to be.

"It's so nice to meet you," Harper said, but her voice got lost in the chatter and shuffle of the customers.

"I believe we had an appointment." Chantel looked at her watch, then at the bifocals and frosted tips circling the merchandise. "Did I get the time wrong?"

"No, you're right on time. Mondays are just busy." Harper extended an arm toward the back of the shop. "Why don't we head into Couture Corner so we can chat." And so Chantel could see a room that hadn't been picked over.

Late last night, right before Harper had finally turned in, she'd had a stroke of genius and turned the back storage space into a private showing room for their more high-end lines.

The transformation was incredible, Harper thought as they entered the room. It was exactly what the Boulder Holder needed to sway Chantel. Bright, bold, breezy, sexy, and of course highlighting the star of the day—the entire Lulu Allure summer line. A detail that Chantel certainly couldn't miss.

Neither could she miss the tufted cream silk panels, silver and black accents, and chandelier Harper had salvaged from the garage and spray-painted to appear vintage. One of the secret tools of any good set dresser was the ability to accomplish high-end looks on a low budget. Harper could turn a fish bowl and an IKEA desk light into a realistic Tiffany sconce with only a glue gun, sea glass, and craft paints.

"This is . . . unexpected," Chantel said, taking a seat, and Harper felt her shoulders lift. Finding sensuality in the unexpected was rule number nine. "It reminds me of this little Parisian lingerie shop I went to last spring. They would bring the customers a cappuccino and croissant while they brought in a selection of their merchandise that was hand-chosen for the customer."

"That's what we're going for, only using selected local wines," Harper said, grabbing a tray of chocolate-dipped fruit with a flight of Napa Valley wines off the shelf. She placed it on the small table separating the two plush wingback chairs she had dragged down from the attic. "We wanted to create an intimate space that would provide a luxurious and plush environment to make the women feel pampered, and to highlight our specialty lines. Also, pairing the perfect wines with elegant lingerie will encourage customers to slow down and really experience the merchandise."

Chantel took a glass and lifted it to her lips. "I didn't get the impression your clientele would be interested in lines like these."

Harper swallowed down the bitter taste of judgment and smiled. "We get a lot of tourists, bridal parties, bachelorette parties, and groups of girlfriends up for a weekend of wine tasting. Our focus is to become the number one destination for bridal parties and girls' days out in wine country, and cash in on the twenty- to thirty-something weekend wine tasters." Harper stood and draped one of Lulu Allure's biggest sellers over herself, as if she were one of those sexy and sophisticated twenty- to thirty-something weekend wine tasters. "Our new look and the Tempting Tastings parties are going to get us there."

"I love what you've done with the shop, this room here, and the front window. And I absolutely adore the Tempting Tastings concept." It was said as if she also absolutely adored Harper. As if Harper was reason enough for Chantel to say yes, and that she wanted to move forward with their relationship.

And that felt good.

So good, Harper actually blushed a little. "Thank you."

"I have to be honest, though." Chantel set the wine down without even tasting it, and Harper felt her blush instantly blanch. She clutched the bra and panty to her as tremors of a big *but* that would no doubt rock the Boulder Holder loose shook the room—and her misplaced confidence. "I'm only here in person because we've had such a long-standing relationship with this shop. The team back home has strong concerns with having the Boulder Holder as our exclusive dealer in this territory—"

"Clovis was the first store in the state to carry Lulu Allure. She has always been a loyal client," Harper quickly pointed out, trying her best to remain calm, but she felt the garments in her hands droop. "In fact, between online and in-store sales, more than a third of the product we sell is Lulu Allure."

"A third of sales in a small-town shop is quite different from a third of sales in our boutique on Wilshire Boulevard."

"The Boulder Holder recently moved to the other end of Main Street, which caused some issues with foot traffic." She tried to keep the desperate edge out of her voice. "But the storefronts in this area have filled up, foot traffic has increased as you can see, and come August, when the harvest is in full swing and wedding parties flood to the valley, the tourists will outnumber the residents ten to one."

"I'm sure they will, but it's not the foot traffic I'm the most concerned about. It's brand protection. There's a reason Louis Vuitton can't be purchased at Walmart." Chantel softened her voice in that apologetic way that gave Harper heartburn. "Look, Lulu Allure is grateful for everything Clovis has done for us over the years, but we are expanding, taking our brand in a new direction with our fall line, and your clientele is not our target."

Harper felt her stomach tighten. "But our online customers are your exact target. Young, edgy movers and shakers of wine country and the greater Bay Area. During the tourist season we are flooded with dot-commers, Hollywood expats, and of course the Silicon Valley elite."

Chantel took in a deep breath and met Harper's gaze. Harper wasn't sure what the woman was looking for, but she gave her best smile, and then, remembering that sexy is a state of mind, pictured herself how she'd felt the other night—her hair down, her lips swollen, and Adam whispering her name—and lifted that lingerie set back up.

"Another show and I didn't get a call? I gotta say, sunshine, I'm hurt."

Harper spun around and found Adam standing in the doorway to the room, dressed in his fitted SHFD blues, displaying his tanned skin and lethal dimples, looking like the cover of a sexy fireman calendar.

Which he actually was.

He was also sipping on a to-go coffee cup while watching Harper model the bra-and-panty set. The spark in his baby blues said he liked what he saw—and suddenly Harper saw the power of *sexy is a state of mind* in action.

One grin from him and Harper felt her inner goddess strap on stilettos and lace, and strut right over her well-devised plans—which were imperative in saving this meeting, and her grandma's shop.

chapter
five

"What are you doing here?" Harper asked in a welcoming tone that was in direct contrast with the *go screw yourself* glare she was shooting him.

"Good morning to you too," Adam said, ignoring her daggers and walking close enough to finger the lace edging of the panties. "Parisian peek-a-boos? My favorite."

Harper felt something strange shift in her stomach. The cause was unclear. Was it some kind of post-traumatic flutters caused from the memory of Adam's hands on her peek-a-boos, or a growing irritation at how his mere presence could cause complete havoc in her world?

Perhaps it was both.

"You're familiar with our When in Paris line?" Chantel asked, surprise and excitement radiating from her tone.

Adam looked over Harper's shoulder and raised a questioning brow at the sight of company. It was good to know he hadn't interrupted them due to rudeness. *Just ignorance,* she thought. He was having way too much fun at her expense, and the gleam in his eyes told her it was about to go from fun to entertaining—for him.

God! How could he push her buttons and *push* her buttons with equal measure?

It was baffling.

"Go away," she whispered.

"And ignore the pretty lady's question?" he whispered back and shook his head. "I wouldn't want to ruin my gentlemanly reputation."

Harper snorted and he frowned. An honest to goodness frown, as if her reaction irritated him.

"I know the line *intimately*," he said, stepping completely into the room and grazing Harper's hip with his hand as he did it, before addressing Chantel like a gentleman. *What a load of BS.* "Although I'm partial to the brighter, party colors."

"Party colors?" Chantel asked, and Adam flashed one of his trademark grins she'd seen him use many a time on many a woman—including her. Last Friday.

It was clear Chantel, with her big-city sex appeal and I-do-yoga body, was Adam's type. If Harper didn't intervene, Adam would likely charm Chantel right out of this meeting and into his bed. Not that she cared who he took to his bed, as long as it didn't impact her plan.

"He is referring to the Moulin Rouge set," Harper said, poking him in the back—hard. "Adam, this is Chantel Larue from Lulu Allure." Harper gave Adam her most intimidating look, the one she used on her students when they needed to keep their hands to themselves, then plastered a smile on her face and turned to Chantel. "Chantel, this is Adam."

"Would you like some wine?" Chantel offered, pointing to the flight Harper had bought specifically to impress her. Not Adam.

"Nah, I've got my coffee," he said, and instead of behaving, he helped himself to a seat—*her* seat—leaning back as if he were right at home. Which, surrounded by women's panties and female fantasies, he probably was. "And I'd go with the Parisian peek-a-boos. In fact, I was thinking of picking some up and I wanted to see if Harper could show me her favorites."

The only favorite Harper was going to show him was her favorite finger. But since this was a meeting, and being professional was of utmost importance, she decided letting her bird fly would have to wait. "I'm a little busy with Chantel right now, but if you'd be so sweet as to wait outside—"

"Ah, but sweet is my specialty."

Didn't she know it. And like sugar, he had addictive qualities that were unexplainable.

"You shop here?" Chantel asked, and the genuine surprise that a man like Adam would buy presents for his girlfriend here had Harper snapping back to what was important: her grandma's shop.

"All the time."

"Really?" Chantel made a note in her little red journal. "Besides the Moulin Rouge, what sparks your interest?"

Harper held her breath, waiting to see just how bad Adam's answer would affect her ability to spin this situation. The amusement in his eyes as they roamed around the room at the garments, then over her body, told Harper it was going to be a good one. Only instead of making some offhanded remark about the sex toys in back, he picked up a chocolate-dipped strawberry and said, "I like everything Harper has laid out today. She has a good eye."

Ignoring the way her thighs tingled, she cleared her throat and in her most professional voice said, "Thank you."

"But what has me most interested is whatever she's got on under that dress."

Harper felt her cheeks flush—and not just the ones on her face.

"What are you wearing?" Chantel asked, as if this were a normal way to sell lingerie.

"Excuse me?"

"I wondered too," Chantel said. "Do you mind?"

Adam smiled. "Of course she wouldn't. Would you, sunshine?"

Harper secretly sent Adam a death glare, because, *poof*, just like that, what little spotlight she'd created with her dress and remodel vanished.

Adam had come with his alluring charm and bigger-than-life persona and made Harper an insignificant part of the meeting. Of her own meeting.

"No, of course not," Harper said diplomatically. "All the employees wear the merchandise. Today I have on the Honeysuckle demi-cup and matching boy-shorts from your summer line."

"Honeysuckle." Adam leaned forward, resting his elbows on his knees. "Is it lace like the one you had on the other night that made your boobs—"

"Could you excuse us for a moment?" Not waiting for a response, Harper took Adam by the arm and yanked him out of the chair—not letting go until she led him out of the room.

She marched through the store and onto the sidewalk, her patience reaching nuclear levels, as he slowly strode out the door behind her. God forbid the man actually move at a normal pace. Not Adam.

He was the kind of guy who liked to set the pace—for everything. Even worse, he only had two speeds: Superman and *How you doing?* The former he used to fight fires, and the latter he used when sparking them. But since Harper was itching for a fight, he was wasting his good moves.

"What are you doing?" she demanded.

He took a leisurely sip of his coffee, savoring it for a moment, while a gentle summer breeze carried the sweet scent of ripe grapes through town. "Helping you sell a Honeysuckle demi-cup and matching boy-shorts," he said, his eyes dropping to the vee of her dress. He ran his thumb over the edge of her dress near her collarbone.

She swatted his hands away. "She's not a customer, and I'm not selling her a bra-and-panty set. She is a sales rep and . . ." Her voice trailed off because Adam's eyes had drifted down. Maybe there was something to the red rule. It was something she could investigate later, after the rep agreed to the original terms.

"What are you doing here?" she asked again, this time annoyingly breathless. Which had zero to do with the way his work shirt clung to his chest and arms. Or that he'd arrived at the store on his big red engine, which was glistening in the sun beside them and making him look bigger than life.

"I came for my jacket," he said, looking into the shop. Harper glanced over to watch the flurry of sunbonnets and man-hammocks swarming the register. "I left it the other night, and I need to get it back. It's my uniform jacket."

"Sorry, I haven't seen it." There wasn't an inch in that shop that Harper hadn't dusted or decorated since last week.

"It was hanging by the dressing-room door."

"Nope."

At her easy dismissal, he leaned in slightly and grinned. "Maybe you can help me look for it?"

"I'm a little busy right now." She pointed inside the store where every bifocaled eye now stared back. A few faces were even pressed to the window.

Completely unfazed, Adam waved to his adoring public, then turned his back on them, getting eye-to-eye with Harper. That's when the phone cameras came out, arthritic fingers ready to shoot. "How about tonight then?"

Adam's gaze dropped to her lips, which immediately began to tingle—stupid lips. Even stupider were her feet. Because as Adam closed in, coming so near that she could smell the hot summer morning on his skin—she didn't step back.

Nope, with a six-foot-plus wall of testosterone and yummy male coming at her, her brain short-circuited, and her feet went the wrong way—they closed the distance instead of creating more of it.

She licked her lips, making the tingling worse, because all she could think about was him licking her lips. Again.

Maybe taking a little nibble of his in the process.

A surprised but positively wicked spark lit his eyes and he laughed, low and rough, as if he knew exactly what direction her thoughts had taken.

Harper resisted the sexual vortex pulling her in, reminded herself of how many ladies his lips had charmed, and suggested, "Why don't you ask Baby? She may have seen it."

"I'd rather find it with you." The man didn't even have the good manners to look embarrassed.

"Sorry. Busy."

Adam didn't look deterred—in fact, he looked determined—but he asked, "Is Baby around?"

"She doesn't work here anymore," Harper said, feeling a heavy dose of guilt push down on her. "She was let go."

Adam's smile fell and his face went slack. "I got her fired?"

"Baby got herself fired," Harper said, because even though Adam didn't help matters, she truly believed people were responsible for their own choices. And Baby chose to put her job in jeopardy. Not Adam. "She was using the shop for personal, uh, *aspirations*, and that goes against shop policy."

"Baby might have invited me, but I said yes to the after-hours party," he admitted, his voice laced with disappointment, surprising the hell out of Harper. "I didn't think it through, and I willingly participated in the against-policy . . . aspirations. And now she's fired."

He sounded genuinely remorseful, appalled even—at himself—and that had to mean something. Maybe it was proof that under the life's-one-big-pillow-fight attitude he had permanently tattooed to his forehead, Adam had a softer side. That his shallow interests in women were nothing more than a cover for hidden depths.

"It all worked out. My grandma wanted her back, but she'd already landed her dream job down the street," Harper said gently, placing her hand on his to reassure him that he hadn't single-handedly led Baby into a life of unemployment and debauchery.

Adam looked down at their hands, and suddenly the friendly gesture felt anything but. "Maybe I could get that private showing? Honeysuckle was the style, wasn't it?"

"Are you kidding me?" Harper removed her hand and studied him long and hard to see if, in fact, he was. *Nope*, she acknowledged as he casually flipped his ball cap around and shrugged. He was dead serious.

"I never kid about lingerie."

"Except you came here to find your jacket." That he'd forgotten after getting his pre-party on. "Not tonight's date."

He also hadn't really apologized. For putting her in a weird situation by sneaking into her grandma's shop for an after-hours play-date with Baby. Or kissing Harper. Or not bothering to call the next day.

Not that it mattered. He'd come with one woman, kissed another, then left alone. Harper had gotten the impression he enjoyed the kiss, but she regretted it all the same.

Clay asking her to babysit Tommy had knocked her off balance, and she'd still been teetering when Adam found her. Otherwise she never would have allowed his flirtations to go that far.

"Problem is, I got distracted by a red dress," he said, dropping his gaze again.

"That is a problem." Because tomorrow he'd be distracted by a bartender in a short skirt, and his world would keep spinning. Thankfully, Harper suffered from severe motion sickness, so spinning wasn't in her best interest. "Just not mine, since I'm not interested in being one of your many conquests."

Adam's eyes took a slow inventory of *her* summer collection, then the corners of his mouth lifted slightly and he shrugged. "Okay. I'll be one of yours."

Harper almost fluttered. *Almost.* Only right at the first sign of wings in her belly, he smiled, big and smug and so full of himself, and the flutter turned to irritation. "Whatever game you think we're playing, I'm not interested."

"Your dress says otherwise."

"This dress isn't for you," she primly pointed out and wanted to look away, but she couldn't. Rule number three clearly stated to maintain direct eye contact—and she wasn't about to let him win. "It's for an important meeting, which you are keeping me from."

"That may be, sunshine. But the hair? Slept-in bed waves, I believe we called it." He reached out and fluffed it some. "That wasn't for the meeting, and it's a game changer. Well played." His tone was a mix of surprise and respect. "Now, when you go back in there, make sure you're a little breathless." His thumb ran along her lower lip, smudging her lipstick, and she felt her pulse skyrocket. "Yeah, just like that."

"Like what?" she heard herself whisper.

"Like you're interested."

A flash went off behind them, someone's camera phone clicking away. Not that Adam seemed to care. With a wink that had her toes curling, he sauntered off toward the engine parked at the curb, his swagger proving rule number one: being comfortable in your own skin was the key to sexual allure. And Adam didn't just feel comfortable, he owned it.

Harper stood in silence, her heart thudding against her sternum as she took in a deep breath. Then ten more to be sure she didn't look as if she were interested.

Which she so wasn't.

"Hidden depths my ass," she mumbled as she watched him drive away. The man was as shallow as a puddle in the summer. Not that this should have surprised her.

St. Helena's notorious playboy made no apologies, no promises, and no excuses for his frat-boy take on life. Women knew it. Men knew it. The whole town knew it. It was only Harper, and her see-the-good-in-everyone outlook, who had forgotten.

Harper turned to walk into the shop and nearly bumped into Chantel, who had come out to watch Adam parade his ego and engine down Main Street. And she wasn't alone in the gawking. A half dozen other women remained crowded around the doorway as well, hollering for Adam to demo his hose for their followers on Facebook. Including Clovis.

Ignoring the crowd, the snapping cameras, and her grandma's catcalls, Harper smoothed down the skirt of her dress and addressed Chantel. "Sorry about that. He was just looking for his jacket."

"His jacket," Chantel said loudly enough to be heard in New Zealand. She took in Harper's newly tossed hair and lips and laughed. "That Honeysuckle must be one hot piece if he's driving up on that engine just to get a peek."

"What?" Harper asked, then saw the amused twinkle in Chantel's eye. "Oh, no, Adam and I were just—"

"Looking for his jacket?" she said again with the laugh. "Look, I have to be honest, I came here to let you know that we're looking to place our merchandise in stores that are trending, that speak to a younger, edgier woman. Our core customer is bold and driven, a trendsetter with a sensual side who's dominating the boardroom and looking to dominate the bedroom"—Chantel pointed to the fire engine pulling down Main Street—"with a man like that."

"Like Adam?"

"Well, not Adam specifically, but tall, built, all-American alpha males who wear testosterone and sex appeal like cologne. The fireman's hat is a bonus." Chantel leaned closer. "I shouldn't be saying this, but Lulu Allure is getting ready to announce a new male line called Swagger. It will complement our new Flirt line for the fall and, unfortunately, with such a limited release and a huge marketing push, we're looking for boutiques that can not only guarantee sell-through, but also generate buzz within the millennial generation. Which was why I was supposed to tell you that we're no longer able to have you on as our Bay Area retailer."

Harper's heart swelled and hope beaded. "*Supposed* to tell me?" As in she wasn't going to renegotiate Clovis right out of business?

"I still am."

"Oh."

"But . . ." Chantel took Harper by the arm and turned her to face the new display. "If you give your catalog the same fresh and flirty feel as you did with this display and the private party room, then find a way to convince my boss that men like *him* are your clientele, I might be able to convince her to reconsider."

"How would I do that?"

"You appear to be a multifaceted artist," Chantel said. "Your grandma showed me the charity calendar you shot with the local first responders."

"Cuties with Booties?" Harper asked, referring to the charity calendar she'd helped create for her friend Shay. It had local heroes showing off their guns posing with adorable rescue dogs in need to help place them in Napa County.

"Real men, taking on real problems, while looking real hot?" Chantel's eyes went wide with excitement. "Golden idea, and I heard it went viral."

It had done more than go viral. Shay's calendar had turned the men of St. Helena into sex-lebrities. Not to mention, it raised enough money for Shay to open her dream rescue center in town and helped place a record number of strays with their forever families.

The photos had become so popular—and effective—every month Harper shot a new set of hot heroes with homeless animals for Shay's blog, and the Cuties with Booties calendar was in its third year.

"Getting the guys to volunteer for a good cause with their shirts off is one thing, but posing in underwear?"

"Well, when Adam comes home tonight, make sure you're serving dinner in nothing but those heels and Honeysuckle. Then when he's ready to play *find the jacket*, ask him if he'd be willing to do a little modeling of his own. In our underwear."

Harper looked around at the crowd of ladies who were feigning interest in the new flowers Harper had planted in the window boxes, and lowered her voice. "You only want Adam to model. In skivvies?" Harper could almost see the amused look on Adam's face when she asked him.

Then her heart sank at the implications and gave a familiar twinge at the idea that she wasn't sexy enough, her star bright enough, her ideas alluring enough. The sad truth was Chantel thought that Harper, on her own, wasn't enough. And that made her replaceable.

A role she was tired of being cast in.

Mistaking her irritation for concern, Chantel added, "Nothing formal, just a few shots of your guy in Swagger to use in a mock campaign for social media or a sample catalog layout. Something Boulder Holder could use to promote our line. Oh, can you capture that same rugged, everyday-hero feel like in the calendar, so I could show it to the marketing team?"

The correct answer was no.

No, Adam was not her *guy*. No, she wouldn't boost his ego by shooting him in his briefs. And no, she definitely did not get a secret thrill at the idea of someone mistaking Adam as her boyfriend.

Unfortunately, there were two things more important than thrills and ego that Harper could never say no to. Ever.

Her grandmother. And a noble cause.

That this was her grandmother's noble cause was the only reason Harper leaned in and whispered, "As long as it's informal, I don't think Adam would have a problem."

After all, he had offered to help. Right after he'd stolen her spotlight.

"Beat the Heat Festival?" Adam asked, his right eye twitching as he looked down at the list of responsibilities that were outlined in the binder—a three-inch binder filled with color-coded tabs, approved vendors, and a phone tree like it was created before the invention of the Internet and e-mail. "No way. I'm a firefighter, not an event planner."

"Have you seen the dent?" Captain Roman Brady sat back in his chair, his feet plopped up on the desk, one ankle crossed over the other, looking for all the world as though this wasn't a big deal. "When Lowen found out it was from a bunch of tampons, he about shit a brick. So when his recommendation was something other than firing you, I agreed. You should be thanking me."

Adam wanted to punch that smile off Roman's smug face, but at the station Roman was his superior, and Adam would always honor that. Come Saturday, when they were boxing at the gym, he'd hand him his ass because Beat the Heat wasn't just a day, it was a destination.

The annual picnic had started out as a laid-back afternoon of fun and games designed to promote fire awareness and prevention. But because it was held in a town that loved its community events, over the years it had morphed into one of the most anticipated weekends of summer. The picnic raised funds for the station's Back-to-School

Pack project, which provided kids with the right shoes, supplies, and books they needed to be successful in school. It was a great pay-it-forward project, allowed firefighters to connect with residents, and was a gigantic headache for the person tasked with its planning.

"I guess all that's left to say is congratulations, Baudouin. You're the official go-to guy for all things Beat the Heat."

"Come on, man." Adam cupped the bill of his SHFD hat with both hands and pulled it low on his head.

He didn't want to do this. It was a responsibility usually tasked to someone's wife or a rookie, not a senior member of the crew. "Give it to Daugherty. His wife loves all that Martha Stewart stuff."

"Daugherty's wife is pregnant, which is why we are short a planner. Plus, you're more connected than Martha and have more game than the entire NBA." Roman snapped his fingers. "Your family owns half the vines in this county. Hell, just a bottle of your sister's wine could raffle off for as much as a thousand bucks."

"I'll call Frankie about the wine," he said, knowing that when it came to his baby sister, it could cost him. Big-time. "But I'm not a party planner."

"You have to have some kind of planner in your phone. Call them."

A hot blonde with big blue eyes and an even bigger rack popped in his head. "Megan," Adam said, clapping his hands. "She would be perfect."

Megan was cute, had a hot little bod, and loved to party—which worked well since she was the senior event planner over at Parties to Go-Go. She and Adam had done a little flirting on New Year's Eve, and a little more after the ball dropped, but she'd been called away for a party emergency before they could get better acquainted. She had apologized, given him her private number, and told him to call—*anytime*.

Maybe now was that time. A chance to be in "it's go time" proximity with Megan for three fun-filled weeks was a tempting prospect—a prospect that should have had him smiling. Only instead he heard himself say, "Give the event to Seth and McGuire. They can share the duty and bond or some shit."

"No can do." Roman rested his folded hands behind his head. "The caterer is already on board, the date is cleared through the city, and the booth preregistration forms have already gone out. Now we just need someone to oversee the event. And Lowen wants the *someone* who dented his engine. So unless you want me to explain to the chief how you couldn't have been driving the engine since you weren't even at the station when the accident happened—"

"Nope."

This was not how he'd envisioned spending his morning, sitting in the captain's office, getting reprimanded for a mistake he'd fessed up to but hadn't committed. Lowen had chewed Adam's head off in front of his entire crew, threatening disciplinary action in the form of a letter to add to the colorful collection already in his file. And unless the chief was talking about an attaboy letter, which the pulsing vein in his temple had implied no, then it would sink Adam's chances of lieutenant.

Roman was right—planning some picnic would be a lot easier than finding a new career. The dent was pretty massive, Seth hadn't taken a step out of line since, and Adam's file wasn't going to get any larger. All in all, it had worked out.

"Didn't expect you would," Roman said with a smile. "Seth will make a good addition. The kid has good instincts."

"When he starts thinking with the right head."

"As the expert in that field, can you let me know when that's supposed to start? Because I've been waiting for that to happen for years." Roman pushed the screen of his laptop with his foot until it swiveled so Adam could see it. "Take this, for example. After the week-long course Lowen put us through on the appropriate and inappropriate use of social media with regards to the house, some jackass let his girl put this up on Facebook."

Roman didn't say anything else. He didn't have to. Adam could tell, even before he peeked at the photo, that he was the jackass in question. Which made no sense since he was girl-less. Then he looked at the screen, and looked hard.

His stomach did a vertical drop straight to the floor.

On his Facebook timeline, right there for the world to see—okay, so his world of 3,287 friends—was a picture of Baby in heels, a floral-patterned G-string, and . . . his missing jacket.

Not that anyone could tell it was Baby, since the selfie was taken from over her shoulder into the dressing-room mirror. To him, though, the platinum ponytail and neon flower-studded floss were a dead giveaway.

"Ah hell," Adam said, fishing his phone out of his pocket and swiping the Facebook app. "My jacket. I didn't let her wear it. I forgot it, and she must have tried it on." He'd been too distracted by that kiss with Little Miss Sunshine to remember to grab it.

"That's some fitting," Roman said, not knowing Adam had missed the show.

"Yeah, I'll take care of it." He gave a few more swipes. "And the picture is already down."

"Make sure it stays down. I would hate for her to post it anywhere else." Roman dropped his feet to the ground and leaned in. "The last thing you need right now is more of the wrong kind of attention. Especially from Lowen."

"I know."

"Do you? Because sometimes I wonder. I mean, I get that you had a rough start with Lowen, made a punk move, and got caught." *In the utility closet, pants down, with Lowen's goddaughter* went unsaid. "But you have worked hard to prove yourself."

Now he had to work hard to overcome his reputation. Many of the stories were pure fiction, and the ones that were true had been embellished over time. Once word had spread about Adam and the chief's goddaughter, and that he had somehow managed to keep his job, he'd become some mythical, urban legend among firefighters.

Adam wasn't looking to point fingers or lay blame. He was as much a part of the problem as anyone. He'd never clarified fact from fiction, and he didn't mind looking like a playboy. Adam was good with women, and they were good to him—because he followed the three A's to dating: always treat women with respect, always make sure they have a good time, and always, *always*, make sure everyone is on the same page—meaning nothing deeper than a night or two. Which didn't exactly scream the kind of commitment and leadership Napa County FD was looking for.

"You are so close, I'd hate to see you mess this up," Roman said, and Adam agreed. He loved his job, but he also wanted to move up the ranks. Be a leader. "They can look past stupid choices made by a stupid kid, but becoming a lieutenant is serious and competitive. And you know damn well Lowen has it out for you. So if lieutenant is still what you want—"

"It is." More than anything, Adam wanted this promotion. He wanted to become the kind of man who didn't make snap decisions, but had the control to think things through and explore every possible outcome before acting.

"Good, then don't give him another reason to pass. Just like California's fire season starts in January and lasts through December, you might work four on and three off, but if the day ends in Y, Lowen is watching you. And he is looking for a leader, not the guy who jumps without looking and gets caught with his pants down in the equipment closet."

"*My* pants weren't down."

Roman lifted a brow and, okay, so hers were. "You took the lieutenant's exam two years ago, Baudouin. You got one of the highest scores in the county, and yet you're still in the same place. Do you ever wonder why that is?"

Every damn day.

Adam had done everything right. Took all the classes, aced the exam, worked more special ops teams than even his superiors, and yet he'd watched other guys climb the ranks while he remained a senior engineer. "Not my time yet, I guess."

"Not your time?" Roman's voice went serious. Dead serious. "Or there hasn't been enough time since Trent?"

It was like a vise clamped on and tightened around his chest at the sound of his friend's name. It was accompanied by the all too familiar burn of guilt. "Trent has nothing to do with me getting promoted or not."

"Really?" Roman sat back. "Because every time you get close to a promotion you do something stupid, almost like you're challenging the universe to see if it's okay to get on with your life."

"You don't move on from something like that."

Roman blew out a breath. "No, you don't. But you also can't let his death stop you from living yours. You're one of the best, Adam. You make solid choices when it counts and crap ones when you're off the clock, like you're giving the department just enough reason to hesitate."

Was that what he was doing? Adam hoped to hell not. He'd busted his ass to become a better firefighter, to assess a situation in seconds with the highest probability of success—to be the kind of firefighter Trent would have been. Then Adam thought about all the stupid pranks he'd pulled, the way he'd lived his life, and knew he wasn't anywhere near the man Trent would have become. "Maybe they have reason to hesitate."

"You act like I wasn't there," Roman said quietly. "Like I wouldn't have made the same exact call."

"But you didn't." Adam had. And even after a decade of playing it over in his mind, reevaluating every possible outcome, forward and backward until they were tattooed to the inside of his eyelids, he still couldn't say with certainty what the hell had gone wrong. One minute they were in control of the fire, the next the wind turned and the blaze swallowed them whole.

"Had I been working on logic instead of raw adrenaline, I would have pulled back to the line the second the smoke shifted."

"We were young, all gung ho and hopped up on FNG invincibility, pretending we weren't scared as shit. And we all made that decision, Adam. So you don't have exclusive rights to carry the guilt."

"I was the senior guy there," Adam bit off.

"By nine months."

Adam gritted his teeth to keep from arguing. Nine months, nine years—it didn't matter. When communication was cut with incident command, the choice to pull back or not fell to Adam. He'd made the wrong one.

In their line of work, courage was as necessary as water. But a good firefighter had a healthy dose of fear when it came to fire. Fear caused them to slow down, think through the situation, and give them time to let their training kick in.

Training that would have noticed the telltale sign of the fire pushing the air up. Training that could have ensured that one of the best firefighters and friends Adam had ever had would still be there.

Giving me shit about kissing the hometown sweetheart, he silently added, knowing Trent was probably in heaven shaking his head right then thanking Jesus, Gandhi, Babe Ruth, and anyone else who would listen that his buddy had hooked up with a crazy cutie.

"You want to know why I'm here and you're still there? Because I didn't let Trent's death overshadow my life," Roman said, making sure Adam knew they weren't just talking about his position in the department.

"I let it fuel me to be better, make smarter choices, grow up. Then I worked my way into a position to where, if I got cut off from incident command, I'd know, without a doubt, what to do. And I didn't wait for the department to move me up to captain—I proved to them I was ready. That I had what it took to go from lieutenant to captain to chief and beyond."

"Because you're the real deal," Adam said. Roman was as skilled, methodical, and honorable as they came. He never hesitated and never missed important facts, even in the middle of a hell-blazer. He was captain for a reason.

"So are you. You're just too busy jumping from one hot spot to the next to prove it."

And wasn't that the heart of the problem? By design, Adam was moving so fast he didn't have time to think—about anything. Which had worked for him in the past, since thinking led to feelings and events he didn't want to revisit. But maybe Roman was right, and his methods were also keeping him from moving forward.

Suddenly, he felt as if he'd spent most of his life running only to find himself in the same place. And if he wanted to make a difference, he needed to focus and show them he was serious. About his career—and his life. If he wanted to be a lieutenant, he didn't just have to prove he was ready for the job.

He had to prove he *was* the job.

chapter
six

St. Helena had three truths Harper could always count on.
Keeping a secret was as realistic as winning the lottery without
a ticket. The only person who benefited from lying was the liar—
until they got caught. And when you challenged the first two, the
only thing left to do was eat your weight in cookies.

Not that Harper had lied to Chantel about dating Adam—it
was more of a half truth. She and Adam *had* gotten hot and heavy.
Once. But it was still a cookies-needed kind of week.

Only yesterday, her favorite confection connection, the Sweet and
Savory, had been closed when she'd walked by for her morning cookie
fix. It was the first sign of impending doom. Then last night, Father
Giuseppe stopped by the Fashion Flower to pick up the donation box
for the family outreach program. Even after telling herself he was just
there for the clothes, and not her repentance, Harper had handed over
the box, her brand-new iPod, and every cent in her purse.

Then promised to see him Sunday in church.

Today, she opened a box of early-readers books that had been
delivered, and on top, staring up at her in big, vintage, circa-1970s

yellow letters was *The Berenstain Bears and the Truth*. The same book her grandmother had given her that first summer Harper had moved in. She had just turned nine, was heartbroken over her mom missing her birthday party, and devastated to learn Gloria wasn't coming back. So when the neighbor kids had asked where her mom was, she'd lied and said she was "filming a movie in Paris with Johnny Depp."

To be fair, Gloria had been dating a guy named Johnny at the time who was the director of a small production of *Oklahoma* in Paris—Missouri. And it had sounded more exciting than the truth: her mother hadn't loved her enough to stay.

Harper slapped the box lid closed and shoved the books under the counter, then busied herself with organizing the antique lace bibs on the front display.

The Fashion Flower was the one-stop shop for everything kids and crafty in wine country. The high-end kids' clothing appealed to the fashion-forward mommy, while the one-of-a-kind handcrafted styles allowed even the smallest of wallflowers to feel unique.

For Harper, though, this shop was about more than popsicle-stick ornaments and kiddie couture. She had done her best to create a space that inspired adventure and imagination, and encouraged children to explore their identity. To make bold choices.

Harper had been bold with Chantel, promising something she had no idea how to deliver. Then she'd gone and made it worse by lying.

"Lying is much harder to keep track of than the truth," she mumbled, repeating what she told her students.

Telling herself it wasn't a lie, just an omission of truth—because that sounded so much better—she stacked the lavender bibs on the top shelf. She was reaching for the poppy-colored ones when the bell on the door jingled and in walked her first customer of the day.

"Welcome to the Fashion Flower," Harper chimed in her sunniest voice. "We have lots blooming today."

Harper looked up and her stomach took a dive-bomb.

Francesca DeLuca, formerly Frankie Baudouin—as in Adam's sister—stood in the doorway. She wore black combat boots, black jeans, and a black tank top that said I BUST MINE SO I CAN KICK YOURS across the front. She also had a fuzzy alpaca on a leash.

"You got any of those Monkey Munchkin teething toys?"

"They're in the baby boutique section."

"Thanks," Frankie said as she and the alpaca located them in seconds. She cleaned out every single ring and headed to the cash register, dropping a dozen of them on the counter.

"Didn't you buy a case of these last month?" Harper asked, ringing up the order.

"Yeah, but Blanket here goes through them when he's stressed." Frankie took one of the rings out of the packet and gave it to Blanket. "Don't you, boy?"

Rump wagging with glee, Blanket took the teething ring with his big horse teeth and rolled it around in his mouth. A low hum filled the room.

"You should ask Peggy at the Paws and Claws Day Spa if she has a chew toy he can't eat through." Harper rang up the last one and put them in a decorated paper bag, then tied the handles with a big blue bow.

"Why would I do that?"

"Because Peggy sells those indestructible dog toys."

"Blanket isn't a dog," Frankie corrected. And her eyes? They skewered. "And he's only going through so many rings because his daddy and I have been hoping for another and he's been feeling left out."

"You're getting another alpaca?" Harper asked because Frankie already had three. Blanket and his alpaca family lived in a custom-made habitat, which was spitting distance from Frankie and Nate's place. Complete with bedrooms, a splashing pool, and a reading loft, it was bigger than Harper's apartment.

"No," Frankie said as if questioning *Harper's* sanity. "Nate and I are trying for a . . ." She mouthed *baby* and pointed at her flat belly.

"Oh my God." Harper clapped her hands. "You're going to have a baby?"

"What part of me not saying the word in front of Blanket did you miss?" Frankie threw a few bills on the table. "And yes, that's the plan. The universe just needs to catch up." Frankie put her hands over Blanket's ears and, even though his humming had grown to white noise, she lowered her voice. "We've been trying since last fall. And, don't get me wrong, the trying is fun—Nate makes everything fun—but I want to get to the next part."

Harper's heart went out to the couple. It might have seemed like everyone was pregnant lately, but she'd met so many women since working at the Fashion Flower who'd struggled with getting pregnant on a timeline. It was frustrating and stressful and Harper could tell that Frankie didn't need someone else telling her things like "It will come in its own time" or "Everything happens for a reason." That would only dismiss her fears.

Whether she'd been trying for ten months or ten years, her fear was real.

Harper knew what it was like to want a family, and what it was like to be unable to create one. She didn't know how to make Frankie's problem disappear, but she did know something that might help.

Grabbing a copy of *What to Expect Before You're Expecting* off the shelf, she handed it to Frankie. "A lot of my clients who wanted to speed things up swear by this book."

Frankie flipped through the book and went straight to the index. "Is there a chapter on Pop-Tarts?"

"Pop-Tarts?"

"Yeah, when Blanket's mom was pregnant, the vet told me to stop feeding her Pop-Tarts, something about the food coloring being enemy numero uno." Frankie looked up at Harper. "I've been eating Pop-Tarts. Do you think that's the problem?"

"I don't know, I'm not a doctor, but I've never heard anything about Pop-Tarts and conceiving." This seemed to soothe the woman. "But I have heard that tossing out the ovulation calendar and getting away from all the pressures of life works wonders."

"There has been a lot of pressure. The second our families found out we were trying, it was like open season on the baby questions."

"Then give this a try," Harper said. "Take a spontaneous trip up the coast. No pressure, no stress, no expectations, and no family. Just you and Nate letting nature work her magic."

Frankie closed the book and rubbed Blanket's head. "I'd need to find a sitter."

"I'm allergic," Harper said in case rumors of her sitting career had spread.

"Bummer. How much do I owe you for the book?"

Harper held up a hand and, whether it was because she felt for Frankie, or because she'd secretly kissed her brother then alluded to him being her boyfriend, she said, "On the house."

Frankie rested her elbows on the counter, getting nose-to-nose with Harper. "You might want to check that whole deer-in-the-headlights thing you have going on. It makes you look guilty. Like you're hiding something. That's just some advice"—she winked and grabbed the bag—"on the house."

It was Adam's first day off this week. Normally, he'd stay in bed until noon, tangled up with a warm and sexy woman, then go for a run and grab a breakfast burrito for lunch.

Only *normal* had taken a hike right around the time he'd been drafted into planning Beat the Heat. Or maybe the problem had started with that dress. The slinky, body-hugging red one. Either way, Adam had woken up at the ass crack of dawn, frustrated and alone—and thinking about that dress. Which was almost as stupid as thinking about what was beneath that dress, because fantasizing about Little Miss Sunshine was a bad idea.

So he'd gone for a hard run until his legs were shaking and his mind was blank, and now he was in town. The breakfast burrito and a woman in his immediate future. Too bad the woman was wielding a knife and shooting him looks that were anything but warm.

The knife made sense. Emerson wasn't only his brother's fiancée, she was also founder, owner, and executive chef of the Pita Peddler Streatery, an award-winning gourmet food truck. The scowl shouldn't have surprised him either, since she rarely smiled at anyone before noon—unless it was at Adam's youngest brother, Dax.

"Sorry, that weekend doesn't work for me," Emerson said, not sorry at all.

Taking a breath, Adam glanced at Dax, who was standing at the prep station fashioning napkin rings out of twine and daisies in his deputy's uniform and apron, using every bro-sign in the book to tell Adam to get out now, while he still could.

Knife or not, Adam wasn't scared. Plus, bro-code was hard to decipher when the signer in question was dressed like Betty Crocker. "You catered the event last year, Em, and agreed you'd do it again this year."

"Were you there?" she asked. "Did I personally tell you that I would?"

"No, but—"

"Then how do you know what was said?"

Adam looked down Main Street to avoid Emerson's smug glare. The food truck was parked in the middle of downtown today, directly across from the community park and the annual Summer Blossom Showcase banner. Although it was barely eight, the sun was already burning up the asphalt, while Emerson's chilly gaze was freezing his nuts right off.

"What's your problem?" he asked.

"The Five-Alarm Casanova," Emerson said, and the reference to his embarrassing-as-shit nickname caused the pressure behind his eyes to grow.

Three weeks.

If she agreed, he'd have to deal with this BS for three weeks. Then again, if she didn't he'd be screwed.

"You proposed a sample menu." Adam flipped to the catering section of the binder and found the order from last year's event and a preliminary menu for this year. He held it up to the welcome window. "See?"

"See?" Dax repeated, sounding disappointed. "Come on, man, that's your big strategy? To tell a woman she's wrong in her own kitchen?" Dax shook his head. "And to think I used to believe you were really the lady-whisperer."

"Don't get upset, Dax," Adam said, looking at his brother's latest flowered napkin ring. "You might bruise the daisies."

Emerson ignored the sparring and glanced over the counter at the menu, then looked Adam dead in the eyes. "That's a great menu."

Adam felt his chest relax a little. He had a meeting Friday to update Cap and Chief Lowen on his progress. Having a caterer and event planner locked down would give him a gold star. If he played his charm cards right, between Emerson and Megan at Parties to Go-Go, he might just wind up throwing the best Beat the Heat Festival in the history of the event—and not even break a sweat.

Wouldn't that be nice.

"All I need is a great chef." Adam slid one of the two to-go cups he'd set on the stainless steel serving counter toward Emerson. "How about we finalize the menu over breakfast burritos and morning beverages?" When she didn't move to take hers, he added, "Fifty Shades of Chocolate latte. Your favorite."

Lucky for him, nearly every woman in town now had the same favorite when it came to hot beverages. The Fifty Shades of Chocolate latte from the Sweet and Savory bistro was bold, heady, and perfectly whipped for St. Helena's female sector.

"You didn't bring me one?" Dax asked, eyeballing the cups.

And apparently his former Special Forces brother.

"You already traded in your gun and holster for an apron. There would be no coming back from this for you."

"Says the man who carries his deflated hose around town," Emerson said, and Dax smiled—as if Emerson giving him shit took away from Dax wearing an apron. "And you know what I get behind?"

"Driving customers away?" Adam said.

"Supporting my friends." She rested her elbows on the counter and leaned in—so close Adam could see just how narrow her eyes were. "Not delivering them a shit sandwich on a lingerie-covered platter."

"Ah man," Adam said, closing his eyes so he didn't have to watch his brilliant plan explode in front of his face. "It was just a kiss."

"Yeah, well your kiss totally screwed with Harper's week, which screwed with mine."

"Really?" Adam asked, because Harper would have had to feel something a hell of a lot more than *Not interested* if the kiss screwed with her entire week. "Define screwed?"

"Easy. Pissing off the only caterer in town who would cater your party for pennies." Emerson gripped the plastic partition above the window and jerked it down. "Enjoy the latte."

"Mine is straight drip."

Adam grabbed both cups seconds before they would have gone flying and crashing to the ground—like his career if he couldn't get her to open the partition. "Come on, Em." He tapped on the plastic. "I need you."

The partition was flung back up and Emerson's eyes glared out. "Yeah, and I needed Harper to help me prep for the big wine convention last weekend, but she couldn't because she was too busy dealing with your mess."

"I wouldn't call it a mess." He'd call it more of a one-taste-wasn't-enough kind of situation, but certainly not a mess. They were both adults, both enjoyed the moment, both, apparently, were still thinking about it. "In fact, I'm pretty sure I rocked her world."

Emerson furrowed her brow in confusion, then rolled her eyes and reached for the partition again.

"Wait." Adam blocked her from slamming it. "Here's the deal—I have to meet with Chief Lowen Friday, and if I don't have you on board then I'm more than screwed." He might find the occupational ceiling lowered permanently.

"Not my problem," she said, but he could tell he was getting to her. Beneath that ballbuster exterior, his soon-to-be sister-in-law was a softie who couldn't turn her back on someone in need.

And he needed her bad.

"What can I do to change your mind? You name it, I'll do it."

Emerson studied Adam for a long moment, and he smiled his most trustworthy smile, then popped that dimple just in case.

Unimpressed, she looked at Dax, who needed to hand over his man card immediately because he shrugged and cocked his head adoringly. That *I'm behind you one hundred percent, baby* shrug/head cock combo that suckers gave their women after they'd handed over their balls for eternity.

Adam threw up in his mouth a little.

"Are you really sorry?" she asked.

No, Hell no, and *No fucking way* all would have been truthful responses, because kissing Harper had been the most exciting thing

Adam had done in weeks. Months. And he'd just worked one of the worst fires of the season.

Knowing she was fixated on that kiss made it even better. But since none of those would win over Emerson, he said, "From the bottom of my heart."

"Which isn't saying much, but fine. You convince Harper that you're sorry you almost screwed the barely legal coed stripper who stole your jacket and I will reconsider catering the event."

"She was an NFL cheerleader not a stripper, and she's a college graduate, which means she has to be at least twenty-two." He hoped to God she was closer to twenty-eight, because he was closer to thirty-five than fraternity, and saying *twenty-two* out loud made him cringe. "And I didn't give her my jacket. I forgot it at the shop, and she was neighborly enough to hold on to it for me."

"She looked a whole lot more than neighborly on Facebook."

"I took the photo down."

"How noble of you." She put her hand over her heart. "I'm sure it was right after you called Harper to apologize?"

"I did apologize to Harper."

"Did you make it a good one?" she asked, and Adam had to think really hard about that. He'd been so distracted by talk of Honeysuckle and her in that red dress that he wasn't sure. "You better have, because we both know that giving up on someone, even when they deserve it, totally screws with that whole *save the world* mantra Harper subscribes to."

Ah, Jesus. He sighed, feeling like a grade-A douche bag. Because *he* was the someone in question.

"Yeah, she spent the entire weekend picking up the pieces, balancing her own job while filling in for the fired coed," Emerson said.

"I didn't know Baby wasn't supposed to have guests in after closing," Adam said, knowing it was a lame excuse. "But I should have."

That he'd added to her stress by crashing her meeting with the rep made him a bastard. Wasn't this exactly the kind of behavior Roman had warned him about? Acting without a care about the repercussions?

It also explained why Harper had been so hostile.

"Don't sweat it, bro," Dax said, smiling. "Harper helped Baby land her dream job down the street. Pole dancing or something."

"Pole dancing?" Adam felt the panic rise up. He knew Baby had found a new job, he just didn't know what it was. Sweat beaded his brow and his right eye twitched with disbelief. "Please tell me that isn't some fancy wine-country talk for stripping."

Could this get any worse?

"Lucky for you, pole dancing is the number one way to stay in shape for the ladies of St. Helena," Emerson said. "The *senior* ladies. Baby teaches classes at a dance school down the street. Unlucky for you is you're still out a chef."

Knowing he needed to make this right, Adam stepped back. "If I make things right with Harper, can I tell Chief Lowen you are on board?"

"Only because I'm marrying your brother and I don't want it to be weird at the wedding. And if I didn't pull out the fire extinguisher when your career was going down in a ball of flames, it would make it weird," she said. "But if Harper isn't cool with it, then you are SOL."

"Not a problem." He knew exactly how to sweet-talk a woman. "Now how about one of your famous breakfast burritos to go?"

This time the partition shut and locked, almost drowning out the sound of Adam's stomach growling. Thankful he still had his nuts intact, and that Emerson's chilly personality hadn't frozen them off, he made his way across Main Street toward Parties to Go-Go. He needed to talk to Harper, but first he had a party planner to secure.

Charm amped to full, he pushed through the doors and was hit by the scent of latex balloons, varnish, and lavender candles.

Megan stood on a step stool hanging brightly colored lanterns from the ceiling. She wore a crop top that crept higher with every lantern hung, painted-on jeans, and a yoga-sculpted ass that promised to clear his mind of all things sunshine.

The door closed behind him, the bells jingling in his wake. At this, Megan attached the last lantern and turned to face him, a welcoming smile on her face. Recognition lit her eyes and her smile grew—uncomfortably big.

"Adam," she said, hopping down off the step stool and swaying her way toward him. "What are you doing here?"

"You said I should call." He leaned a hip against the counter. "*Anytime*, I believe was your phrasing, but then I couldn't have brought you this." He held up her latte. "It's from next door."

"That is so sweet." She leaned over to sniff the steam. And groaned in ecstasy. "Fifty Shades of Chocolate? My favorite."

"I know," he said, kicking that Baudouin grin up a few notches. "Which is why I made it a large."

She didn't say thank you, didn't acknowledge that *anytime* worked in today's agenda, didn't reach for the cup—or him. Instead she sat poised behind the counter. And that weird vibe Emerson was giving off was in full effect here too.

"So what can I do for you?" Although there was genuine warmth to her voice, there wasn't the usual heat-laced undertones he was used to with women.

"I'm looking to throw a party and am in need of a partner."

"We already had our party," she reminded him sweetly, and images of New Year's popped into his mind.

"That was more of a pre-party," he clarified. "But I was hoping you could help me with this." He set both cups on the counter and held up the binder.

"Beat the Heat isn't just a party, it's *the* party of the summer," she said, taking the binder.

Every page she flipped relieved some of the weight Adam had been carrying. He'd flipped through those same pages over a dozen times and was no closer to figuring out how to plan something of this magnitude than when Roman had drafted him. But Megan, flirty and sexy Megan, looked as if she understood everything and knew exactly what steps needed to be taken.

"Are you planning it?"

"Long story short, yeah," he sighed. "And I need your help."

"I helped plan Beat the Heat a few years back, when I was first getting started, and gained a lot of new clients from it."

He rested his elbows on the counter, slid the latte a little closer. "Think of how much more you'll gain planning it with me."

He winked.

She looked at the cup as though it were common drip from the convenience store.

Adam tapped his cup to hers and gifted her with his best *Mr. July* grin—and waited.

It took longer than expected, but he knew the second he had her. Two cute pink spots appeared on her cheeks and she placed her hand around the cup, batting those long lashes his way. Then she— slid it back toward him?

"This is weird, right?" she said in a hushed tone. "The coffee, you here, wanting to plan this event with me?"

"I don't think so," Adam said, not sure if she was mad that he hadn't taken her up on her *anytime* offer sooner. Or maybe something in the air was making women weird-sensitive. "It's great exposure for you, and you would be helping me out big-time. That's what friends do, right?"

She looked around the store, and even though it was empty she lowered her voice. "We're more of *friends waiting for something to happen.*"

"Is that a problem?" When she looked as if, yeah, it was a big freaking problem, he changed tactics. "This is a real job offer, Megan. One that comes with a paycheck. Not a big one—it's probably what you received last time—but a legit check."

"I want to help you out. I do. But you know how people talk in this town." She rolled her eyes, then went serious. Dead serious. "I mean, that new pole dancing teacher just wore your jacket to class and all the biddies at the studio were sending her the stink eye. Not that I ever would have shipped you two."

"Shipped?" he asked, because obviously this was one of those Mars versus Venus moments—and he didn't even want to think about that jacket.

"You know *ship*, short for relationships, couples to get behind," she said, as if that clarified things. "At first, when I heard whispers about Hadam, I didn't get it—"

"Hadam?"

"Your ship name," Megan said, clearly unaware that Adam's understanding of this conversation was out to sea. "I mean you two are so different. Like never happen in a million years with you being strictly a friends-with-benefits kind of guy. A total BBD," Megan said, and it didn't sound like a compliment.

"BBD?"

"Bigger better deal, always looking for the next thing."

Wow, was that how people saw him? As a guy who was unable to focus on something long enough to see it through to the end? Because if that was the case, then he had a whole lot more to prove than being lieutenant quality.

"And she's that all around awesome, super sweet, best friend who guys want to marry," she said, and Adam choked at the last word. "So I, like everyone else by the way, thought there was no way it would work, but then I read on Facebook this morning about the whole 'Hadam at hello' and I have to admit"—she reached across the counter and patted his hand, as if he were her gay best friend—"I'm totally Team Hadam."

"Who the hell is Hadam?"

"Harper"—she held up one hand, then the other—"and Adam." Then she married her fingers together and smiled. "Hadam."

Adam felt the floor shift.

"Me and, um—" His windpipe collapsed and choking didn't even cover the sensation.

"Harper," Megan said in awe, as if she were talking about unicorns, Mother Teresa, and her favorite sorority sisters all wrapped up in one sunny package. Then she patted his hand. Again. "She is the sweetest. When my brother-in-law walked out, Harper stopped charging my sister for her kids' art classes until she was back on her feet. She also helped me land my first client when I started working here, and never asked for anything in return. She's just . . ."

"Awesome?" Adam deadpanned.

"Totally. I can see why you'd fall for her. It doesn't get BBD than Harper."

Adam wanted to ask if Harper gave birth to Jesus as well. And what the hell? He hadn't fallen, and that kiss—although surprisingly hot—didn't constitute a ship name. Not in his world anyway. But Megan wasn't done.

"And since you and I, um, *partied* a little . . ." She threw up air quotes around the word and grimaced. *Grimaced!* "Well, working together now would just be weird, you know?"

No, Adam didn't know. Because women didn't grimace when recalling their time with him. And nothing about his parties were ever little. Pre-party or not, he was a closer. A fact he wanted to point out, except Megan was already closing the binder.

"Good luck with Beat the Heat," she said. "Oh, and you should get your jacket back. Harper's too sweet to be the crazy jealous type, but people are talking and it's a total douche move."

"Douche move?"

Placing the two cups in his hand and the binder under his arm, Megan ushered him to the door. "Tell Harper I said hi!"

The door slammed behind him, leaving Adam with no caterer, no planner, and no one to drink his Fifty Shades of Chocolate.

However, he had a few choice words to tell Harper. The first one was a heartfelt sorry for screwing up her week. The second would be exactly where she could stick all of her sunshine. Adam wasn't the only one with some explaining to do.

He might have messed with her week, but she'd destroyed his game.

chapter
seven

Later that day, Harper moved carefully through the rows of easels, taking the time to study each and every student's Picasso-inspired self-portrait. Some had crowns, others had capes and laser guns, but all of them told a unique story.

It was why she loved art so much. Almost as much as she loved her pint-sized artists. Each and every one of them touched her heart—even the challenging ones. Especially the challenging ones. They usually had the most important stories to share, but were often overlooked.

Not by Harper. She glanced around the Fashion Flower, at the bright and expressive clothes cheerfully displayed, then to the Budding Artists Gallery that filled the shop's windows, and a sense of pride welled up.

She understood that every superhero smock worn and finger-painted canvas made was a purposeful statement that her little customers were too young to put into words. It was important that their art was seen and appreciated—that the *children* felt seen and appreciated.

Harper was well aware of the connection between her job and her personal life. Growing up with an actress for a mother, who was happiest when center stage, and being overshadowed by her had become a way of life. No matter how boldly she behaved or dressed, Harper had never managed to find her own spotlight.

Something she was determined to change.

The shop door opened and in blew a warm gust of summer air—and her second chance. Clay was no longer in the dark suit and tie he'd been wearing when he'd returned home from San Diego a few hours ago. It seemed Dr. *GQ* had shed his professional attire for something more date-like—dark jeans, blue button-up, and a to-go bag from the Sweet and Savory bistro—too big for a party of one, but not big enough to be leftovers.

"Hey," she said, walking over to meet him, happy she'd worn her favorite dress. It wasn't red, but it was a bold teal and bohemian, and it made her butt look amazing. Not that he was looking at her butt right then, but if he did she knew it would look its best.

He smiled and then the most wonderful thing happened. He leaned in and kissed her. Not on the mouth, but on the cheek. A sweet and charming greeting that felt safe and warm—and encouraging.

"Am I interrupting?" Clay asked quietly, taking in the ten sets of eyes curiously aimed in their direction.

"Eyes on your own canvas, I'll be right back," Harper said, and after some disappointed grumbling, paintbrushes were moving again. She slipped off her smock that read FLOWER POWER, in case Clay wanted a better view, and ushered him outside. "They should be fine for a few minutes."

"As long as they know you can see them, you mean," Clay said, and Harper had to laugh.

"Yup, as soon as I turn my back, paint will fly."

"If Tommy is doing a craft, I can't turn my back for even a second without fearing the glue will wind up in his mouth and the house will explode in camo-colored paint bombs."

"Tommy's a smart kid with a big imagination, and he's very talented," she said, knowing it must be hard to keep up with a kid as high-energy as Tommy. "And you're a good dad for indulging him."

"Thanks. Being a single parent wasn't how I imagined this all going, and this last year has been rough, but I finally feel like I'm getting a handle on things. San Diego got me thinking that I should find a way to carve out some time for myself again. Like you said. Maybe even get back out there and start meeting people like—"

People like me? Harper wanted to ask, because when Clay had returned from his trip earlier that day, she may have only imagined the way he'd looked at her when he'd seen her in his bed watching cartoons, but she wasn't imagining how he was looking at her now. As if he wanted to kiss her.

But a squeal erupted from inside, and Harper turned to find two students mixing all of the colors into one.

"You'd better handle that."

"Yeah." Harper stuck her head in the door. "William. Violet. What are the rules when we use acrylics?"

Both kids stopped to look at her, then their hands went behind their backs. Too bad their brushes were dripping paint all over the floor.

"No mixing," Violet said innocently.

"Then what are you doing at the supply table?"

"Mixing black paint," William said. Violet held up her brush and smiled in agreement.

"You both have black paint"—she lifted a brow—"at your easels. Which is where you should be standing."

"Yes, Miss H," they said in unison, then moped back to their respective places.

Harper closed the door. "Sorry about that."

"Not a problem." Clay laughed, a warm and understanding laugh, and she felt everything inside her go soft. Clay understood kids, understood her job. Being a single dad made him the perfect match for her. Yet she didn't feel any tingles today. "I came by to say thanks for watching Tommy today. He really had a great time."

"I did too. Tommy's a great kid and we had fun."

"Which is why I wanted to give you this." He held up the bag and smiled. "I asked around and found out that you have a sweet tooth. And since you've been so slammed, I wanted to indulge *you* a little, for saving my hide."

"I do like sweets. A lot."

Blaming the lack of tingles on stress and knowing it was now or never, Harper licked her lips to bring Clay's attention there, then thought of a sexy scene from a book she'd just read and flicked her hair. Because, according to rule six in creating lasting appeal, feeling sexy makes one appear sexy—and with being covered in finger paint and glitter glue, Harper needed a little help in the allure department.

She wanted Clay to see her as more than a friend who was good with his son. She wanted him to see her as a sexual being who would be good in his bed.

Lowering her voice, she leaned in and rested a hand on his arm, making sure her head was tilted in case he wanted to aim that cheek-kiss somewhere more central. "You know what else I like a lot?"

Clay shook his head.

"When it's a little dirty?" a voice cut in.

Before Harper could respond, she was spun around and two full lips crashed down on hers. Hard and demanding and with enough irritated male to have her staggering back. Because it wasn't Clay cashing in on those benefits she was so eager to dole out—it was her very own kissing bandit there to steal more smooches.

Smooches meant for Clay.

Harper pushed back, surprised to discover just how many packs Adam had under his shirt. A twelve-pack for sure.

"What was that?" she demanded, wiping her hands across her lips, painfully aware they were tingling.

Dang misfiring tingles.

"Me, missing my girl," Adam said, holding up a to-go bag of his own. He also held the paintbrush that had been holding her curls back, which meant her hair probably looked like an electrocuted Q-tip.

"Your girl?" she asked, a sinking feeling settling in her gut.

"According to Facebook you have some big status change you're dying to announce."

Harper felt her hands start to sweat. There was no way he could know she had a favor to ask. A favor she had been putting off asking because she didn't know what she'd do if he said no. A favor that, if she asked in front of Clay, would make everything awkward.

She looked at Clay's expression of shock and snorted. After that kiss, awkward would be a welcomed state. "It's nothing, really."

"Huh," Adam said. "Aunt Luce has placed ten-to-one odds that it is a ring-required kind of status change. Which is why I thought I'd drop by and let you know I'm a size fifteen." He wiggled a brow. "Special order."

"You wish," Harper mumbled.

"Ring required?" Clay said, not as horrified as Harper would have liked. In fact, he seemed excited to be chatting with Adam. "I didn't know that you two—"

"We're not," Harper clarified, right as Adam said, "She had me at hello."

Clay's eyes bounced between the two of them like he was watching the final set at Wimbledon. Adam's eyes? They were firmly affixed on Harper's cleavage.

"One look at her Parisian peek-a-boos and, *pow*, it was like witnessing a goddess being born."

"Parisian peek-a-boos?" Clay asked, his brows folded in on themselves.

"You *peeked* at my Parisian peek-a-boos," Harper clarified.

Adam grinned, wicked and with purpose—and Harper's knees wobbled. "I did a lot more than peek."

"He's kidding." When Adam didn't comment, only twisted one of her loose curls around his finger, she elbowed him in the ribs. "Tell him you're kidding."

"No can do, sunshine. Parisian peek-a-boos are powerful stuff," he said, slinging his arm around Harper's shoulder. "Plus, some girl was seen wearing my jacket and was nearly mobbed. I can't imagine what would happen to anyone who spoke out against Hadam."

Oh God. Harper's stomach constricted—Adam had seen the post. Not wanting to get into it in front of Clay, Harper used her best teacher tone and said, "Cut the bologna. This is about the jacket, isn't it?" Without giving Adam the chance to respond, she turned to Clay. "Can you give us a minute to straighten this out? I promise this is not what it seems."

Clay looked at his watch. "Actually, I have to go. I just wanted to say thanks for babysitting. Enjoy the gift." He handed her the bag. "Nice to see you, man."

"He kind of walks like a girl," Adam said as Clay headed down Main Street toward his car.

"He does not. And what was that? Payback for me interrupting you and Baby?"

He laughed. "No. *That* was nothing like me and Baby. What happened with me and Baby was a gigantic cock block. *That*"—Adam wiggled his fingers in an animated wave as Clay drove by—"was just me interrupting some friendly chitchat."

"That was not friendly chitchat! You totally co—" She looked in the shop's window at the kids, who were looking back, ears peeled. "Well, you know what you did."

He grinned. "Maybe you should explain it to me."

She grabbed a pencil out of her apron and resecured her hair into a messy bun at the back of her head, ignoring the flyaway curls. "Clay was about to ask me out and your kiss was to chase him off."

"He wasn't about to ask you out, sunshine," Adam said in a gentle way that made Harper question herself. She hated questioning herself, even though she did it often when it came to the opposite sex.

"You don't know that." But somehow she got the really sick feeling that he did. That she was the one misreading the situation—again. Which was impossible. She was sending the right messages this time, and receiving them.

She opened the bag and wished she had the ability to make herself disappear.

Inside wasn't a set of pastries and napkins for an impromptu sweets break. Inside was a gift card and a pencil drawing of a big stick figure with a paintbrush, holding hands with a smaller stick figure. They were both smiling, only the bigger one had a halo of curls that took up most of the page. At the bottom, in hard-won scribbles was a big #1 followed by the word SITTER.

"Maybe he's just not ready to start dating," she said quietly, reminding herself that his divorce had been finalized just last year, and twelve months wasn't all that long to mourn the loss of a dream. So she'd be patient. Not that Clay would forget her and Adam locking lips on Main Street.

"Maybe," Adam said, but he didn't sound all that convinced.

"What do you mean *maybe*?"

"I know guys, and he's not the guy for you."

Humiliating moment complete, Harper closed her eyes and took a few deep breaths, trying to get the burning red embarrassment to recede from her cheeks. It didn't help.

"I bet this will make it better." He held up his bag with two fingers and shook it. Harper could hear a pastry tumble around. The grease stain on the side of the bag told her whatever was in there was frosted. The size of the bag said there was more than one.

Maybe cupcakes? Or a dozen cookies? She was an equal opportunity consumer when it came to baked goods, but cookies were her favorite. Especially ones with enough butter to stain a bag. But this bag made her uneasy, because this bag felt like a bribe.

"What's going on, Adam?" Her gaze fell to his chest when she asked, "And why did you kiss me?"

"You looked like you needed to be kissed, and dumbass wasn't perceptive enough to see that," he said in a tone that had Harper looking up and, *holy smokes*, Adam was looking back.

It wasn't the look she expected—it was protective and hungry, if not a tad bit confused.

Welcome to it, Harper thought. Two minutes ago, she was so focused on Clay's chaste kiss she had convinced herself he was going to ask her out. Now she couldn't seem to remember why she wanted to go out with him.

"He needed to know that it wasn't you missing out on something amazing. It was him who was missing out."

"Oh," she whispered, her stomach clenching a little. "I thought you kissed me as payback for, you know . . ." She waved her hand at his fly and groaned. God, she was so awkward. "So you kissed me to save me from embarrassment?"

He chuckled lightly. "You really need to work on reading signals, sunshine."

"I don't understand."

"Exactly," was all he said. Then his posture shifted, and so did that easygoing smile. "Now that we got that taken care of, want to explain to me why you keep blowing my game?"

"What are you even talking about?" she asked, although she had a bad feeling she already knew, and silently debated whether to just fess up. She knew it was the right thing to do, even had a pretty good idea he was already in the loop, but wishful thinking held her back.

For all she knew, she was misreading signals again. And he was just there to confront her about Emerson playing hardball with her catering skills.

"Because of you, there will be a huge sex deficit," he said, sounding genuinely concerned.

"If this is your idea of how to charm me into forgiving you so Emerson will cater Beat the Heat, then I gotta tell you, your game-sucking has zero to do with me."

"That came out wrong," Adam said and ran a hand down his face, and at least two days' worth of stubble, which made him appear sexier and somehow vulnerable. Two things that had her pausing.

Adam didn't do vulnerable. But the longer she looked at him, the more she wondered what was wrong. The life's-a-beach ladies' man was gone and in his place was a worn soul.

"I came here to apologize about the other night."

"It all worked out," she said. "And thank you for apologizing. It really means a lot."

Adam nodded, a single jerk that was male for *welcome*. But when Harper thought he'd walk off, he continued to stare. At her. Not saying a word, until the silence grew and Harper felt more tingling. This time it was from unease, twisting around in her stomach.

"Now, you want to tell me why everyone seems to think we're dating?" he said, and that twisting went Category 5.

"Not really. I'm good."

He laughed softly, then moved forward until she felt enveloped.

And for one ridiculously stupid, amazing moment she thought he was going to kiss her again. Not the hard smack to the lips he'd given her a moment ago, but a gentle, languid kiss that would have her knees melting.

It had been so long since she'd had a good public knee-melting that she found herself swaying closer. Their bodies brushed and she realized she'd stopped breathing.

"Even if I said I brought you a present?" He opened the bag and held it beneath her nose.

Harper closed her eyes and breathed in mouthwatering vanilla and rich cinnamon. Knowing it was a bribe, and refusing to give in, she shook her head. "Even then."

He pulled one of the cookies out of the bag—a confetti cake batter cookie, her favorite—and took a bite, moaning, the big jerk. "You sure? There's plenty."

Cursing her weakness, she reached into the bag, telling herself that sometimes a cookie was just a cookie. Only then she realized that the bag was full, busting at the seams with enough cookies to feed a small army—or her entire class—and she knew the gesture was so much more.

She looked up and Adam gave a shrug which came off as more boyish than dismissive. "My mom used to bring cookies to my Mighty Mites meetings when I was a kid. So when I saw the sunshine-painted sugar cookies, I grabbed extras."

Harper's heart rolled over and showed its soft underbelly. "Thank you. That was very sweet."

"Sweet enough to tell me why Nora Kincaid posed the question on Facebook about why my status still says single?"

Harper hesitated.

"I guess I can always just go see Nora."

"No, wait." Nora Kincaid ran the gossip rag in town. It was hosted on Facebook, all of the photos were amateur, but her word was golden. The last thing Harper needed was Nora catching wind that there was more to the story.

"Remember the meeting you interrupted with the sales rep?"

"You mean the lingerie lady?" He gestured to his chest as a way of identifying that yes, he remembered everything about Chantel. "She had great merchandise."

Harper ignored this. "Well, because of how we were acting, she thought we were dating."

"You mean, me asking to see your panties and you shooting me death glares indicates that we're a couple?" He shook his head. "This is why I don't date."

Harper guessed there were a lot more reasons why he didn't date, deeper reasons that explained a lot of the crazy, and often dangerous, decisions he made, but she left it alone. "I didn't exactly say we were dating, but I didn't correct her either." Harper felt her face redden further. "And I guess someone overheard. I never meant for it to go this far."

"My guess? It was Nora, since she posted a picture of us talking on the sidewalk, which looked very cozy by the way. Then she shipped us as the summer couple to watch."

"Shipped us?"

"Ha-dam," he said, not bothering to elaborate more. "As for lying by omission." He grimaced. "It's a slippery slope, sunshine. But you already know that, so why?"

Harper took in a deep, calming breath, but it didn't work. Admitting this to anyone would be humiliating. Admitting it to Adam was going to be unbearable. But he deserved the truth.

"My grandma's shop is in trouble, and the only way to save it is to get one of our manufacturers, who is trying to phase us out, to reconsider and re-up our contract."

"The lingerie lady?"

Harper nodded. "I spent all weekend giving the shop a complete makeover, making it perfect for the meeting. I even researched what's sexy and bought a new dress. No matter what I did, though, it wasn't enough to convince her we were hip, edgy, and *alluring* enough. Until"—Harper looked Adam square in the eyes—"she saw I had landed a guy like you. She thought that if I was sleeping with someone as"—she paused to throw up some air quotes—"*beefy* and hot as you, then there must be more to me than she was seeing. So she gave me a second chance, contingent upon me convincing her boss that I have what it takes, even though I don't appear to."

"You mean that the store has what it takes?"

"Same thing."

"Not really," he said softly, and so full of concern that Harper had to close her eyes.

This wasn't as bad as she thought it would be. It was so much worse. Because Adam saw more than she'd wanted him to, picking up on things most people would look right past.

Harper wasn't only determined to get her grandma the contract and save the shop—she secretly wanted to be seen as someone who brought a special uniqueness to the project. And Adam wasn't saying a thing, not even a smart-mouthed jab, taking this moment from awful into the vortex of the worst day ever.

Harper Owens was too pathetic for the hometown tease to tease.

When the silence grew too thick to breathe, she opened an eye, just one, enough to see his expression. Only he didn't look as if he was pitying her. His face was gentle, understanding. No, it was deeper than understanding. There was empathy. As if it came from a place of personal experience. Which was ridiculous since Adam was the most seen man she'd ever met.

He walked into a room and all eyes went to him like white on rice. But in that moment, with the way he was looking at her, she wondered if the person people saw and the person Adam was deep down were in direct conflict.

"I really didn't think it would get out," she admitted.

"This is St. Helena—everything gets out." Adam let out a breath as though someone thinking they were dating was the worst thing in the world.

Letting that sting settle, she asked, "Is it really that bad? People thinking you dated me?"

"What? No!" And even though her head was telling her he was just being nice, she really wanted to believe him. "The truth is, I've had my eye on lieutenant for a while. I've put in the time and the training, and now I need to prove to my superiors that I'm focused and dependable, the kind of guy who brings honor to the badge."

The statement threw Harper. Sure, Adam played it fast and loose in his personal life, but when it came to his job, it was clear he took it seriously. "You're a great firefighter and the other guys admire you."

"Tossing back a few with my buddies and effectively leading my crew are two different things." He shook his head as if disgusted. "And having some girl post a photo in nothing but a G-string and my work jacket isn't the best way to prove I'm ready for a promotion."

"Especially when a few days later you are rumored to be hooking up with me." Guilt filled Harper's chest. "I'm so sorry, Adam. I had no idea."

"The misconception seems to be county-wide," he said, and a powerful surge of protectiveness sparked. "Normally this whole thing would blow over as a big joke, another locker-room story about the Five-Alarm Casanova, but . . ." He shrugged, his expression so full of embarrassment, Harper wanted to hug him.

"I will clear everything up. With Emerson and Chantel. I will call her as soon as my class ends and tell her I lied."

A strange expression settled on his face. "Won't you lose the account?"

Harper didn't want to think about that. "I don't know. Maybe." *Probably.* "Chantel might look past it."

Adam glanced down Main Street toward the firehouse. "Look, we both messed up, but I don't want you losing the account. So as long as you tell Emerson and Megan it's okay to work Beat the Heat, I can handle the rest."

"What about Chantel?"

Adam shrugged. "Chantel lives in San Francisco. It's not like she's privy to St. Helena gossip. So what if she thinks we're dating?"

Harper shrugged, then stared at her shoes. "Actually, I may have also implied that you'd be willing to model their new line for a campaign for Clovis's shop, and maybe a sample page for the online catalog?"

"Like the pictures we took for Shay's calendar?"

"Just like that," Harper said, picturing Adam in his turnout pants holding a rescued bulldog. She felt her cheeks flush. "Only . . . you'd be wearing nothing but underwear."

Adam drew in a startled breath, and she knew right then that it didn't matter if they were silk or cotton, posing in underwear wasn't lieutenant material.

chapter
eight

"Why didn't you tell me he was going to be playing?" Harper asked, glancing out at the baseball field as she placed a stack of food tickets in the window of Emerson's food truck.

"If by *he* you mean your *boyfriend*, it was because I wanted to see you squirm," Emerson said, dropping several pita wraps onto the hot griddle.

"He's not my boyfriend," Harper said in a hushed whisper. "I don't even know if we're friends."

"Sounds complicated," Shay Baudouin said from inside. She was standing next to the prep counter, eating baklava straight from the tray.

"Worse," Harper said.

It was Thursday night and the weekly Napa County Sheriff's Department softball game. With Dax geared up and on the field, Emerson was short on backup for her food truck. It was deputies versus firefighters, and with Harper running orders in the stands and Adam down on the field, it seemed as if the entire town had come out for the game.

The stands were heavy on the sixty-five-and-older crowd, all vying for Nora Kincaid's fifty-dollar reward for the best candid shot of St. Helena's Miracle Match. The fine print clarified the fifty dollars was to be paid in double-day coupons to the local pharmacy, but since Bottles and Bottles was a pharmacy *and* a wine shop, the coupons were a hot commodity.

And if that weren't complicated enough, the rest of the stands were filled with twenty-somethings, and a few bold cougars, all wanting to see with their own eyes if the Five-Alarm Casanova was really off the market.

Something Harper intended to clear up when she went to talk to Megan. Which she was totally going to do—tomorrow. She'd already come clean with Emerson, who had agreed to cater Beat the Heat as long as Adam agreed to keep his hose out of trouble. Now Harper needed to admit to a woman who was everything Harper would never be that it was all a big joke. Which made *her* feel like a big joke.

"I told you it was all a big misunderstanding, but actually I lied and got caught." Harper strategically avoided her friend's glare, instead paying particular attention to arranging the mouthwatering baklava. Sweet and gooey and drizzled with enough honey she nearly forgot that it was after seven in the evening and she still had several hours of inventory waiting for her back at the Fashion Flower.

"And I believed you," Emerson said, "but then someone told me they saw you kissing Adam on Main Street." Emerson might be dressed in pink sparkly high-tops and an apron that said KISS THE COOK, but beneath the recently engaged glow was a ninja master, with knives and at doling out guilt.

"How do you know that someone wasn't lying?" Harper asked, confident she could honestly say she hadn't kissed Adam. He'd kissed her. Big difference.

"Well, since that someone was me," Shay said, "I feel pretty confident stating that you were locking lips with Adam Baudouin on Main Street." Shay eyed Harper, and Harper resisted the urge to run. Barely.

Emerson and Shay were watching her, waiting for her to spill, so Harper zipped her lips and stared back.

Long, tense moments passed. Harper felt sweat bead between her shoulder blades and drip down her back, but she held strong. Until Emerson crossed her arms and dug in for the long haul.

Her bestie wasn't big on gossip—in fact, she wasn't all that talkative—but if she felt like someone was hiding something from her, she was a master at ferreting out the truth.

Being under that intense scrutiny made Harper's stomach go wonky and she found swallowing difficult. Like Emerson, she hated secrets—hated keeping them almost as much as she hated uncovering them. Which was why she never kept any. She knew just how harmful they could be.

Tightening the band on her ponytail, which made her feel sporty and flirty, she said, "Fine, he kissed me." Her friends exchanged knowing smirks, so she added, "But it was just a kiss. Nothing else happened."

"Then why didn't you tell me?" Emerson asked.

It was a good question, and one Harper didn't have an answer for. But then she caught a glimpse of number nineteen playing shortstop and she knew. Knees bent, ready to go, his game face dialed to destroy, Adam looked strong, capable, and ready to handle anything that came his way. And that, more than anything, got to her.

"Because it happened twice," Harper admitted, leaving out the part that she wanted it to happen again. "And if I told you guys about the second kiss, then I'd have to tell you about the first one, which took place after I caught him in my grandma's shop, and before I fired Baby." She dropped her head to the counter with a thud. "I am such a hypocrite."

"Because you got cozy with Adam in your grandma's shop, then fired the coed for doing the same thing?" Emerson asked.

Harper groaned. "And worse, I liked it." Harper took a minute to choke on that truth, while her friends did that whole glance-slyly-at-one-another thing again, which actually wasn't sly at all. It was kind of annoying. "I was kissed by the Five-Alarm Casanova. And I liked it. Not that it is happening again." She looked her friends in the eyes when she said it, as though having witnesses would create accountability and ensure it would never happen again.

"You sure?" Shay asked. "Because you said it wasn't happening again, and then you checked the field for him."

Harper realized she was not only scanning the field for him, but her eyes had zeroed in on his mighty-fine butt in two seconds flat. Like a moth to a flame.

"I'm sure." She took one last look, then turned to her friends. "I asked him to model for the Boulder Holder, and he said he'd have to think about it. Not that I blame him—posing in underwear isn't really in his best interest—but if he doesn't do it, then I am so screwed."

"It's not like St. Helena is short on good-looking men," Shay said.

Shay had a point. For such a small town, St. Helena seemed to have a surplus of man candy walking around. Between Shay's Cuties with Booties blog, which was filled with hot men posing with animals in need, and her yearly calendar, Harper had shot most of the hotties in town. Only no matter how rugged or sexy the cuties of St. Helena were, none of them had the swagger Chantel was looking for. Except Adam.

Adam had a charisma about him, that something special that made it hard not to stare. In fact, the photo of Adam in SHFD turn-out pants and suspenders, holding Large Marge the bulldog, had been the most talked about month in the calendar. Mr. July wasn't just the calendar's centerfold, he was also an instant hit. Then her grandma had uploaded it to her Pinterest board and it went viral, making Adam a bona fide Internet sex-lebrity.

Gaining him the exact kind of notoriety he was now trying to avoid. And creating the exact kind of buzz Chantel was looking for. God, this was a mess.

"I'll ask a few other guys I've worked with in the past," Harper said, "but Chantel is stuck on Adam. He's my ticket in. So I can't dump my not-boyfriend for another not-boyfriend and expect Chantel to give me another chance."

"Chantel sounds like an idiot," Emerson said. "You don't need some guy to prove you are perfect for this."

"Yeah, well, she has her heart set on him."

Emerson lowered her voice, uncharacteristically soft. "I guess I just want to know where your heart is at?"

"Firmly locked in my chest." Which was beating a little faster when she thought back to yesterday, how Adam had seemed more concerned with the welfare of her grandma's shop than chiding her for complicating his life. "I promise."

"As long as you're sure, because I would hate to have to explain to Dax how I ran over his brother for being an ass. It would make for an uncomfortable wedding, and I'm already stressing about wearing heels."

"You won't have to kill Adam, I've got this."

Shay didn't look convinced that Harper was in control of anything, so Harper added, "A quick reminder that I was the one who told you Jonah was a good guy." She turned to Emerson. "And I supported you when you were sniffing around Dax. Encouraging you to jump his bones and go for the golden O."

"Which he delivered on, then walked out and broke my heart," Emerson pointed out.

"Yes, but he came back."

"Only because he was afraid I'd hunt him down and kill him."

"He came back because he loved you," Harper said, and even she could hear that her voice had a dreamy quality to it.

She was thrilled that her friends had found amazing men and were living amazing lives. She really was. In fact, she couldn't think of two women who were more deserving. Most of the time, Harper believed she deserved that kind of happiness too. But sometimes, when life's silver lining hid beneath the shadows, Harper wondered if she would ever find that kind of connection.

Love, passion, a family—she wanted it all. She just hoped she'd find someone who wanted those same things—with her.

"He did," Emerson said, and a rare grin escaped. "And now I have a ring on my finger."

"Well, I'm not looking for a ring, just someone to pose scantily for a catalog."

The last time she'd been trapped in her small studio with only Adam and body oil, she hadn't known what his kisses tasted like. This time she would know exactly what she'd be missing out on when they kept everything aboveboard and professional. Which they would.

If he said yes.

"Good, because you aren't the kind of person who treads lightly, and Adam is smooth," Emerson said. "He's even figured out how to sweet-talk me from time to time, and I don't do sweet." Emerson sounded horrified at the admission. "You, on the other hand, are so sweet you make Disney movies look seedy. You collect people like others collect stamps, but don't mistake Adam's easygoing charm for more than it is, because he isn't looking to be collected."

He was too bright and shiny for Harper's taste anyway.

"Strike!"

Swearing, Adam loosened up on the bat and stepped out of the batter's box at the umpire's call. It was the bottom of the ninth, two outs, and the bases were loaded. SHFD was tied with the sheriff's department, which was why they'd called in Adam.

He was the closer—on and off the diamond. Something he needed to remember.

"Come on, man, it's like you're not even trying," Jonah heckled from the mound.

A former homicide detective for the San Francisco Police Department, Jonah had traded in his big-city problems to become the keeper of Mayberry. He also liked to keep tabs on his younger brothers—and give them shit when necessary. Which was why he turned the bill of his hat around backward, so Adam could clearly make out his smug grin, when he shouted, "I mean, that was right up the middle."

"A gnat was buzzing around my ear," Adam said, shooting a look at Dax, who was also grinning smugly beneath his catcher's mask. "Next time, I'll just squash him."

"Someone's sensitive," Dax said, throwing the ball to the mound, not the least bit intimidated by Adam's threat. Not that he should be. Dax might be the baby boy of the family, but he had a good three inches and fifty pounds on both his brothers. And he knew it.

Adam kicked the dirt up, then stepped back in the box and choked up on the bat. Focusing on Jonah's hand, he slowed his breathing until he felt his heart rate drop and his mind begin to settle—and all he saw was the ball.

Jonah pulled back and Adam watched as the ball slid off his finger, right up the center and—

"I mean, I would be too if a pretty girl wouldn't return my calls," Dax said, blowing Adam's concentration.

"Strike two," the umpire called.

Adam glared down at his brother, wondering if he'd be expelled from the game for punching a member of the opposing team in the nuts.

"I'm just saying that new picture on Facebook is a pretty big sign that you struck out big-time on closing that deal." Dax flipped his mask up and laughed. Adam clenched his jaw. "No way. You haven't even seen it, have you?"

"Nope." He'd been too busy trying to figure out why he'd gone in for the save yesterday.

Adam might be a firefighter by trade, but in his personal life he didn't do the savior act. Never had. Being someone's personal hero only led to complications and disappointment. And he'd delivered enough disappointment in his lifetime. Yet, when he'd normally pull back, with Harper he'd stayed. Gotten involved.

The shit of it was he'd do it all over again, if it meant saving her from another humiliating moment with Dr. Dumbass. Yup, Harper with her coat-of-many-colors fashion, bright smile, and big doe eyes got to him. Bad.

Then again, maybe he was the dumbass in question. Watching Harper flutter around the bleachers, greeting every person she came across like they were an old friend, he knew going any further with her would be an exercise in extreme stupidity. They were a train wreck in the making, yet he couldn't seem to stay away.

Instead of focusing on what was important—cleaning up his reputation—he'd somehow missed Baby posting a new photo of her in his jacket. Which took his current situation from annoying to disastrous. When Roman found out, and he would, he'd blow off Adam's left nut.

And if Lowen found out, he'd blow any hope Adam had for making lieutenant right out the fire station door.

"I've called Baby a dozen or more times," he admitted. "I can't get hold of her."

"Man, that's rough," Dax said, shaking his head. "Wanting some kind of closure and only getting radio silence? Total dick move."

"I don't want closure, I just want my jacket back," Adam clarified and, sure, at the first signs of complication or drama he simplified things by dumping plan A and moving on to plan B, and eventually plans C, D, and E when necessary. But he always made sure when it ended there were no hard feelings. So what if he'd avoided a few calls from time to time in his day? That didn't make him a dick.

That made him smart. Although he didn't feel so smart right then.

"Her generation texts," Dax explained as if he were slow. "Did you try that?"

Adam's face went slack. "Her generation? How old is she?"

Jesus, he really needed to get his jacket back and clarify that when she said she was a graduate she meant college and not high school.

"I don't know, text her and find out," Dax said. "Add one of those emojis to it. The one with the googly heart eyes. Girls love that shit."

"She's twenty-four," Jonah said, coming off the mound. The second his feet hit the grass the "Final Jeopardy!" theme song came though the speakers—indicating that a powwow was taking place on the field. "Something you should have known before you slept with her. Now can we get back to the game?"

"I didn't sleep with her," Adam said, breathing a sigh of relief that Baby was in fact not jailbait.

"How about that event planner Megan?" Dax asked.

"I didn't sleep with her either."

"What about your girlfriend? You sleep with her?"

He didn't have to ask who the specific *her* in question was—the stupid grin on his brother's face said it all. "I'm not dating Harper. And no, we haven't slept together."

"Facebook says otherwise. On the dating," Dax clarified. "Because it's obvious by your pissy attitude you haven't gotten laid in a while."

Try more than a month. Between training and everyone thinking he was in a relationship, he was practically a virgin again.

"Not that it's any of your business, but I am helping her out with some stuff for her grandma's shop. There was a misunderstanding, that's it."

Adam stopped, not comfortable with going any further. First, because when he was with Harper it felt like a whole lot more. It felt good. Mostly though, he kept silent because it wasn't his place to explain to anyone what had transpired between Harper and the doctor. Or between Harper and Adam for that matter. "It's complicated."

"You don't do complicated," Dax pointed out, as if Adam weren't well aware of this fact. "Especially with someone you'll have to see around the family table."

It was the main reason to steer clear—Harper was going to be around for the duration. Jonah's marriage to Shay increased the potential for weirdness, but the moment Dax proposed to Emerson, the line was officially drawn. Crossing it would be more than complicated.

He was sure there were a million other reasons, but he was too busy imagining all the ways to get complicated with Harper to think of any.

"Oh man." Dax gave a sad shake of the head and rested a hand on Adam's shoulder. "You're losing your touch, bro."

"He's losing something," Jonah said dryly. "Otherwise he wouldn't even consider telling his superiors that his proposed event planner, for a department-sponsored event, is a girl he tried to sleep with but didn't quite close the deal. Now he wants to use department money to pay for the girl's services. It doesn't get more complicated than that."

Adam cringed because when put that way he could see how it might be construed as a problem. But Megan was his ace in the hole. The meeting was tomorrow morning. And if he went in there without a plan, Lowen might just demote him to the FNG and he'd wind up answering to Seth and McGuire.

"Megan is my best bet at this point," Adam admitted, wondering what the strange tightness was in his chest.

"Well, that is a bet I don't think you should take, because the only outcome of mixing business with pleasure is getting fired," Jonah said.

"What if I make it clear that there will be no pleasure?" God, he was totally losing his touch.

"As long as you're using department funds to pay someone you've hooked up with, it's a bad move."

"Shit." Jonah was right. Adam needed a new plan, and fast. He couldn't walk in there with his New Year's hookup on his arm, just like he couldn't walk in there without some kind of plan to prove to Lowen that he had this thing handled. "I'm so screwed."

"Just not in the right way, bro," Dax said with a shit-eating grin. "All you have to do is find someone in town who knows how to plan a party who you haven't slept with."

"We going to play or stand around clucking like a bunch of girls?" McGuire yelled from third base.

"You ever see that movie *Anaconda*?" Adam hollered back, and McGuire zipped it. He had no qualms whatsoever referencing the python incident in front of a crowd to keep McGuire in line.

Adam rubbed some dirt on his hands and went back to the batter's box. Finding someone he hadn't slept with to plan the party shouldn't be that hard. Especially with the current drought going on.

Then again, the budget was practically nonexistent, the schedule impossibly tight, and St. Helena was a small town.

The music stopped and the crowd stilled. Jonah returned to the mound while Adam and Dax returned to the batter's box. Jonah chalked his hands, stared down Adam, wound up, and released the ball. Adam saw it speeding toward him—not toward the plate, but *him*. At an alarming rate. He was so lost in thought that he didn't step back in time and the ball smacked him in the thigh, making a loud thud and no doubt leaving a mark.

"What the hell?" Adam asked.

"Whoops," Jonah said, not pissy in the slightest for just costing his team the game.

"Whoops?" Adam threw the bat and stalked toward the mound, the tightening in his chest growing with every step. "No whoops. That was on purpose. You just threw the game."

"Did I?" Jonah shrugged as McGuire made a big show of prancing over home plate and throwing his cap in the air as if this were the fucking World Series. "Guess you needed the win more than we did."

chapter
nine

Harper had once read that the best way to eat an elephant was one bite at a time. And since there were too many elephants in her life to address, she decided her first bite of the day would be a cookie. Which was how she found herself at the Sweet and Savory—instead of at the fire station.

A girl needed a hearty breakfast before tackling her problems. She also needed a cute dress, something she'd justified as she'd slipped on a little strapless summery number she'd kept at the back of her closet, just waiting for that perfect event to wear it to, like say, facing a certain funny, gorgeous, sex-lebrity.

Checking her makeup in the bakery's window, she touched up her lipstick, Sensual Seduction, then practiced eye contact. It was bold and direct and—

"Oh God." Everything inside her stilled. Everything except her heart, which pounded as she took a closer look at herself—surprised at what she found looking back. Scared even.

The dress was silky and flirty and spoke of a woman who knew what she wanted. More importantly, a woman who went after what she wanted—and got it. Which was why it had sat at the back of the closet for so long. Once she took it out and wore it for the world, she'd never be able to put it in the back again.

The dress was designed to be noticed, and deep down Harper wanted to be noticed. But what if she put herself out there for the world to see, stepping directly into the glare of the spotlight, and was still overlooked?

Telling herself that it didn't matter, that being recognized for who she was and how she cared for others was more important, Harper dug deep for confidence and pushed through the door. Immediately she felt her nerves settle as she was greeted by a warm blast of vanilla, fresh baked pastries, and home. The smell of baking cookies reminded her of summers with Clovis in the kitchen. Safe, cherished, loved.

Helping herself to a sample of peach scone, which sat on a tray held by a cardboard cutout of David Hasselhoff in board shorts—a leftover from before the renovation—she bypassed the usual suspects in breakfast pastries and went right for the cookies.

Face pressed against the glass display window, she considered her options carefully. A friendly lemon scratch cookie was calling her name, and nothing said breakfast like fruit, but somehow she knew her day needed a buttered-rum blondie.

After her talk with Emerson last night at the game, Harper realized she was being selfish. Counting on Adam as the quick fix to her problems, when it could land him in trouble with his boss, wasn't a friendly thing to do. And Harper was, above all else, a good friend.

Who always did the right thing.

So why did her stomach hurt? It wasn't just thinking about the dress or the evening that was causing it, but thinking about Adam. Before she could really process that, an instant smile appeared on her face as if on automatic.

As if a small part of her thrilled at the thought of doing the wrong thing—with the Five-Alarm Casanova. He'd opened up to her, showed her a part of the real Adam, a guy who wanted to become more than people's perceptions, and she couldn't look past that.

"You're early today," Lexi DeLuca said, coming out of the kitchen. Lexi balanced a tray of éclairs in one hand, a rolling pin in the other, and had matching toddlers with blonde pigtails and freckles hanging on to each of her legs like monkeys. Both baker and daughters were speckled with chocolate.

As owner and mastermind behind the most popular French bakery on the West Coast, Lexi was the local sugar supplier. She had three daughters, one of the hottest husbands in town, and a way with buttercream frosting that could only come from divine intervention.

"I actually counted to ten after you flipped the sign to OPEN before I came in. I didn't want to look desperate."

Lexi laughed and grabbed a paper bag. "Inventory time at the shop?"

"Among other things," Harper said, nibbling her fingers because choosing was impossible.

"Sounds like a half-dozen kind of day." Lexi traded in the bag for a pink box, then reached for a confetti cake batter cookie. "The usual?"

Harper shook her head. "I'm trying to live outside the lines and try new things."

"So I've heard," Lexi said with a mischievous grin, and Harper blew out a breath.

"You heard wrong," Harper said. Lexi smothered a laugh behind her hand.

"If you say so, but *new things* is a good look on you." Lexi took inventory of Harper's zigzag lime-green backpack with little lemons on it and smiled. "In fact, I have a key lime kringle that would match your backpack."

Although that sounded delicious, Harper wanted something decadent. Something flirty and bold. Something that told her she was more than the town's #1 Sitter—she was a sexually attuned woman who could handle her world on her own.

Just look at her hair, she thought, leaning forward and letting it slide over her shoulder. Thanks to some nuclear-grade straightening gel and a YouTube tutorial, it was now straight, sophisticated, and so full of allure she couldn't help but run her fingers through it. Or swish it back and forth as she walked.

"I'll try a black velvet whoopie pie with cherry-cream frosting." Then she looked at the bright orange frosted cookies on the next tray. "And since I would hate for that bad boy to get lonely, throw in two of those sangria sunrise minis."

After all, it was morning, and she did love sunrises. And the last two *were* minis, which everyone knew meant calorie-free. Plus, a little liquid courage couldn't hurt.

"You got it." Lexi loaded up the order in a box that could hold another three goodies at least. "How about a few firecracker fudge bars to match that glow?"

"I'm not glowing," Harper said.

"It's a firehouse favorite," Lexi said, all singsongy.

Not even a bite of cookie and already the inquisition had begun. "Contrary to the current gossip, Adam and I are just friends."

"Friends," Lexi said, her face taking on an expression that was impossible to translate. With a smile, she filled the last three spots with firecracker fudge. "Then I guess Adam's the one trying new things. Interesting. And telling."

Before Harper could ask what was so interesting about Adam making friends with the town's friendliest person, a bony finger jabbed her in the shoulder blade.

"Excuse me, dear."

She turned around to find Peggy Lovett, owner of the Paws and Claws Day Spa, clutching her phone. She wore jeweled high-tops, a yellow pantsuit, an orange cardigan, and enough dog hair to cause acute asthma.

"Aren't you going to say hello?" Peggy asked and thrust her cell, which was set to record, in Harper's face.

"Okay, uh . . ." Harper leaned into the phone and gave a self-conscious "Hello?"

The older woman's brow furrowed with disappointment. "Not with a question mark, but how you would normally greet a customer. So I can practice my greeting and get the inflection down."

"Inflection?" Harper asked as Peggy moved closer, and that was when Harper noticed the grapefruit-shaped buttons on the sweater. "I have a cardigan just like that."

And wasn't *that* lovely. She and her grandma's best friend had the same taste in clothing.

"Oh this," Peggy said sheepishly. "I actually borrowed it from your closet."

"She saw it at yesterday's Panty Raid, and I told her you wouldn't mind," Clovis said, walking over in a black-and-royal-purple corset and matching broom skirt. A Panty Raid was the equivalent of a Tupperware party for Clovis, only instead of selling plastic storage with matching lids like other grandmothers did, Clovis threw pleasure parties for the town's geriatric sector. "She's trying to impress that new fella Roland down at the senior center. The one who, if he weren't a retired dentist, I'd think had teeth that are too white to be real."

Jabba plopped at Clovis's feet, his sides heaving as if he'd just run the Boston Marathon, not waddled five storefronts down.

"Roland came into the shop asking about our Better Breath Biscuits for his Maltese, canine," Peggy explained, "and we started talking about the importance of doggie dental care. When he left, he said he hoped to see me at Singles Night next week, and I figured if I walked in wearing your sweater, it was like saying I'm bringing sexy back," Peggy said, then gave a little shimmy that sent her grape-fruits swaying.

"It looks lovely on you, Peggy," Harper said, and the older woman blushed. To her grandmother, she said, "And explain how your Panty Raid ended up in my closet?"

"We didn't go in your closet," Clovis said, sounding appalled. "Shame on you making it sound like I'd violate your privacy that way. We had it in your bedroom."

Harper choked. "My bedroom?"

"Worked like a charm," Clovis said. "It was my biggest moneymaker of the year so far. I even managed to get those starched blouses in the active living community off Vine Street to agree to start looking locally to satisfy their needs. Plus it skews our average customer age lower."

Harper didn't bother to mention that the development off Vine was a fifty-five-and-older community and still skewed their average way too high. "My bedroom is a mess."

She couldn't remember just how bad it had been since she'd fallen into bed after 2:00 a.m. and gotten up before the sun, but if memory served, her entire apartment was a mess. Between testing out Mother's Day craft ideas and trying to singlehandedly save her grandma's shop, Harper's apartment looked as if a lingerie and glitter piñata had exploded.

"We tidied up a bit, because what better place to sell sin than in the private sleeping chambers of our very own Hometown Temptress?" Clovis paused as if she'd had an epiphany. "I coined a phrase."

Peggy clapped delightedly, and before Harper knew what was happening the two fist-bumped like homies, even adding little explosions at the end.

Harper rubbed the headache growing between her eyes. "What are you talking about?"

"Didn't you know that orange is the new black?" Peggy said, running her hands over the sweater, her voice all atwitter. "And you are the new sexy?"

"In what world?" Harper asked, because the last male she'd made direct eye contact with had freckles and a milk mustache.

"The one where you landed yourself Mr. July," Peggy said in awe, and Harper realized she had somehow landed herself a fangirl.

"Mr. July?" Oh God, this was the last thing she needed today. She was supposed to be clearing up the rumors, not encouraging them.

"So many have come before, most only getting a few nibbles, but my granddaughter reeled in the Moby Dick of men." Clovis took a moment to let that settle, then fanned herself. "Although if you want Moby rearing out of the water you might want to consider new sheets. That's not the kind of kitty he wants to snuggle up with, if you know what I mean."

Unfortunately, she knew exactly what Clovis meant. An official Panty Raid had been thrown on her Grumpy Cat sheets.

If this was anything close to what Adam had been experiencing the past week, then she needed to put an end to it. Immediately. Then let him off the hook. She might need him for the shoot, but she wasn't willing to sacrifice his promotion to get a photo.

"Look," Harper said in her best inside voice, then remembered that Clovis only had one volume. And it was "Can I get a witness?" She took the ladies by the arm and led them to a quieter part of the store. "Adam and I aren't dating."

"Labels are so passé," Clovis said. "I told Giles that we didn't need to DTR in order to get DND."

"DTR?"

"Define the relationship," Peggy said. "And DND means to get down and—"

"Got it." Harper held up a hand and tried not to picture her grandma and Giles getting DND.

"Harper, order up," Lexi said from the counter where she was dangling Harper's box of courage.

"We aren't DNDing or LH6ing or sexting or any of the other terms you might come up with." Although they had been KISSing. "Adam and I are just friends. F R N D S."

"Say what you want," her grandmother said, "but I know women, and I know lingerie. No woman wears Luscious lace cheekinis for a friend. Especially when that friend ranks a solid fifteen on the man-candy meter."

Harper didn't bother to ask how her grandmother knew her lingerie of choice—the woman had a God-given gift. But she also had a mouth the size of the Grand Canyon, so Harper needed to make herself clear. "We. Are. Not. Dating."

"But Facebook—"

"I lied. Okay?"

Clovis tsked. It was a sound that always managed to make Harper's throat fill with guilt, even if she hadn't just confessed to lying.

"Oh, honey, you're a horrible liar. You always look like you're going to cry when you fib." Clovis patted her on the arm, and if she weren't Harper's grandmother, Harper would say it was condescending in nature. "Kind of like now. But a word to the wise, even if Facebook is saying you had him at hello"—Clovis looked at Harper for so long she felt her ears heat—"if you want to have him screaming *Oh*, you might want to be more forthcoming with your cookies."

There wasn't much Adam couldn't handle. From jumping out of planes to charging headfirst into some gnarly situations, he tackled problems balls-out and head-on. The bigger the risk, the bigger the rush, and the greater the thrill.

So then why did he feel as if he was about to pass out just looking at a book of party themes?

"How about this one?" Seth said, pointing to the page with black tablecloths, poker table paraphernalia, and fuzzy dice table decor.

"It's a family-friendly picnic, not a bachelor party," Adam said, wondering how, out of everyone he knew, he'd managed to get stuck with the FNG as his party planner.

Right, because the universe was bitch-slapping him for his past indiscretions. So when Seth mentioned he'd planned all the poker nights for his fraternity, Adam drafted him as the decorations committee. A decision he should have made before they'd ordered their second round of beer.

"If this is a picnic, then can't we just buy some hotdogs, paper plates, and chips? I mean, everyone likes hotdogs and chips."

"The handbook says we have to have games and craft tables and an overall theme. I don't think *tailgate eats* counts as a theme." Adam flipped to the next page, which had everything one would need to throw a clambake engagement party. And slammed it shut. "I'm screwed."

He had less than an hour before his meeting with Lowen, was thirty minutes from town, and outside of securing a caterer, who wasn't talking to him, he had accomplished jack shit on his massive to-do list.

"Maybe we should just go back to St. Helena and ask the cute girl at the party store to help us plan it," Seth suggested, and Adam was tempted to give in.

Megan had approached him this morning, explained how Harper had cleared everything up, and said that she would be happy to help with Beat the Heat. Only, Adam had politely declined, then lied, telling her he had it all under control. Because (a) she wasn't all that forthcoming on what *everything* meant, (b) Megan looked exactly like what Jonah had said—a bad decision—and (c) Adam was tired of making bad decisions.

If he wanted to prove worthy of the badge, then he needed to start acting like it. And that did not include spending the next two weeks flirting with a pretty party planner on company time. So he'd driven right past Parties to Go-Go, and all the way into Napa to the party store there, where he asked a lovely saleslady in her sixties for help. She'd directed him to the party themes book, and that's when the panic had started.

He didn't know a centerpiece from a sash, had not a clue as to what kind of kid-friendly activities to plan. Should they match the theme? Were water guns a bad choice?

As a kid, he'd never missed Beat the Heat, yet he couldn't remember a single thing about it except when the firefighters pulled the engine out to the middle of Main Street and threw the ladder, then picked a lucky awestruck kid from the crowd to climb it.

One year, when Adam had just turned seven, he'd been that lucky kid. And it had rocked his little world. At the first rung he'd been hooked. Not much had changed—firefighting was his life, and his days were still spent hanging around the engine. Only instead of watching from the sidelines, he was the one who got to run the show and rock some kid's world.

"How about a fireman theme?" he said, flipping to the back of the book to where the kid-themed parties were. "We can swear in little honorary firefighters, give them a plastic hat and sticker badge."

"You mean like what we do with the school kids during their fieldtrips to the station?" Seth said.

"I see your point." He was so screwed. "Okay, tailgate it is."

Adam grabbed a cart full of red plates, cups, and matching paper napkins. If he couldn't do fire hats, at least the color would be firefighter approved.

Seth and Adam loaded up the rig and headed back toward town. He hit Send on his Bluetooth and called his sister.

"I'm busy," Frankie said in greeting.

"Then I'll make it quick," Adam said. "I'm heading up Beat the Heat and was hoping you and Nate would donate the wine this year."

"Even if we weren't sold out for the next decade, you couldn't afford me."

The stress of the day settled behind his eyes. He'd assumed as much. After his sister's Red Steel was crowned Cork King a few years back, which was pretty much like the Oscars of wine, her label had become one of the most sought-after in wine country. Which meant he needed to contact another winery.

Not that his family didn't own a bunch, it was just Adam had never really been a part of the family business. Hell, he didn't even like wine—he was more of a beer kind of guy—so sniffing around for handouts always felt wrong.

"How about donating a bottle or two then for the raffle?" he asked. "And asking Grandpa to provide the wine for the event?"

Frankie was quiet for a long moment. "I'll donate a case for the raffle and ask Nate if DeLuca Vineyards is interested, but it will cost you."

"Jesus, Frankie. If you could pull that off, I'd do anything."

And he meant it. Owing Frankie was like owing the mob—if you didn't pay up, she'd come after you with a bat. But walking into the meeting with the caterer and wine locked down?

Totally worth it.

"Nate and I are going away for a few days and we need you to come and stay with the alpacas."

"I meant anything but that," Adam said, his nuts already turning in on themselves. "You know that Mittens hates other men in his space. And the little one always goes after my boys."

"He's just sniffing you out. It's all normal male behavior one would find at a sporting event or bar," Frankie said. "And that's the deal. Take it or leave it."

Adam weighed his options, and they weren't good. Impressing Lowen or pissing off Frankie. He blew out a breath. "Fine, just let me know when and I'll check my work schedule."

Adam hung up and prayed he'd find himself stuck with overtime.

Half an hour later, he pulled into the engine bay to find that either he was late or Chief Lowen was early. Adam glanced at his watch. "Shit. Lowen is early."

"And he's talking to that sexy sweater set chick," Seth said.

Adam paused from grabbing the bag off the floorboard to peer through the windshield and nearly choked. Because Lowen was indeed talking to a sexy chick, but she wasn't wearing a sweater set. At least not today.

Nope, everyone's best friend, Harper, was holding court with his boss and crew, decked out in a flowy sundress that hugged her curves and flirted around her thighs. It was soft yellow with little white flowers and exactly zero straps, leaving her silky shoulders completely bare, and him begging the question of exactly what she had on beneath.

A question that fucking McGuire was probably also asking himself. He was using Harper's trusting nature to peruse more than just the items in the big pink pastry box she held.

McGuire said something, Harper said something back and touched his arm, then laughed. Real and loud, throwing her head back in a way that tempted the elastic holding up her dress.

Jesus. The guy was practically drooling all over her. And Chief Lowen was no better. The man seemed completely disarmed, smiling at Harper as if she were the most charming person on the planet. Which she was.

Harper had this way about her that was warm and welcoming

and, as he was discovering, compelling. But when she smiled, *man oh man*, he couldn't seem to stay away. Which only made him wonder why he had never noticed it before.

Sure, he'd noticed Harper around town. It was hard not to with her bright clothes and *everything is awesome* attitude. But somehow he'd overlooked just how sexy she was. Or maybe it was that she was finally letting her sexy show, and he was lucky enough to witness it.

Either way, he wasn't about to let a prick like McGuire witness any more than he already had.

"McGuire, I need you to help Seth empty the engine," Adam said, and all four sets of eyes were on him. "Hey, Cap. Chief." His gaze met Harper's, and that buzzing inside that was constantly set to *Go* shifted. It was still there, but if felt softer somehow. "Harper."

"Hey, Adam," she said, gifting him one of those bright smiles that made everyone's day brighter. "I stopped by to drop these off." She held up a box of cookies, but her hands shook slightly, telling him she was nervous.

And he knew why. She needed his answer on modeling for her grandma's shop. An answer that, two seconds after he said he needed to think about it, he'd made up his mind about.

Posing shirtless in a calendar for charity was one thing, but posing in silk boxers and a man's leisure robe would invite Hugh Hefner jokes. If word ever got out about the shoot, and it would, then his guys would call open season on him and the wisecracks would be never ending. That was saying nothing to how it might weigh in on Lowen's morality meter.

Seeing her in that summer dress, looking like a breath of fresh air, didn't help his resolve. In fact, it took his *No way in hell* to a solid *As long as you wear that dress* in two seconds flat.

"What is all of this?" McGuire asked, holding up the red plastic cups as he unloaded the engine. "Is this for our beer pong rematch next weekend?"

McGuire might not technically still be the FNG, but he sure as hell acted like it.

"They're for Beat the Heat," Seth defended.

"You bought drinking game glasses for a family event?" Chief Lowen asked.

Adam wanted to explain this in Cap's office, with Emerson's menu on display, but now Lowen was looking at him as if he'd better explain immediately or there wouldn't be a meeting and come tomorrow he'd be on trash duty for the rest of his career.

"I went with a red theme, like a, uh . . ." He almost said *tailgate party*, then realized that was one step away from beer pong. "Like a picnic."

"Beat the Heat *is* a picnic," Lowen pointed out. "So the theme you picked, after a week of planning, is the event itself?"

When said that way it sounded as if he'd half-assed the project. And maybe he had. He'd spent the last week trying to figure out how to get someone else to do his job, rather than put in the sweat equity toward a promotion. And spent this morning realizing he was ill equipped in the party-planning department.

That unfamiliar tightness in his chest was back. Adam realized it was panic—a strange sensation to have for someone who feared nothing. But looking his superiors in the eye, knowing that he'd screwed the pooch yet again, Adam knew this failure would cost him.

He didn't do failure, but somehow he'd managed to get himself pretty close.

A gentle hand came to rest on his lower back, and he immediately felt the heat.

"An old-fashioned picnic," Harper said, her fingers subtly moving on his back in a way that was meant to soothe. And damn if it didn't work. The tightness disappeared, only to reappear when he looked over at her and found that from his angle, he could see right down her dress. And cream-colored strapless lace was the answer of the hour. "The town would love it, and it would go perfectly with the menu Adam and Emerson hand selected. Cold lemonade and a selection of different sweet teas, red-and-white checkered tablecloths—"

"Ah, these are solid red," McGuire said, and Adam shot him an *Are you fucking kidding me?* look.

To which McGuire lifted a *What did I do?* brow.

You were born. That is enough to screw with my day.

Are you PMSing or what?

Harper ignored all of this and said, "I can just see the mason jars hanging from the trees, filled with candles." She reached out with her free hand and tapped the chief's shoulder lightly, as if physically bringing him to her vision. "Battery operated, of course. This is in honor of fire safety after all."

And just like that Lowen was there, in the picture she was painting, buying into red Solo cups and Adam's ability to make this event memorable. She'd also managed to distract from the fact that Adam thought hotdogs and Solo cups were a brilliant idea, and make him look like a guy who had his shit together.

It's her gift, Adam thought with a smile, the ability to draw out the best in people, make them feel as if they belonged in her magical world. Everything about her was magical.

A scary thought because when she was no longer there, he was pretty sure the magic would fade to a strange emptiness.

Lowen looked at Adam and showed some teeth beneath his mustache. Adam wasn't sure it was a smile, but he didn't growl so Adam counted it as a win. "I like the direction, Baudouin. And I'm pleased you have come so far with the event." He looked back at Harper. "The young lady was telling me earlier how inspiring you were in her art class this week."

Adam looked at Harper and lifted a brow. "Inspiring?" Because the only inspiring thing he could remember was that kiss to show up Dr. Dildo, then their talk, then how he wanted to kiss her again.

Her ears turned pink and he smiled.

She did too, sweet with a little undertone of sass to let him know he was on the money.

"It was all the kids could talk about, seeing a real-life hero up close and personal," Harper said. "They were so excited that I decided during the week of Beat the Heat, I would do a lesson on heroic portraits and hang them in the Budding Artists Gallery."

"You should bring them by," Lowen said. "Give them a tour of the station."

Harper looked at Adam, her eyes filled with excitement and uncertainty. It was obvious she wanted to say yes, but didn't want to put him in a weird position. Adam smiled. "I can have Daugherty set something up for you."

"That would be amazing." Amazing didn't even begin to describe what happened next. Harper smiled, and man what a smile. It was bright, joyful, and contagious as hell, because every damn guy in the room smiled back—including him. "Maybe we can even have you visit the shop on the Saturday of the event and judge them, Chief Lowen."

And wouldn't you know it, Chief Lowen, the tightest ass in the entire department, actually blushed. "I can't tell good art from a ketchup-smeared napkin, but I can wear my uniform and award a trophy."

"The kids' work is more about telling a story and sharing it with others," Harper said, placing a hand on Lowen's arm so that her comment came off as genuine sharing of information, a connection rather than a correction. "If you could say something nice about each artist's work, it would make their little days. Especially when they see how smart you look in uniform."

Adam was quickly learning that Harper wasn't concerned with conforming to society's standards of beauty, like most people he knew. Her mission was to make sure every one of her kids felt special and that their uniqueness was celebrated.

"I don't see why not."

"Wonderful. I was hoping to set up a display at the event this year, maybe by the stage, since the focus of the piece is real-life heroes. So maybe you and Adam"—those soulful blue eyes were aimed his way—"could judge it together. Our very own fire chief and the man who inspired the project would be the talk of the kids for months to come."

"Inspired the project?" Adam asked, unsure who was blushing more, him or the chief, but it was obvious why this town was so protective of Harper. She wasn't just a resident, she was their bright light.

"When you dropped by the other day with cookies and talked to the kids, they couldn't stop talking about how exciting meeting a real hero was."

"As long as my wife can come along," Lowen said, sending a relieved smile Adam's way. "She wants to meet the woman responsible for taking this one off the market."

"So the rumors on Facebook are true?" McGuire asked. "*You're dating Five-Alarm?*"

Everyone looked surprised, except for Chief Lowen, who looked surprisingly pleased by the news. Pleased that the guy who was gunning for lieutenant was spending his private time with someone the department could get behind. Someone other than his goddaughter.

Then there was Harper, mouth open, trying to form the word *no* only nothing came out. At first he thought she was just embarrassed being caught in a fib. But then her eyes went wide with panic, her face flushed fully, and Adam watched, knot in his stomach, as the embarrassment quickly turned to humiliation.

"No. Adam and I aren't, um . . ." She cleared her throat and sent him a small smile that was all apology and agony. "I lied," she finished, then threw her shoulders back, and damn, if her courage in the face of utter mortification didn't cause something inside of him to rear up.

"You lied?" McGuire asked, and there was something about his humorous tone that had Harper fidgeting with her hands.

She was taking in every surprised look, every questioning glance through a skewed filter. A filter that was the unfortunate side effect of expending energy and too much heart on a guy who didn't deserve it.

Harper nodded, her smile small and tight, as if it were the only thing holding her together. The last time she'd tried to look this brave had been when Dr. Dildo made it clear he wasn't interested in what she had to offer. Which was a hell of a lot, if you asked Adam.

Her hurt over the rejection was so deep it tore at his gut then, and he sure as hell wouldn't let her go through that again. Not in front of a station full of guys.

"She lied about when we started dating."

"I did," she said at the same exact time McGuire mumbled, "She did?"

"She did," Adam said, slinging an arm over her shoulder and pulling her to him, as if she was his. Funny thing about that, she kind of felt like his. Had since their first kiss. "I realized how special she was a few months back, when we were shooting the latest Cuties with Booties calendar. Then I bumped into her at her grandma's shop, and I couldn't stop thinking about her, so when she asked if I would do some modeling for her grandma's shop I said, *Hell yeah*. A chance to spend time with her? That was a no-brainer."

"You don't have to do this," Harper whispered, and he could hear her voice crack.

He looked down into her eyes and felt himself drowning in the emotion he saw there. "I know. I want to," he said gently.

"Well done. The way to a lady's heart is always through her family," Lowen said, looking at Adam as if reciting the eleventh commandment. He turned to Harper. "I guess that's how he sweet-talked you into helping plan Beat the Heat."

Now it was Adam's turn to gasp.

Harper, however, looked as if she was going to throw up. Or bolt. Not that he blamed her. She'd come here to help him out, and her quick thinking on her feet, outlining a vision that Lowen could get on board with, had somehow caused her to be drafted into his shit storm. Not his intention.

"Harper is one of the most creative people I know," Adam said. "She's friends with just about everyone in town and would no doubt throw a party that reflects the town's wishes."

"Slippery slope," Harper quietly said to Adam, referring to his own lie by omission, and pushed through a smile that was so big it could have been seen from space.

With a look that said he had this, Adam added, "Even though it was the perfect solution, we realized that our private relationship would be a conflict of interest."

They may not have slept together, but the whole town had seen their kiss. So no one was more surprised when Lowen shrugged, as if he hadn't delivered a three-day training last spring on the negative impacts of mixing department business with personal interests, and said, "I don't see the problem."

The man sounded relieved at the information that Adam wouldn't be left to his own devices. Harper looked horrified, whether it was over the idea of coming clean about their relationship after his big speech—and tanking his shot at lieutenant. Or being drafted into planning Beat the Heat—and spending the next two weeks with him. He wasn't sure. All he knew was that the direction had changed and someone was about to feel the heat.

"In fact, I think it's a great idea. The papers will love it. 'Local art teacher brings small-town traditions back to St. Helena's Beat the Heat.'"

Harper took in a deep breath and he saw the word *no* forming on her lips, then she looked at him and *slippery slope* didn't even begin to describe what Adam felt. Suddenly, he didn't want to be

Five-Alarm or the guy who played beer pong on his days off. Hell, he was too old for beer pong.

He had no business having a girlfriend and wouldn't even know what to do with one. But he liked who he was around her, and how he felt. And the idea of spending a little more time with her seemed right.

Harper's eyes went soft, just like his heart, and she tightened her hand around his, a little too tight for comfort, but a show of support all the same. Then smiling at their audience, she said, "What can I say? He had me at hello."

chapter
ten

W hy did you do that?" Harper asked when they stepped outside of the fire station away from prying ears, still shocked Adam had publicly claimed her as his girlfriend.

Correction, he'd said *private relationship*, which now that she thought about it wasn't very far from *private dancer*, but she knew exactly how his boss had taken the news. "Now they all think we're really dating."

His brows lowered over his eyes. "As opposed to the pretend dating we were doing before?"

"That was different. It was before our deal." And before that second kiss. And before he'd said all of those sweet things about her. Which, having an actress for a mother, she knew was for authenticity of his role. But in that moment, when he'd said them, she'd started to believe them. And that was the most terrifying part. "The deal where I would clear things up with everyone? Which I did, right before I came here to let you off the hook for modeling."

"The deal changed," he said, casual as can be. "And now you have a model for your shoot."

Harper set the cookie box on the hood of her car and turned to face him. "I told my grandma this morning that we weren't dating. I told her that I'd lied. Which is pretty much like admitting it into a blow horn in the middle of town."

Adam smiled. "How did that go?"

"She didn't believe me. She said I was lying about lying." Harper rolled her eyes. "In fact, no one believes me. It's like they're all convinced I can't handle a casual relationship. Something about a bad habit of collecting people."

Adam was quiet for a long moment, studying her. "Do you want to collect me?"

Whoever succeeded in stealing his heart would be an incredibly lucky lady, but Harper wasn't that lady. She was struggling to get the safe bet interested—there was no way she could lure a man who passed through people's lives like smoke. "I only collect people who want to be collected."

"Then why are you looking at me as if you want me to kiss you again?"

"I do not." If anything, *she* wanted to kiss *him*. Wanted to kiss him until that troubled expression vanished and he looked like the guy who could handle anything again. Because he might be acting calm and as if what happened back there was no biggie. But it was.

And they both knew it.

Watching his plan fall apart in front of the one man he needed to impress was heartbreaking. Not that anyone else noticed. Adam hid his disappointment well, adopting a fireproof exterior. But Harper knew what being discounted felt like, knew how bad it stung. Adam was rarely, if ever, overlooked and she felt the urge to comfort him. What a ridiculous notion that was, wanting to comfort a guy who considered himself indestructible.

"And we will not, so if it looks that way, just know it's not on purpose, and walk away."

"Walk away from kissing my girlfriend?" His brows lifted and he took a step closer. "That would look odd."

"I'm not your girlfriend. And—what are you doing? Back up." She put her hands out to stop him from getting within lip-smacking range, her hands settling on the hard planes of his chest. It didn't help. He was closing in fast. Almost as fast as her heart was pounding.

Unsure if he was going to kiss her because he wanted to, or to prove a point, she added, "Although I'm sure there are many girls in town who would love you to kiss them."

He paused a scant inch from her mouth. "Just not this girl?"

"Sorry."

Challenge lit his eyes and he tilted his head lower until his lips were right there. A whisper away from touching hers. And all of the air whooshed out of her lungs. "You're a terrible liar, sunshine."

He pulled back and with a wicked wink turned to prop a hip against her car. He opened the box of cookies, settled on a confetti cake kringle, and offered her one.

Her stomach did a backflip at the thought, but she declined. "I've already had three this morning. A fourth would come off as greedy. Plus if I'm helping with Beat the Heat, I'm going to want to fit into my shorts."

"I prefer the dress anyway." They both looked down at her dress and she decided that maybe it was time to toss out her shorts. "And you know you want another."

There were a lot of things she wanted. Some things were better for her than others. Telling herself that carrots are a vegetable, and therefore healthy, she grabbed a caramel pecan carrot cookie and took a bite. Her eyes slid shut in pure ecstasy as the sweet and salty combo of the caramel and nuts melted on her tongue.

She heard a light chuckle and opened her eyes. "Just because you're my boyfriend doesn't mean you know me," she teased.

He didn't laugh. In fact, his smile faded and he let out a slow breath. "I didn't plan it to go down like that, it just came out," he said. "Lowen wasn't buying anything I was selling, McGuire was being an ass, then you started talking about jars, candles, art projects . . . me. Turning what was a shit idea into something amazing and real. So amazing that Lowen became interested." Adam slid her an uncertain look. "And by association, he became interested in me."

"So you decided to take that interest and lie to him about being in a relationship with me?" Harper said quietly.

"Slippery slope, remember."

As if she could forget. That one little lie had complicated an already complicated situation. Then again, it had also given her a chance to get to know Adam, someone she'd known her entire life, but never really *knew*. The more time she spent with him, the more layers she uncovered, and the more she liked what she saw.

But did he? Or did he find himself in a jam, needed an out, and she was the closest willing female? If so, and this was another one of his on-the-fly solutions, then what?

"What happens when your chief finds out we lied?"

"Who says he has to?"

Harper choked on her cookie, because surely he didn't intend on keeping up the façade. "Fibbing to a sales rep who lives two hours away is one thing, but lying to the town would be impossible."

He stared at her for a few beats, then turned to face her, placing one hand on either side of her hips, pressing her between her car and his body. "Then we won't lie."

"What do you mean?" she breathed.

"This." He placed his hand on her hip, and she moved slightly from the spark. "Don't move, just stand here for one minute."

"This isn't a good idea."

"One minute, Harper. That's all I'm asking."

She didn't remember agreeing, but she didn't move either. Couldn't. Adam's hands were cupping her hips. They were standing so close she could smell the sugar from his cookie.

He didn't kiss her, didn't give her some sweet line to sway her decision, or sweet-talk his way around her common sense. He didn't do a single thing from the Five-Alarm Casanova handbook. He just stood there, as the cars passed by on the street and a light breeze stirred her skirt against his thighs, while he silently stared into her gaze. And what she saw staring back made breathing impossible.

It also made saying no impossible.

Respect, humor, friendship, and connection—it was all there. So was hunger. A hunger so intense she could feel it heating her skin until her dress felt constricting and her heart pounded as if to escape.

"Whatever this is between us," he said, his voice a rough whisper, "it's real."

"It's just chemistry," Harper said, then wanted to laugh. She hadn't felt chemistry like this—ever. At least, not reciprocated.

"I've felt chemistry before, sunshine, and this is something different."

For the first time in her life Harper didn't mind being different. Because whatever this was felt exhilarating. Sensual.

Alluring.

And God knew she wanted to allure, and be confident she could do some alluring on her own. "So I help you with the picnic and you what? Hold my hand in public?"

His face carefully blank, he said, "You want me to pose half-naked for Clovis's new campaign, and the only way Lowen would ever sign off is if it were done as a favor to you—the town's favorite sweetheart, who happens to be my girlfriend."

"*Chantel* wants you to model for the line," she said, because, *wow*, that sounded very contractual, and not the least bit chemical. Or alluring. "Men's underwear."

"Like David Beckham for Armani?"

"More like Michael Jordan for Hanes," she lied, because his expression was turning too smug for her liking, and her heart was a little too soft to agree to this deal. "And I've changed my mind. This won't work."

Obviously stuck on comparing himself to Beckham, Adam leaned down and licked the caramel off her cookie. "You, me, under the hot lights in nothing but silk undies? It will work, I promise. And if you're still unsure, I'll take it slow."

She set the remainder of her cookie in the box and pushed at his chest—only he didn't move. "I just said I changed my mind. I told you this won't work, and your solution is to talk about sex?"

"I'm a guy. Every solution includes sex," he said, as if that were written on one of the tablets Moses brought down from the mount. "As for this not working out, your hand proves that wrong." She looked down to find her palm had slid down that stone stomach of his, to tangle in his waistband.

Horrified, and a little turned on, she snatched it back. "You're not my type."

"Then you won't want to collect me," he said, but something about the way he said it had her wishing she could take back the words.

Five-Alarm Casanova with his panty-melting wink and ladies' man charm wasn't her type. But funny, focused, and slightly vulnerable Adam with his quick wit and contagious smile got to her. And that was who she was talking to right then—not the playboy, but the layers beneath.

"Adam—"

"No, it's okay. The truth is you don't need me," he said, tucking a loose curl behind her ear. "You think you do, but you don't. You're so good at reading people, bringing them into your world. Every time, you deliver on your potential. God, you're so damn real, Chantel will want to re-sign with Clovis with or without me." He got quiet. "But I need you, Harper. You saw the look on Lowen's face. I'm bound to fuck this up without your help, and I'm so damn tired of fucking up."

chapter
eleven

It had been four days since changing her Facebook status to "In a Relationship," and the closest Harper had come to sensual was tagging Fireman Saves the Day dildos at the Boulder Holder. A huge order had arrived from their largest "toy" suppliers, just in time for their midsummer sale, and since Clovis was off hosting a Panty Raid, Harper had spent her morning restocking the shelves.

Now she was back at the Fashion Flower, folding Lollypants ruffled bloomers for the front display, her ear cocked toward her phone. She had texted Adam earlier that day that the samples from Lulu Allure had arrived, but since he was still on shift she hadn't heard back. That didn't stop people from asking about their "relationship," though.

Harper couldn't go anywhere without someone weighing in on her romance status, and the shop had never been so busy. Even her students wanted to know about Hadam. It seemed the only person who hadn't wanted to talk about her and Adam was Adam.

He'd texted her a few times over the weekend, and she'd swung by the station to pick up the Beat the Heat binder, but other than a few pleasantries, it was as if they'd gone back to normal.

Something that should have come as a huge relief. But it didn't. Harper had managed to snag herself the hottest catch in town, and it was strictly platonic.

Not that there was an interest in blurring the lines with Adam. But it would be nice, for once, if a man wanted to blur the lines with her. Especially a man who seemed to live to defy the rules.

The shop bell jingled, and in walked Liza Miner. As the founding member of the town's most prestigious mommy-and-me craft co-op, Crafty Mamas, and owner of *Whining, Dining, and Diapers,* the top mommy blog in wine country, there wasn't a toddler trend or kid craze that she didn't create—or capitalize on. She was sophisticated, driven, and one of the biggest voices in the mommy community. She was also a single mom to Brooklyn, one of Harper's Sprouting Picassos.

Her intense competitiveness was rivaled only by her black book. There wasn't a parent group she hadn't infiltrated or a PTA seat she hadn't won—and her daughter was only in the second grade. Which made her the perfect outreach mommy for Beat the Heat.

"I got your message during the Crafty Mamas' meeting today," Liza said, adjusting her designer clutch and getting straight to business. "We're interested in running a booth, theme and age appropriate, all proceeds going toward the firefighters' Back-to-School Pack fund."

"That's fantastic." Harper set down the bloomers and barely resisted the urge to pull Liza in for a hug. "I can't believe it."

Liza placed her purse on the front display. "I thought about just e-mailing you, but when I heard you were working here today I decided to see you in person. To ask you a favor."

"Ask away, I am the favor fairy." To prove it, Harper put on her friendliest smile.

"Actually, it's more of a requirement."

A small part of Harper's heart sank. She didn't understand why people couldn't just do things because it was the nice thing to do. And since when had goodwill become so costly?

"I'm sure whatever it is, we can work it out." After all, that's what Harper did. Worked hard to make things work, make people happy, and make them smile—although, she was having a hard time holding her own smile.

"First . . ." Liza held up a manicured finger, and Harper held her breath.

Here come the negotiations. Liza hadn't become one of the most powerful momtrepreneurs by playing nice. She had markers out all around town, and now she was calling in Harper's two seconds after she'd doled one out.

"For *Whining, Dining, and Diapers,* I need to get sole credit for handling all of the marketing and PR for this event."

"Are you offering to handle all of the marketing and PR?"

Liza snorted. "Lord, no. I'm too busy to handle all of that, but if I'm going to bring in the mommy demographic, then I want to put that on my site when I cover the event for my next post, 'Goodwill Makes for a Good Jack and Jill.'"

"I have equal access to the mommy demographic," Harper pointed out.

"You teach finger painting to kids," Liza corrected.

This was not the first time Harper had heard this, and as long as she was spending her days teaching kids' art classes, it wouldn't be the last. Not that Harper didn't like teaching—she loved it. But she also loved creating her own designs, and she missed combining bold colors with varying textures and light to make sets and displays that came to life. It was one of the reasons she was putting her heart and soul into saving her grandmother's account. Aside from helping Clovis, of course, Harper was loving the artistic process and getting back to her own roots.

At one time she was considered an up-and-coming set and window designer. She'd started making a name for herself as a live artist who told her stories through people and everyday pieces of furniture, fabrics, and paint.

But there wasn't really a market for her kind of talent in St. Helena. Besides the Boulder Holder and the Fashion Flower, there wasn't another clothing shop in town with a big enough window for her to work with. But St. Helena was the only home she'd ever known, and every person in her patchwork family lived there. And that was what was important.

After a lifetime of watching her mother put her art before matters of the heart, Harper knew she wanted a different life. She valued things like connections, security, and love above all else.

"That may be, but giving one person sole credit when there will be so many people helping out doesn't seem fair."

Plus, she wasn't sure what Adam would say to that. Or the department, for that matter. She didn't mind if Liza capitalized on the event, but she didn't want to diminish other people's hard work.

Liza looked at her as if she were slow, and maybe she was. Maybe that was why she was still folding ruffled bloomers instead of pursuing her passion for visual arts. Then again, she didn't hate her job, but she'd hate herself if she bulldozed over people.

"Well, other people wouldn't be able to get Vintage Elementary to send out flyers offering extra credit to every student who participates in the event. They also couldn't get every mommy blogger in Northern California to get on board with a grassroots marketing effort to ensure that parents all over the greater wine country know that this is *the* family event of the summer."

Harper was pretty sure, if given the time, she could do the same. But she didn't have the time. And she'd promised Adam she'd help.

"What's the second requirement?" Harper asked, and immediately Liza's face went flush.

"This one is actually a favor." The woman who was always cool and collected—a Stepford in every sense of the word, sans the wife part—smoothed down the hem of her skirt and self-consciously looked around. "I need advice on picking out something sexy."

"For Brooklyn?" Because ruffled bloomers was as sexy as the Fashion Flower got.

"For me." Liza lowered her voice, even though the shop was nearing closing time and there wasn't another soul in the store besides the two of them. "I'm stopping by the Boulder Holder on my way home, to pick something up. And I needed your advice first."

Now it was Harper's turn to flush. "You need my advice?"

"I have a date tonight. A real date. Time with a man who isn't my brother, father, or elderly relative." She shook her head. "God, I haven't been on a first date since I married Brooklyn's dad, and even then I think he took me to his favorite college pub with his dorm mates." Liza laughed, a little self-conscious, a little bitter, and a whole lot sad. "Pathetic, right?"

"No," Harper said, placing her hand on Liza's. "I think it's a real situation for more women than you'd think. And wearing pretty lingerie makes us feel sexy, and everyone wants to feel sexy when they go on a first date. It's not pathetic at all."

"Yeah?"

"Yeah," Harper said. "What are you looking for?"

"Well, that's why I came to you," Liza admitted. "My mom was in the shop the other day and overheard Adam talking to you about some bra-and-panty set." She shrugged. "I figured if he liked it enough to request it by name, then it must be pretty sexy. And I need all the sexy I can get."

It was an odd statement for someone who carried herself as

though she had it all figured out. A woman couldn't get trendier or more put together than Liza. She dressed for world domination, moved with purpose, and yet she was nervous about what kind of panties to buy. Nervous enough to ask Harper.

Or maybe, like Liza, Harper carried herself differently than she thought. Perhaps the way she perceived herself and how other people saw her didn't match.

Or maybe, she thought with a secret smile, she carried herself differently since Adam. She felt different. Lighter, edgier, more relaxed.

Whatever the reason, it felt good. Liberating.

Sexy.

"It's called Honeysuckle," Harper said, thinking of what her grandmother would say. "It's elegant without being uptight. Sophisticated without being stuffy. I think it will look lovely with your complexion and will help with your inner goddess."

"Thank you," Liza said, the words sounding a little rusty from lack of use. "For the advice and . . . well . . ." And there went the fidgeting again. "If it hadn't been for you, I wouldn't be going on a date at all."

"Why is that?"

"His son is in Brooklyn's art class," Liza said, and Harper got a really bad feeling in her gut. "I've noticed him looking at me for a few weeks now, but he never approached me. Then the other day after class he asked me to dinner, told me about how you encouraged him to get back out there, make some time for himself." She waggled a brow. "Cute, sweet, and a doctor to boot."

Harper felt sucker punched in the gut. She would have let loose a grunt from the pain, except her smile was so tightly frozen her lips couldn't move.

"Are you talking about Clay?"

"If you mean Dr. Walker, then yes."

"My Dr. Walker?" Harper asked, her voice a little shrill.

"He's lots of people's doctor," Liza said, then seemed to realize that wasn't what Harper had meant. Her eyes narrowed, taking all the warm fuzzies in the room with her. "We're meeting at the Cork'd N Dipped at seven for wine and a chocolate tasting."

Okay, so Clay wasn't Harper's anything. But she felt as if he were. Even if she hadn't felt the tingles.

Harper had noticed him first, before he'd lost the dazed failed-marriage look, the outdated goatee, and twenty extra pounds. She'd been there when he'd needed a friend, talked to him at the same wine bar, babysat his son so he could recapture some much-needed alone time. Well, she'd babysat Tommy because she loved that kid, but also because she wanted to help Clay.

And now Clay was ready to carve out a little time for himself—just like she'd encouraged him to do. Only he wasn't interested in sharing it with Harper. She was just his fill-in friend.

Adam had gone into the new week with a mission: win friends and influence people. Not with his easygoing smile and charm, but through hard work and exemplary behavior—a real nose-to-the-grindstone mentality that spoke past his fast-and-loose reputation and more toward a respected lieutenant-in-training.

It was only Wednesday, and already it had become clear that there was a conspiracy to screw with his mission.

"A condom vending machine?" Adam slammed the request form on the kitchen table in front of McGuire. "Want to explain how this ended up on Cap's desk?"

McGuire looked up from his bowl of cereal, his expression one of pure confusion. "You told me to fill out a request form for a new helmet, and when I saw your form floating around I thought I'd do you a favor and submit it for you."

Adam couldn't tell if the guy was being serious, or if he was really that narrow sighted. "What was it about the phrases *condom vending machine* and *hose safety* that made you say, 'Yeah, Cap really needs to see this completely legit request'?"

"The Wrap Before You Tap It safety campaign did seem odd," McGuire admitted. "But I figured that whether it was a joke or a real request, Cap would think it was funny."

"He did when I showed it to him as an *April Fool's joke*. Off duty. But when you submitted it officially, it somehow bypassed Roman's desk and went straight up the line," Adam said.

McGuire pushed his cereal bowl back. "Ah shit, man, Lowen saw it?"

"No." *Thank God.* That would have been the final nail in Adam's career. "His secretary saw it, noticed it was dated April first, and sent it back to Cap to deal with as he pleased."

"How does Cap want to deal with it?"

"He doesn't." Not that Adam blamed him. Roman wanted to clean up another one of Adam's messes about as much as Adam wanted to mess up. Which was why he mentioned that if Adam wanted to be a lieutenant, then he needed to start thinking like one. His first lesson?

Doling out adequate punishment for submitting a dickheaded request.

"He scrapped the form, agreed to let me talk to you about it, and wanted to offer his congrats to the newest member of the Beat the Heat planning committee."

"That's my punishment?" McGuire asked, his eyes dark with dread. "To help plan a stupid picnic with the Fucking New Guy?"

It was actually Adam's punishment. One he gave himself—and one he would feel every second he was stuck with Seth and McGuire. But working with two dickheads seemed a fitting sentence.

Beneath the pain-in-the-ass pranks and bonehead decisions, McGuire was a natural. All the kid needed was some careful handling and solid direction and he would be able to go the distance. Roman had given Adam that direction, helped him transform from an adrenaline-seeking daredevil to a top-notch firefighter.

Now it was Adam's turn to pay it forward, and hopefully do some more transforming of his own in the process.

"You and Seth will work together to make sure that all the posters are hung around town and that the *Sentinel* runs the ads for the event. Plus, you'll run the engine station, talk to the kids about what being a firefighter means to you, and help a few of them climb the ladder."

"With Seth?"

Adam pressed his hands flat against the table and leaned in. "You and Seth will be so close when this is over, people will think one of you puckered your lips too hard and swallowed the other. Got it?"

"Yes, sir," McGuire moaned.

"Good." Adam straightened. "Now I need to go apologize to a lady about being a dick."

By the time Adam's shift ended and he'd made his apologies about the condom prank to the appropriate parties, he was in desperate need of a hot shower, a cold beer, and a solid eighteen hours of sleep in his own bed.

Make that a cold six-pack. In his bed. With a hot woman.

He was SOL on one and two, but only because of option three. A hot woman—one with a camera and a sweet smile who might not have a bed but wanted him in bedtime attire.

Laughing at that ass-backward scenario, he showered at the station, threw on some jeans and a shirt, and made his way up Main Street.

The sun had long since disappeared, so Adam allowed the gaslit lamps to light his way. When he arrived at the Boulder Holder the CLOSED sign was flipped, but the door was unlocked. He let himself inside and breathed in the feminine scent of jasmine and lace.

A light humming came from the back of the store.

Adam followed the sound and discovered Harper in the back room, rifling through a box. Face down and ass up in a pair of cutoff shorts that rode high enough to show the beginning curves of her sweet cheeks—which swayed as she hummed.

Adam felt a small smile lift his lips and his mood.

She had on one of those multicolored tops he favored, maybe tie-dye. It was baggy in nature, cinched in the back by a big bow, and if she thought it made her look more temptress and less art teacher, she was wrong.

He watched her for a few moments, enjoying the show, then cleared his throat when the humming turned into singing "Sexy and I Know It."

When she didn't stop singing, or moving that swaying backside, he realized she'd known he was there all along.

"You're late." Her voice was muffled through the box, but he was pretty sure she ended the greeting with, "Drop your pants."

"Well, if that isn't the best 'welcome home' in the history of mankind." He might be going for upstanding citizen, but he was still a man, and from what he could see of her backside, she was all woman. And right about then, he needed a cute, curvy distraction. "With fair play being what it is, I say the next article to disappear is that top of yours."

Harper straightened and gifted him with a big smile. Not flirty or overstated. Just real, as though she were happy to see him. And a smile like that, man oh man, it cut through all the BS to ease that twisted ball in his gut that was a tangle of stress. And Adam didn't know what to do with that—an unusual situation for him.

"I meant, so you can try these on." She dangled a pair of silk undies in his direction. They were red, tiny, and looked like a thong for superheroes.

"No amount of manscaping will get me in those," he said. She dropped them in the box and pulled out another pair. Boxers. Pink, pinstriped, and not happening. "Pink clashes with testosterone."

"After a drink or two, you might change your mind," she said hopefully, pointing to a bottle of Scotch to be used as a prop poised next to the chair.

"You got another bottle?" he asked, and she shook her head. "Then I promise you I won't reconsider. No man wants to be seen in those, and no woman wants to see a man in those."

"More manly underwear. Got it." With a dainty little huff she dug back in, and after several seconds came up with a pair of boxer briefs. They were kind of manly, not made of silk and, "They're purple."

"Seriously?" She dropped her hand to her side. "Okay, what's wrong?"

He cleared his throat. "Nothing."

"Then why are you acting all pissy? See, there. I can't shoot you when you're pouting." She cocked her head. "Well, I could shoot you, but it wouldn't be with my camera."

"I'm not pouting." Since bitching about his day or having a heart-to-heart with his girlfriend was firmly on his *not in this life-time* list, Adam flashed her the dimples. Double barreled with all the pearly whites showing. It had been called sexy, mesmerizing, endor-phin inducing. "Here's a grin. My way of saying fair is fair, and if I lose the pants, you lose the top."

"We don't have enough Scotch, remember?" She narrowed her eyes and studied him, really hard. Until he was afraid she was seeing more than he wanted her to—and he began to sweat. Then she pointed to his lips. "Yup, that smile's missing the whole *let's get drunk and screw* vibe you normally put off, and you're looking a little soul battered." Her face softened. "Sure you don't want to talk about it?"

He shrugged as if he had not a clue as to what she was talking about. But the sweating didn't stop, because if there was one thing Adam had learned over the past week it was that Harper was a master of the unsaid. She could read body language and translate silence like a professional interrogator. So when she gave a disappointed smile, then bent over to grab a different pair of boxers, he knew she was letting him off the hook.

Which was what he wanted, right? No complications, no confusion, just a whole lot of chemistry mixed with a *I'll rub your back, you rub mine* pact.

Only now, he was here and everything felt complicated, and he was more than confused. In fact, his heart was racing and his face felt hot, and—*Jesus Christ*—he was nervous.

It wasn't the studio lights, or the too-metro-to-be-manly underwear, or even the elaborate Calvin-Klein-meets-Hugh-Hefner man cave she had created from fabric, a leather chair, and raw talent.

It was the unimpressive shirt, the bare feet, and the genuine concern that had his brain checking out. And that smile. One flash of those teeth and he knew he'd come here tonight needing something. He wasn't sure what, but Adam didn't do nervous.

And he sure as hell didn't do needy.

"I was just wondering if you gave Chantel my measurements," Adam said, toeing off his boots and bringing this party back to where it should be.

Fun with a side of flirt.

"She sent a few different sizes. I'm sure it will be fine," she said.

"Size fifteen is usually a special order," he said.

Her expression went from confused to understanding as she recalled his offhanded remark the other day in front of Clay about ring sizes.

"We're not using any accessories," she said, "just pajamas and underwear." She held up his first outfit again.

He grinned big and bad. "Sunshine, when I said my ring size was a fifteen, I wasn't talking about my finger."

chapter
twelve

A dam didn't want to talk about what was bothering him.
Noted—and understood. After the day Harper had had, it
was probably a good thing. She was still reeling from her accidental
matchmaking disaster, so partaking in a kumbaya moment in the
middle of her grandma's shop wasn't a smart idea. Even if Adam did
look as if he could use a real friend.

Only Adam didn't do real—he did frat-boy-meets-beefcake.
Which worked for her since Harper never did the sorority thing,
and she wasn't a big fan of red meat. Plus, they weren't supposed
to be getting to know each other better. Sure, he'd walked in looking sexy and strong and strangely lost—and Harper, being Harper,
momentarily forgot the deal—but he wasn't looking to be found.

And she wasn't looking to add one more platonic guy to her collection. Only instead of taking a step back, like she should have, she
stepped forward and into him, ignoring every warning bell blaring in
her head. His face creased with confusion and a vulnerability so genuine that she wrapped her arms around his waist and just held on.

Adam might not want to talk about whatever was bothering him, but it was obvious he needed a hug.

She felt him freeze and everything in that moment stilled, as if the gesture were so foreign he wasn't sure what to do next. It was a strange reaction for a guy who had canoodled with half the town's female population.

Harper knew all too well that canoodling and connecting were two vastly different things. Mastering one didn't mean receiving the other, so she rested her head against his big chest, right over his heart, and waited. Waited for him to give in, to take what she was offering.

Support and understanding.

She felt him let go, release a breath that seemed to go on forever as his body pressed in closer and closer around hers. When he didn't have anything left, he rested his cheek on the top of her head and locked his hands behind her back.

Neither of them moved. They didn't speak or think. Just accepted the give and take of energy as it passed between them.

A minute or fifteen might have passed before she realized that her eyes were closed, that his arms were holding on to her as if they were the only things keeping him grounded, and Harper wondered what would happen if she never moved, if she decided to stay right there. In his arms. Forever.

Reminding herself that connection and commitment also weren't exclusive to each other, she gave a final squeeze and stepped back.

"What was that?" he asked after a long moment, his voice thick and raspy.

"Us not talking about it." To make sure she didn't do anything stupid—because hugging was one step away from loving in her world—she turned around to focus on the placement of the leather chair, positioning a glass of Scotch on the arm. "Now, go put those on. I cleared out the first dressing room for you."

After Adam had texted her he could stop by after closing, she'd spent the evening turning Couture Corner into a studio, knowing it would take her mind off what was going on at the wine bar next door on her date with the doctor—though Liza was the one on it—and the space would work as the perfect backdrop for the shoot. It was sexy, sensual, masculine. Not that Adam needed any help in any of those departments.

He'd walked through the door wearing jeans, a T-shirt, and yesterday's stubble, and managed to flip every one of Harper's female switches. The man wore sexy like it was a cologne.

"I'm good."

Harper looked over her shoulder as Adam fisted his shirt with a single hand. He drew it over his head in a move that was all bad boy and swagger, tossing the shirt to the floor and leaving him in boxers, bare feet, and enough male confidence that Harper forgot all about Liza and Clay flirting right then at Cork'd N Dipped.

In fact, she forgot a lot of things. Like how photographers shouldn't openly gawk at their subjects. Or why taking a little time for pleasure was bad for business. Heck, she couldn't even remember how to breathe.

Or why Adam was a bad idea.

Adam was gorgeous. Mind-blowingly so. He had miles of toned muscle and tanned skin that rippled as he moved. His chest was covered with just the right amount of hair, which fell into a vee before disappearing beneath a pair of boxers. They were more boxer briefs, which, like every other uniform he wore, he filled out to perfection.

And that stomach, *sweet baby Jesus*, those abs looked to be cut from stone—or perhaps they were from lifting ladders or parked cars, or whatever it was firemen did to keep in shape. He rested his hands on his hips, and his six-pack became an eight, rippling down and tightening, then a twelve—

Harper snapped her eyes to his, beautifully blue and twinkling with amusement. "You did that on purpose," she said.

"Looked like you were waiting for a show." He flexed harder. Damn, the man was built. A fact she'd accepted the first time he'd posed for her. But this time felt different. More intimate. "Who am I to deny a lady?"

A bead of sweat rolled between her breasts from the heat of the lights. Then again, maybe it was the heat Adam was putting off.

Regardless, it was time to get to work. "I was admiring the new men's line."

"I've been told I have an impressive line."

"The lines of the design," she clarified, and he chuckled. She threw her hands in the air and struggled for a way out. "And the color. It matches your eyes."

"The shorts are purple. My eyes are blue. And they're up here, sunshine."

Harper's eyes flew to his—again. This time they were lit with humor. "The boxers are merlot, not purple, and everyone knows that merlot complements cobalt blue."

"Everyone, huh?" Adam stepped into the lights and sat down on the chair. Careful not to knock over the Scotch, he sprawled out, leaning back deeply in the chair, resting his elbows on the arms while making himself right at home on her set.

"My turn, then. Your cheeks are pink, or would that be flushed?" He made the word sound sinful. "And they match your eyes, which are heated and dilating as we speak." He looked down at his boxers and waggled a brow. "Does that mean the boxers will impress the female board members at Lulu Allure?"

Harper rolled her eyes and then picked up her camera, bringing everything into focus, and took a few shots to make sure the lights synched up.

Good to go, and Adam looking stunning on her LED screen, she snapped several more. His hair was mussed just enough, his stubble cast the perfect shadow, and his tan skin glistened against buttery leather. He didn't need to be told how to move or how to sit—he was the embodiment of rugged allure. A real *GQ*'s Sexiest Underwear Model.

A great thing for a successful photo shoot. Not so good for her elevated heart rate.

She tilted the camera slightly, stepping in closer to frame him perfectly, then pushed the button only to stop after one shot because his cobalt-blue pools locked on hers through the lens. And he grinned—one of those full-wattage, flirty grins that was part bad boy and part sex god, and completely heart-stopping.

Harper lowered the camera and looked at the boxers. "You don't need help impressing females, and you know it."

"Life's too short to be ordinary, sunshine."

And wasn't that the worst thing to be? Ordinary.

Harper's throat tightened and her stomach did a familiar dip down. She'd lived an extraordinary childhood, with an extraordinary mother, traveling from one stage to another—never managing to find her own spotlight.

Every cast became family, every set became home, and every time Harper threw her little self into making it fun, making people happy. Ultimately, the final performance would come, her mother would take a bow, and then it would all disappear. Her family moved on to bigger and better sets, her mother moved on to another role, and Harper felt as if she was always left waiting in the wings. Waiting to be noticed.

An irony that didn't escape her.

"Like me?"

Adam leaned forward and took the camera, setting it on the arm of the chair. Then he took her hand in his and tugged her closer.

"Not like you," he said quietly. "Nothing about you is ordinary, Harper."

Around Adam she didn't feel ordinary, or overlooked, or as if she were destined to be everyone's go-to friend. She felt seen—not only as a woman, but as the only woman in the room. And yes, she understood, right then she was the only woman in the room. But the way he watched her and touched her made her feel unique.

Wanted.

"Whoa," he said, giving her hand a soft squeeze. "Dating 101 states you aren't supposed to cry when a guy pays you a compliment. You're supposed to smile and say thanks in that mysterious way that neither confirms nor denies your interest so he's inclined to buy you a drink in order to solve the mystery."

She blinked back the forming tears, then bent over and kissed his cheek, the stubble tickling her lips as she whispered, "Thank you."

"You need to hold your cards a little longer," he said quietly when she pulled back. "Going in for the kiss with one compliment is too easy, even for me."

She choked a little on her tears. "It was the perfect compliment and a perfectly disastrous day, so it deserved a kiss."

"Want to talk about it?" he asked, repeating her earlier words.

"Not really."

"Yeah, well, me neither," he said. "But since I just broke every rule known to man about women and asked you, while wearing merlot undies by the way, the least you can do is indulge me."

"It's stupid, really." And completely humiliating.

"Then we'll both laugh." He took a sip of the Scotch and handed it to her. "Which, if you ask me, beats the shit out of crying."

A small chuckle escaped, and he was right, it did feel good. In fact, it felt so good she did it again.

He palmed her hips and drew her even closer, leading her between his legs, until their thighs were brushing "See, it can't be so bad if you're already laughing just thinking about it."

Harper took a sip, then cringed as the liquid courage burned a path down her throat. When she could pass air through her chest again, she said, "Liza Miner stopped by to tell me Crafty Mamas would run a craft booth, and the elementary school is on board as well."

"That's great. Better than great. It means we actually have a booth filled."

"And she'll fill more booths," she said. "As long as her mommy blog gets all the credit for hosting the event."

Adam laughed. "I don't care what she says on her blog. As long as she helps fill tables, and all the proceeds go to the Back-to-School Packs fund, we're golden."

"She'll be happy to hear that," Harper said. It was still unfair, and extremely petty, but if Adam was okay with it then who was Harper to deny Liza? It wasn't as if boasting about fake accolades was any more dishonest than convincing an entire town of a fake relationship. Which gave Harper fake street cred in the allure department. "She asked my advice on lingerie for a date she has, right now, actually. She said she wanted to feel sexy."

"Lingerie? Sex? Hell, if I knew this was what women talked about, I would have asked to chat it out a long time ago," he said, only half joking. "What did you recommend?"

She felt her cheeks flush. "Honeysuckle."

"Ah. Great choice." He lifted his hand to tug at the neckline of her shirt over one shoulder. "Is that what you're wearing under here?"

She smacked his hand away with her free one. "No."

"What?" he said, sounding like the offended party. "I'm in my skivvies and I don't even get a little peek of lace?"

"You're the subject, not me."

"What are you going to subject me to?"

She ignored this, but didn't move her shirt back up. "Liza wasn't shopping for just any date. It was a first date. With Clay Walker."

"Ouch."

"I guess my pep talk on how he could be a good dad and manage to find some time for himself really inspired him. To ask Liza Miner out."

"Classic dildo move." His gaze drifted over her mouth, as his hands drifted well below the belt loops on her cutoffs. "Guy's a moron."

"Yeah, well, I wanted that moron to want me." She closed her eyes because they felt suspiciously wet. "Here I am, trying to reinvent sexy and alluring to attract the attention of one of the most sexy and alluring designers in the world, and I can't even attract the attention of the guy I've been crushing on for almost a year. How am I supposed to save my grandma's shop?"

"The same way you save everything else in this town." He tilted her chin up until she opened her eyes. "With your entire heart and soul."

"Maybe that's the problem," she said. "I still have my whole heart and soul to give, because no one wants a piece of it."

"Ah, sunshine." He touched her cheek. "You give a piece of it every day to everyone you meet. The kids in your class, the people around town, the moron who wants to start dating and misses the perfect woman standing right in front of him. Even the asshole who can't manage to plan a picnic."

"You aren't an asshole."

"See, right there, you see the best in everyone. You're warm and quirky and sunny and so damn open and giving it blows my mind." His gaze tracked down her body and back up, making her shiver from head to toe. "And that, Harper Owens, is alluring and addicting and sexy as hell."

Harper couldn't remember anyone calling her sexy before. Coming from a master woman-whisperer, she should have discounted it. But she couldn't. He seemed so genuine, and she could tell he believed what he was saying.

Distracting herself from how heavenly his hands felt on her body, she played with a string dangling off the hem of her shirt. "A year, Adam, and he asks my advice on dating, then asks someone else out on *my* date, and I'm stuck here. Working."

"Correction, sunshine," he said, taking her hand and tugging her onto his lap—his nearly naked lap, which her short cutoffs did little to protect her from. "You're here with your boyfriend, who happens to be Mr. July. And everyone knows that July is the hottest month of the year, reserved for the hottest *subjects*."

She laughed. She was feeling silly and rejected and like a fraud, and he still managed to make her laugh. "Everyone knows that, huh?"

"Yup."

Just like everyone would know the second Mr. July burned out on this faux-mance. People wouldn't ask him if *he* was okay, or if *he* needed to cry it out. Because everyone would assume that *he'd* dumped *her*. Harper Owens. The ordinary woman who caught the most extraordinary fish in town, but couldn't reel him in.

And wasn't that going to suck.

She drained the last sip of Scotch, noticing that her belly was delightfully warm, and handed the glass back. "Thank you for listening to my pathetic day, but I'm all talked out."

She went to stand, but he pressed his palms down on her thigh, holding her in place. "Oh, honey, my day will make your pathetic one seem like a trip to Disneyland."

She snorted, because she'd been to Disneyland. It was her senior trip, and she was in love with the captain of the water polo team. Curtis was sweet, smart, going Ivy League in the fall—and gay. Not that Harper knew. It came as a complete shock when he decided, during the big Happiest Place on Earth photo beneath Sleeping

Beauty's castle, to kiss the captain of the football team. Well, a shock to Harper—her friends were only shocked Harper didn't know.

"Impossible," she said.

"It's a second-glass kind of story." He took the bottle off the stand next to the chair and refilled the tumbler. "One I promise will have you laughing."

She crossed her arms.

"Fine, if by the end I convince you mine was worse, then I get a peek at what's under that top of yours."

Convinced there was no way his day could have been more embarrassing, and wanting to get off his lap before she went in for another hug—and pressed herself against that twelve-pack—she said, "I think this is just your *mine is bigger than yours* mentality kicking in, but go ahead."

"As an April Fool's joke, I submitted a request for a condom vending machine, which was accidently passed up the chain of command."

Harper's hand flew to her mouth. "Oh my God."

He gave her a look. "It gets better. I had to go apologize to the chief's secretary, in person, for writing the word *dick* seventeen times in a formal request."

Harper felt Adam cringe, so she had to ask, "Who is the chief's secretary?"

He handed her the glass. "Mrs. Franklin."

Harper choked on the whiskey. "Mrs. Franklin? She was my first-grade teacher."

"Mine too. I had to look straight into the eyes of the woman who taught me the importance of penmanship and explain the importance of proper hose safety." Adam took the glass back and drained it.

"What did she say?"

"That she was so impressed with my use of innuendo she didn't feel the need to hand it over to her boss." Adam leaned back against the chair, and Harper felt herself slide a little closer. Her heart followed suit. "I've screwed this promotion thing up a few times now, been passed over for lieutenant more than that, but I need to get it right. This is my last chance to prove I'm more than my reputation."

Harper knew it was none of her business, but sitting on his lap, listening to the frustration in his voice, she felt herself being pulled in. Becoming invested. "Prove it to yourself? Or to the chief?"

"What do you mean?"

"Love interests aside, I'm pretty good at reading people," she said. "But I can't figure you out. It's clear to me how much you want this promotion. You're planning the biggest headache of the year, and you even took yourself off the market to impress your boss. But you still picked up Baby in a bar, while in uniform, came here having no idea who she was, then two minutes later you kissed me, and have probably kissed a dozen other girls since—"

"I haven't kissed anyone."

"—even though you knew it would look bad." She stopped, along with her heart. "Wait, you haven't kissed anyone since me? But that was like two weeks ago."

"I know. I haven't even gone looking," he said, sounding equal parts surprised and proud. She understood the first emotion, but the second confused her. It had only been a week that people thought they were dating, but he'd already taken himself off the market before that.

Why?

Was she that bad of a kisser that he'd gone into hiding? Or was she that good and he'd felt those darn tingles too? Not that she got the chance to ask, because he said, "Thinking back to that night with Baby, you were right, it was a stupid move"—his voice dropped to a low rumble—"but haven't you ever needed to let go? Drop all of the BS and escape for a while?"

"Yes." Harper had spent most of her childhood pretending that the sets in the play were real, that the cast was her family, and that she belonged in that extraordinary world.

"So you go out, meet someone, there is heat and zero expectation beyond mutual pleasure. And there it is, the chance to get lost for a while, blow off some steam, and before you know it, you're in a ladies' dressing room, caught up in the moment, waiting for the rush to take you over, like you're free-falling from thirty thousand feet without a chute, and . . ." He paused, the look on his face one of confusion. "Really? Never?"

Harper realized she was shaking her head. Because embarrassingly enough, she'd never experienced anything like what he was describing. Even worse, she didn't know it existed outside of books.

She'd had boyfriends. Some even knew how to make her hum. But to be so caught up in the passion of it all that she felt out of control? *Thirty thousand feet without a chute* out of control?

Sadly, no.

She had serious doubts that she'd ever elicited those kinds of feelings in her partners either.

"Well," he continued, "I was a little slow in learning that the rush isn't always worth the repercussions, and the only thing thirty thousand feet without a chute can get you is dead. So I'm changing, because I want this promotion. I need it."

"I believe you." She just didn't understand why. She didn't think he did either. But being sworn in as a lieutenant seemed to represent more than a promotion to him. It was a defining moment of some kind.

"But I still confuse you," he said. If anything, that seemed to make him more frustrated than the thought of not getting the promotion.

"One minute I think you're an overgrown frat boy," she said softly, "but then you do something incredibly selfless and sweet and . . . you surprise me."

"I'm not sweet, sunshine," he said, cupping her face, "and very little of what I do is selfless."

"You brought me my favorite cookies."

"Because I needed to figure out why I was being shafted by every single woman in town."

"You were sweet enough to ask what my favorite was. And you didn't out me in front of Clay for lying, when you had every right to."

"I wanted to kiss you."

"You put your life on the line every day," she said, and he gave an *all in a day's work* shrug, but she saw the tips of his ears pinken. "You love to make people laugh, but when it really matters you do the right thing, always. Even when it's hard. You're loyal and protective of those you care about, which is why you took the blame for the rookie crashing the engine."

He stilled. "How do you know about that?"

"I'm the oracle," she joked, not wanting to rat out Emerson, who'd mentioned Adam was with Dax at Stan's Soup and Service at the time of the accident. "I know everything and I know that hiding beneath that reputation"—she poked his pec—"is a sweet man."

One who wanted to make amends for his past and build himself a better future. One who was determined to move forward, no matter how hard. From what, she wasn't sure. But it impressed her almost as much as it turned her on.

He turned her on. Made her want to ditch the chute and free-fall. Heck, the way he was looking at her, as though her thinking him sweet made his day, made her want lots of things. A kiss for starters, which would lead to another, then another, then the dressing room and that rush she couldn't stop thinking about.

Her stomach was already in a free fall, and her heart wasn't too far behind, which was why her head was yelling to pull the ripcord before she got hurt.

Harper straightened, enough so she didn't feel as if he were surrounding her. "And when a lady pays you a compliment you're supposed to say thank you, then walk away to keep her guessing." Still being sucked into his vortex of charm, she stood. "As for your day versus mine, you win, but you have to admit that my introducing Liza to the alluring powers of Honeysuckle for her date with Clay is a close second."

"Clay doesn't deserve to see your allure," he said, his gaze lowering over her body until her nipples went hard. "But I do. A deal is a deal."

Harper looked down at herself and saw casual—uninspired in her flip-flops, jean cutoffs, and a strategically picked tribal shirt. Sure she'd added some lip gloss and a few swipes of mascara before she'd texted him back, but that didn't warrant the hunger she saw on his face.

"I'm not wearing anything sexy under here," she lied. Beneath the crazy artist look, she was wearing nothing but lace and silk— enough to do her own lingerie shoot.

"Did you know that when you lie your eyes go all misty as if you think you're killing unicorns?" He tsked softly, standing to face her. "And there you go, misreading signals again. It wasn't the bra and panties that got me the first night." He was looking at her mouth again. "It was you. And you deserve a man who can see that."

He took the tumbler, then backed her into a side table, setting the glass down. Without a word he framed her face between his big, rough hands and pressed their bodies close. So close she had to place her hands on his chest for balance.

Which only made things worse, because his body was solid and unforgiving, nothing soft or vulnerable to grab on to. Yet, he was holding her with a gentleness that stole her breath.

"What are you doing?"

"Something I sure as hell don't deserve, but can't seem to stop."

That gravelly midnight DJ voice he had going on went a long way toward making those pesky concerns vanish. And whatever little worry she was clinging to disappeared the second his mouth came down on hers.

Not hard like before, but soft feathering kisses that skated across her top lip, then the bottom one, before capturing them both in a way that had her knees melting. That was to say nothing for what was going on in her panties.

Adam coaxed and teased, sliding his fingers into her hair and pressing in as close as he could, until all of their good parts were lined up. And the man had a surplus in the good part department. Hard muscles contrasted with the gentle way he held her, and suddenly she forgot how to breathe. She simply didn't have enough brain cells left to figure out how to get enough oxygen to her lungs.

Then he whispered her name and breathing was the least of her problems. Her bones liquefied, her knees buckled, and her heart turned over. And over again. Before she knew what was happening she was wrapped up in a warm man cocoon, sitting on Adam's lap, her arms locked around his neck.

She dug her knees into the leather of the chair as her thighs settled around his. Adam seemed to like the direction she was taking because he moaned and took the kiss deeper, took everything deeper, until she didn't know what was up and what was down, even though it felt as if the ground were rushing up to meet them. And Harper let go.

Let go of the fear and the worry. Let go of that damn parachute string, since it was impossible to hang on so tight and live up to her end of the bet. Because fair was fair, and Harper wanted to fall.

"What are you doing?" This time it was Adam who asked, his voice so thick she could barely make out what he said.

Tugging the bottom of her shirt up to show her belly, she said, "Life is too short to be ordinary. And I want extraordinary."

Harper pulled her shirt off and, no, she didn't have on Honeysuckle. But she did have on a see-through demi that was guaranteed to heat things up. Although when she tossed her top to the ground, Adam gave her a look she couldn't quite decipher. A look that had her wanting to cover herself. "What do you see?"

It took him a long moment to speak, but when he did, his voice was gentle. Almost as gentle as the finger tracing her cheek. "I see a woman who is so extraordinary that she makes everything else here seem ordinary."

Which was the nicest thing anyone had ever said to her. Only instead of kissing her, showing her how incredibly intoxicating she was, he tucked her hair behind her ear and said, "Which is why I have to go."

chapter
thirteen

Adam was buttoning his pants and nearly to the shop's door when Harper came around the corner. Still in nothing but teal lace and cutoffs, she paused by the counter and crossed her arms.

Her hair was a mess of curls from his fingers, her lips bruised from his kisses, and her nipples were hard because he was that good.

"Wait. You're leaving?"

As fast as humanly possible, because it was the strangest thing. As he stood there, holding her gaze, something inside of him shifted. Something massive and sharp that had his chest doing a whole one-two jab combo to his ribs. The one would be peeling those cutoffs right down her legs and having a lose-yourself moment that he'd been going on and on about.

Except he'd gotten his hands on her, tasted just how sweet she really was, and now he knew he'd get lost—only it wouldn't be for a moment. He'd want more.

Yes, by more he meant sex, but he also meant talking and laughing and not feeling as though in the morning it would all fade away. And that was where the second jab came in.

"I want to leave before it gets too late."

"It's barely nine," she said, challenge lighting those eyes. "And I need more than one pose."

Yeah, well that would have to wait. Because what he wanted and what he *wanted* were not lining up. So before he did something stupid, like follow her back inside, he said, "Another night. I promise."

"But it felt like a tonight thing to me," she said so quietly he wanted to punch himself. "The chair, the kissing . . . it all felt . . ." She looked up at him and, *God*, it broke his heart. "Was I misreading something? Because it seemed like . . ."

"No. I mean, yes." Jesus, his mind was all over the place. Opening up to her about his day had been expected. That's what Harper did, she talked the truth right out of people. But the way he felt talking to her, as if she really heard him, that was as refreshing as it was terrifying. "I was giving you all the signals, Harper. Loud and clear."

She looked down at his pants, and the tent he was sporting, and shook her head. "Then why are you running out of here?"

Adam let out a breath. "Because I only have a couple weeks." Of her. They only had two weeks and then their time would be up and they'd most likely part ways. That was how it went for Adam—people came and people left, and life moved on. Not that Harper would move far, she'd still be in town, her smile appearing around every corner, but things between them would be different.

They wouldn't be required to see each other. So what then?

Harper was open and genuine and the connection they shared felt, well . . . nice. Something that normally scared him off, but with her it was addicting. He didn't want to lose out, lose her, when this was over. And he would if he took her in her grandma's shop as if she were just another fleeting rush.

She deserved more.

The strange thing was, around her, he could almost convince himself that he did too. "I don't want to screw this up," he admitted.

"So it's not me, it's the situation?" she asked and, *holy shit*, she was serious.

Adam laughed because it *was* all about her, but not in the way she thought. He closed the distance, took her hand, and placed it on his pounding heart. "Feel that?"

She nodded.

"That's all you. Not the lace or the setup in there. You," he said. "And if this were a few weeks ago, I would have had you naked the second I saw you in those ass-hugging shorts," he said softly. "Then I would have had you on that chair, the counter, wherever I could."

"But you could've had me, just a minute ago."

"Yeah?" he asked, embarrassed that he sounded like a seventeen-year-old on prom night.

She smiled, small but sweet. "You know you could have."

He did, but hearing her say it made him smile. It also made him cautious.

In his line of work, the ability to quickly assess a hot spot was imperative. Smokejumpers operated on worst-case scenario and worked their way backward. From the time the chute deployed, there was approximately sixty seconds to identify the biggest threat, come up with a strategy, and locate an exit route—just in case. Because once you touched down behind the fire line there were no second chances. No do-overs.

No time for mistakes.

Even the most controlled fire could go from squirrelly to shit-just-got-real in no time flat. And this thing with Harper, it wasn't just squirrelly, it was so damn combustible he was afraid someone was going to get burned. Based on his past, it wouldn't be him.

"I want you, Harper, but I don't want to complicate a good thing."

"So you're saying you *want* me, but you can't have me because you want to be friends more?" she asked sourly. "Oh my God, I must be totally cursed."

"You're too sweet to be cursed, and I want both," he clarified, leaning down and kissing her on the cheek. Then because her lips were right there, pouting and sad, he kissed those too. Pulling back only after they were both breathing hard. "See you tomorrow."

Only he didn't move toward the door.

"To clarify, you're saying that if I took off my bra, right now, it would be a waste of time, because this is not going to happen?" Her fingers played with the strap, driving him right out of his mind.

With a pained groan, he headed for the door. "Not tonight."

"So then you aren't going to kiss me tomorrow?"

He paused at the threshold and thought about that long and hard. Thought about what it would be like to wake up in the morning and kiss her until bedtime. Then thought about how she deserved extraordinary. "Nope."

"It's not nice to lie. It kills innocent unicorns," she called out.

"It's not a lie, it's a fact. And I won't see you tomorrow since I'll be at the sheriff's station finalizing the booth locations and handing out registration forms." He opened the door. "But put on the Honeysuckle and I might reconsider. Night, sunshine."

Adam remained true to his word.

The day was almost over and he had not kissed Harper. Not when he spotted her at the Sweet and Savory getting her morning sugar fix, nor when he saw her walking her grandma's dog down Main Street. He hadn't even called her over for a quick peck when she pulled two of her students outside to have a nice "chat."

A chat with boys who were three feet tall, which, with Harper wearing ridiculously adorable heels, had her bending over to get eye level. An action that, from a distance, brought her hips to Adam's level—and the hem of her flowy dress inches from exposing whether she was wearing Honeysuckle.

But since he was in the sheriff's department, surrounded by his brothers and a bunch of pistol-toting guys, mapping out booth placement for Beat the Heat, he didn't think he was in much danger of breaking his word.

"That's never going to work." Jonah reached over Adam's shoulder to flick the quarter off the map and onto the floor. "It puts the second generator too close to the St. Paws booth. Shay won't have it."

"I'm not moving a generator to increase the odds of you getting laid," Adam said.

Jonah shrugged. "Your call, but last year, Ida's pet duck waddled too close and burned off its tail feathers, blowing the generator. This year, Shay's bringing that flock of geese that got lost in the migration last year."

"And we can't move Shay?"

Jonah laughed. "She had to bribe last year's planner to get a corner spot, so unless you are offering her street-facing property, no way will she give it up."

"Could you at least ask her?"

"Do I look like I want to sleep on the couch?"

"You look like you should trade in that gun for your Deputy Pussycat hat," Adam mumbled, then pulled another quarter out of his pocket and placed it by the stage.

"Too close to the coffee stand. The ladies will complain about having to talk over the noise," Jonah said and flicked it off the map. "Plus, it blocks the walkway to the porta-potties, which is never a good call."

"Where do you learn this shit?"

"Planning a wedding teaches important skills."

"What? Like how to make a table decoration of out fishbowls and where bathrooms should go?" Adam pulled another quarter out and placed it by the oak tree.

"Don't underestimate the power of event planning." With a flick, Jonah sent it flying.

"Seriously, you knock one more quarter on the ground and you'll understand the power of my fist," Adam said, running a hand over his face.

He'd been at this for hours. Trying to map out a hundred vendor booths, a half dozen games, eating areas, and porta-potties in their small community park was harder than he'd originally thought. He had the basic layout from last year, but over the past week they'd grown their vendors by ten percent and added a food truck—which meant two more generators. The public bathrooms were closed for renovation, hence the porta-potties, and Harper had managed to convince some guy who owned a party games rental company to donate a few of the smaller casino games for the weekend—free of charge.

The woman was magic.

"Just because you're not getting any doesn't mean you get to hate on the rest of us," Dax said from his desk a few feet away. He was flipping through a file, his boots kicked up on his desk. And he was grinning.

"Who says I'm not getting any?"

Jonah and Dax both burst out laughing. Flipping them the finger, Adam walked behind the counter to pick up the quarters.

"The way you were hobbling down Main Street was a pretty good indication," Dax said, pushing farther back in his chair. "Your balls were so neglected they were singing the blues."

Adam paused for a beat before setting "generator three" on the counter. "You might think spying is charming, since that's how you managed to snag Emerson, but it's not, man. It's just creepy."

"Call it what you want, but I'm not the one with the neglected nuts," Dax said. "And I didn't have to spy. My fiancée lives above the Boulder Holder. She's also besties with your girlfriend."

"More like sisters," Adam mumbled, regretting the statement the moment it slipped out of his mouth, and Jonah and Dax exchanged a look.

And, yeah, Adam knew he sounded like an ass, but Harper sharing the details of last night with someone else, when he didn't even understand what had happened, didn't settle well.

To say he was thrown by how everything went down would be an understatement. The scene was set, the invitation extended and accepted. It was go time. And he'd gone home.

Alone.

Adam realized right then that it was a damn good call. From an early age, Harper had to create the family she was denied. Clovis stepped in for mother, the other biddies great-aunts. Emerson was her sister, and every guy she'd ever come across became a brother. Harper collected people to fill a need.

And Adam didn't want to be another fucking brother figure in her life, just like he didn't want to go home alone. But he sure as hell didn't want to be one more disappointment.

He'd had plenty of practice at that, and she'd had enough of those.

"So you played the friend card, huh?" Dax asked, dropping his feet to the floor and coming to stand by the counter. He picked up the quarter and placed it by the back row of booths. Then he placed another by the other side of the stage.

Adam didn't ask how he knew where the perfect spots were, since he was pretty sure it had something to do with a woman. Or a wedding. Or both.

"I didn't friend-zone her." Adam pulled out a stack of Post-it notes with carnival games written on them. "And even if I did, there is nothing wrong with being friends. Nothing."

"Oh, it's something, all right," Dax said, laughing. "You have a sweet and pretty woman, who wants something casual I might add, and you put on the brakes so you can become friends first."

Well, hell. When put like that, Adam was the one who needed to wear the Deputy Pussycat hat. "How much did she tell you?"

Dax shrugged. "Not much. She didn't have to. Those walls are so thin, Emerson and I can hear Harper hold her breath when she watches those end of the world movies. So when you two started hollering in the store downstairs, it was like we were in the room with you. Emerson wanted to fillet you, but I made some popcorn and listened as you embarrassed yourself, then told her it was good news."

"How is invading a private conversation good news?" Adam asked.

Dax shrugged. "Wanting to take it slow means you like her."

"Everyone likes Harper. She smells like the beach and birthday cake." She was also funny and genuine and one hell of a friend. He'd seen it in the way she treated others, and now that he'd been on the receiving end of that gift, he didn't want to jinx it.

"Yeah, but you *like her* like her," Dax said.

"How does any of that *Harper told Emerson who told you* BS equate to me liking her?"

Dax took the stack of Post-its out of Adam's hands and, without asking, staggered them around the park, while Jonah stood there silently for a while. Tense. Assessing. Calling on every little trick of the trade he'd learned in that fancy detective school he'd attended.

It worked—sweat beaded on Adam's forehead.

"Women have been chasing you since you were old enough to buy condoms," Jonah began. "You always let them catch you. At least for a night or two. Then you somehow charm them into thinking that being friends was their idea."

"'No ties, no one cries,'" Adam repeated what had become his mantra over the years. Only, now when he said it, it felt odd. Like he was spouting off a lie.

"Yeah, I never really thought you believed that BS," Jonah said. "Just like I don't think you believe that all you want from Harper is friendship."

"There is nothing wrong with being friends," Adam argued, which only made his brothers smile bigger. The assholes. "We're just having fun."

Even saying it made him wince, because yes, Harper was different and with her he always had fun. But when he was around her he was different too. Lighter, happier, grounded.

Able to experience the rush of the jump without the impact of the landing that usually followed. But the landing would come if he wasn't careful—with Adam and relationships it always did. This meant he needed to tread lightly, think before he jumped, because when he did jump, he was pretty sure he wouldn't be jumping alone.

Everything Harper did in life was in tandem, and he'd meant what he'd said last night. Life was too short to be ordinary. Which was why he lived balls-out, chasing the next high. This time though, if he had to deploy the chute, then he wanted to make sure that neither of them walked away burned.

Because with Harper, there wouldn't be a reserve chute.

His brothers exchanged concerned looks. "Well, while you're braiding each other's hair or talking about favorite boy bands or whatever else girlfriends do while having fun, you might want to ask her advice on this map," Dax said, picking up the Post-it for Dr. Harvey Peterson, the town's podiatrist, and sticking it to Adam's forehead. "I might not have been back for very long, but I know enough about this town to understand that stationing Handsy Harvey's Complimentary Two-Minute Foot Massage station next to the Ladies' Baptist Choir is an epically stupid decision."

Adam had already met his quota of epically stupid decisions for this lifetime, plus he'd told himself he wasn't going to kiss Harper today, which was why he was dead set on avoiding her. At least until he'd had twenty-four hours to clear his head—and get that image of her straddling him out of his mind. So when he received a text a few minutes later, asking him to pick up a shift, Adam decided that the map could wait.

"Gotta go to the station," he said, gathering his things. "Daugherty's wife isn't feeling well, his kid's got the flu, and he needs someone to fill in until his mother-in-law can get here from the city and play house nurse."

And since Adam had no wife, no kid, and no good reason to ever turn down overtime, he had become the official go-to guy when it came to covering shifts. Normally it didn't bug him, that was how it worked, but for some reason this time it caused a weird tension to build behind his shoulders.

"What about these?" Jonah held up a stack of forms.

Shit. He was supposed to be at the station anyway to hand out forms to vendors and answer any questions. "Can you cover Beat the Heat duties for me until Seth gets here around three?" he asked Dax.

Rolling up the map, Adam headed for the door and decided it was a good thing, because going to the station meant not going to see Harper about logistical problems—or anything else, no matter how epic it might be.

"You bet, as long as you drop Violet off at class on the way," Dax said, and before Adam could ask what class, a three-foot-tall girl in Converse and pigtails ran out from the lunchroom and climbed in Dax's lap.

And Adam got a really bad feeling. Violet Blake, Emerson's kid sister, was six years old, and could literally blind you with her sweetness. She was also a damn fine artist when it came to glitter.

"What class do you have today?" Adam asked.

"Sprouting Picasso," Violet said, swinging her legs contently as though she hadn't just complicated everything.

Not a big deal, he thought, assessing the possible outcomes. "I can walk you to the door and watch you go inside, but then I have to get to the station."

Violet jumped off Dax's lap, then ran over to wrap her little arms around his middle. "That's where I'm going! On a field trip to the fire station to see real heroes in action for our project, like Miss H promised!" she squealed, confirming that, yeah, he was totally screwed.

chapter
fourteen

I thought your hose would be bigger."

Harper smothered a laugh as Tommy walked over to the deflated fire hose and nudged it with one of his shoes, which were "the Flash" themed, blinked red when he stepped, and hadn't stopped moving since arriving at the station. Neither had Harper's heart.

She had barely gotten two words out to her students about being on their best behavior—and not touching any red buttons—when their tour guide had emerged from the kitchen. It wasn't Daugherty, the nearing-fifty father of seven who had a handlebar mustache and a keg in his belly.

Nope, their tour guide was over six feet of hard-won muscle and charm, wearing yesterday's scruff, delicious SHFD work blues, and enough testosterone to melt the sun. And just as unexpected as Adam's appearance was his date for the day.

Adam strode in holding hands with a travel-sized cutie, dressed in pink, pink, and more pink, who looked up at him with total and complete awe in her eyes. Violet wasn't the only one mesmerized.

Adam had charmed every person in that room—parents included—with a single smile.

Everyone except Tommy, who had his hands in his pockets and his eyes firmly affixed to Adam's awaiting the correct answer, like he had for the last ten thousand questions he'd already asked.

Adam hunched down a little, putting his hands on his knees and getting eye level with Tommy. Harper noticed he did that a lot, talked to the kids instead of at the kids. "We rolled it out so you guys could lift it and see what it feels like. Want to hold the nozzle, buddy?"

"I want to see it big, like how Red's is on *Cars.*"

"When that hose is hooked up to water and cranked to full pressure, it gets so heavy it takes three of those guys just to control it," Adam said, pointing to Sam Lopez, a firefighter who Harper had gone to high school with. Sam was good-looking, built like a tank, and lived to make people laugh.

He flexed his muscles and the kids oohed, beyond impressed.

All except, Tommy, who stuck his hand in the air, even though he was already standing. William made a sound that translated into Tommy being the most annoying person on the planet. The rest of the kids were not quite as vocal in their irritation, but Tommy got the point all the same. They wanted to get to the fun stuff, like sliding down the pole, climbing in the engines, checking out what kind of candy was in the vending machines—and he was prolonging their lesson.

Tommy shoved his hands in his pockets, and Harper could almost see the internal debate play out between pleasing his curiosity and pleasing his peers. For a kid who had an IQ of *Shut the Front Door* and a twenty-thousand-questions-a-second brain, it was a hard decision. So when he looked to Harper for help, she smiled softly and said, "Why don't you take your seat and let Fireman Baudouin finish his demonstration? There will be time for questions at the end."

Tommy's shoulders sank even more and he started walking back to the group.

"That's okay," Adam said, sending Harper a wink that had her knees wobbling. "Questions mean he's interested." Adam looked at Tommy. "What's your question?"

"Are you going to hook it up so we can see?"

Adam got down on one knee and held the nozzle for Tommy to look at. "There are a lot of components when it comes to working the hose, so we use it just when we're fighting fires."

His hand went up again and Adam, once again, entertained him. "If we start a fire, you'd have to put it out, and we could hook it up and turn on the water."

William's hand shot up, but he didn't wait to be called on. "That would be awesome! Miss H said we have to visualize what we want to paint and the hose looks like a spaghetti noodle, so all I can visualize is spaghetti, and I'm not allowed to eat spaghetti."

Adam didn't even bat a lash at the ridiculous train of ideas. Instead he straightened and looked at the group, all twelve of them, who were looking back expectantly, their little bodies quivering with excitement as if waiting for him to light a blow torch, then crank the water to high and make their day as fantastical as a Disney movie.

"That is what our imaginations are for," he said. "Real fires are dangerous. Even the smallest ones can get out of control quickly, which is why you should never play with fire. And if you see one, you go to safety and call . . ."

He put a hand to his ear and the kids all yelled, "Nine. One. One."

"My dad starts fires on our property." This was from Tommy, who was now pacing in front as if he had the floor. "And he holds his hose all by himself."

"Your dad would have gotten permission from the city to burn things on the property. And his hose is probably your average garden-variety, easy to handle," Adam said, then looked right at Harper and she felt a little fire start in her belly. "This hose here pushes water out at a force of eight hundred to two thousand kilopascal units a second. That's fast enough to stop a bullet."

"Like the Flash?"

Adam looked back at Tommy and that fire in Harper's belly warmed its way clear to her chest. Because Adam put his hand on the boy's slim shoulder and said, "Just like the Flash. Which makes you the perfect guy to help me." Even though he was juggling a dozen kids with a dozen different expectations, Adam was aware enough to understand the moment for what it was. This was a chance to connect with a kid who had a hard time connecting with people. "Who wants to go inside the engine?"

Every arm went in the air with so much gusto that most of them had to be supported by the other hand.

"Well, you need one of these first." Adam grabbed a stack of plastic fire hats off the back of the engine. "And to get one you have to come up and hold the hose, then tell the class something you learned today that you didn't know before."

"About fires and hoses?" Violet asked.

"About anything. It just has to be something you learned today that you think is cool."

"Like if a cat gets stuck up in a tree you will come rescue him, but if there is a bad guy at the door I should call Mister Dax?"

"Something like that," Adam grumbled. "Now I need an honorary fireman to demonstrate how to control the nozzle, so everyone can see what it looks like." He made a big deal about studying each kid, up close and scratching his head, so that they giggled, then his eyes landed on Tommy. "You up for that, Flash?"

Tommy nodded, so hard his shoes blinked as if giving off Morse code for *Holy smokes.*

"Great, put your hand here." Adam took his time, guiding Tommy's hands, moving his feet to a stance, slowly instructing him how to hold the nozzle while his classmates looked on in awe. Then Adam did the one thing that could make Tommy cool—he pulled his own fire helmet from a closet and slid it on Tommy's head. "Now who wants to come up here so Tommy can show you how to properly hold the hose?"

A cacophony of excited *Me-me*s filled the room, and Adam pointed to a red X taped to the ground. "A good firefighter knows that being a team player and knowing how to follow directions are important to everyone involved. So let's start the line here. Girls first, then boys. And we go in order of youngest to oldest."

"That's lame," William, the oldest boy in the class, said, folding his arms over his chest.

"That's called being a good guy," Adam said, not an ounce of waver in his voice. "And it's up to the big guys like you, who are older and have more experience, to make sure the littler ones don't get lost in the shuffle. Help them figure things out."

William's chest puffed, then he took to guiding the kids into the line, making sure the little ones were up front. Then Harper watched as, one by one, Tommy showed each kid what he'd learned, pointing out the different parts and talking about the fire safety points he'd learned along the way.

Harper was touched at how invested Adam was in the kids' feelings. He quickly assessed their strengths and weaknesses, giving them all a job that would challenge them while allowing them to succeed. And when they all finished with their turns, he let Sam take them to the outer bay to see the big ladder engine.

"Really? Clay has an average garden-variety hose?" she asked, rising to her feet as he walked toward her. She dusted off the back of her dress and pretended that her hands weren't shaking.

"Facts are facts," he said, not stopping until he was so close she had to take a step back—right into a wall. "Is that a new dress?"

"No, I just never wear it." Its slim-cut and belted waist had always felt like too much, but when she'd put it on this morning it had felt just right. "And the last time you said *facts are facts*, it was to convince me I wouldn't be seeing you today."

"I didn't think you'd be wearing this dress when I agreed to fill in." He planted his palms flat on the wall above her head. His eyes? Those were firmly on her mouth. "And you should wear it more often. It goes well with Honeysuckle." His lashes lifted. "You wearing Honeysuckle, sunshine?"

"Are you still just interested in being friends, Smoky?" she asked. "Because I have a lot of friends, and they aren't privy to what I have on underneath."

"They're not your boyfriend," he said playfully, but she wasn't feeling playful at all. She was suddenly feeling confused and a little scared over how his words sent butterflies racing in her stomach.

"And you walked out of my place last night, so you can see why I want to clarify things."

"I said a lot last night," Adam said.

"You did." There was also a lot that went unsaid, and that was what had the butterflies flapping their wings against her ribcage. "Like you weren't going to kiss me today."

He hesitated. "I thought I needed space, to clear my head."

"And now?"

"The only time my head seems to be clear is when I'm with you. Like this."

Still holding her caged between the wall and his mighty fine body, he stared down at her for what felt like an eternity, as if unsure about what he wanted to do. And while he was thinking about how he wanted to play this moment, Harper wondered just how long she could go without oxygen before passing out.

"Stay for dinner, Harper."

She blinked. Twice in fact because a *Let's get naked later* invitation or *There's a party in my pants, wanna come* would have been less shocking. An invite to dinner was not what she was expecting. At all. And it confused her as much as it thrilled her. "Are you asking me on a date?"

"A date would be the two of us alone and, unfortunately, I'm still on the clock until Daugherty gets here, which means I come with seven other guys." A little of the thrill faded. "But I'm cooking tonight and I would love for you to stay and have dinner. With me."

Harper swallowed the hurt rising in her throat. "And seven other guys?"

"Who will all love you *and* give me a hard time for bringing a girl to dinner, which has never happened before. The girl thing, not them giving me a hard time," he stumbled, and if Harper didn't know any better, she'd think Adam "Five-Alarm" Baudouin was nervous too.

"Is this because you want to see my Honeysuckle or because you want to be my friend?"

He studied her for a long moment and Harper felt her heart race. Not just from the fact that she could smell the summer heat on his skin, but from nerves. She had to know why he was asking. Otherwise her mind wandered down a path that always led to disappointment and heartache.

And her heart was tired of aching.

"Can't it be both?" he asked, his voice a low rumble, his blue eyes locked on hers. Open, genuine, uncertain—and filled with heat. He wanted her, it was right there—and Harper couldn't seem to look away. "Can't it be as simple as I want to spend time with you?"

"So Baudouin hears *secret weekly strip poker party* at one of the big Victorians near the college campus and, boom, he's gone. Goes charging in the house like some kind of self-appointed savior for sorority girls everywhere," Sam said, smacking his palms against the table for effect.

Not that he needed to. Every guy on duty was gathered around the kitchen, hanging on every word of the Adam-inspired story—even though Harper was pretty sure they'd all either been there or heard it a thousand times before. The only one who looked as if he wanted it to end was Adam, who stood by the stove tending to dinner.

"Sorority and strip poker?" Harper said, picking up her glass of lemonade and sending Adam a reassuring smile over the rim. "I'd even go in to check it out."

Adam returned that smile, only his had a touch of embarrassment to it, which added a touch of adorable to the sexy. "See, guys, just doing what anyone would do. My job," he said, magically appearing at her side to fill up her lemonade.

He was good. Charming, smooth, and never missing a beat. Even when the guys were razzing him. That was how it had been ever since she'd taken her students home and walked back in the station. They'd been surrounded by a group of people, but the way he'd looked at her, tended to her every need, made it feel as if they were the only two people there.

"Maybe, but not even two seconds go by and panties come flying out the window," McGuire added. He stood next to Adam at the counter, slicing vegetables for the salad. He set down a tomato to give the story his full attention. "Lace and silk and all kinds of catcalls erupted."

"You weren't even on the crew yet, freshman. In fact, *none* of you were even there," the resident panty-whisperer said, sending Harper a wink as he stuffed cheese and homemade pesto into each piece of chicken. "Otherwise you'd know I only went in alone because I was the first to arrive, and it was a false alarm."

"A false alarm?" Harper asked, leaning her elbows on the counter, her attention solely on Adam, doing her best to maintain eye contact, which was impossible since he was a pro at making her blush.

"False alarm or not," Sam said, leaning in to look Harper in the eye, "Adam came out with lipstick on his cheek, digits in his pocket, and every single lady calling him their own personal hero. Said he saved their lives."

Adam gave the room a mischievous smirk, easygoing and not fazed in the slightest. "Again, just doing my job. What can I say? Women love me."

"Women?" Sam barked. "They were more like pinups from what I heard, wanting a taste of the legend." He turned to Harper, and she began to realize why Adam never brought girls to the station. "That's how he got the name Five-Alarm Casanova, because he can walk into a simple false alarm and walk out with five hot honeys on his arm."

The barrage of innuendos and stories didn't slow down, and Harper noticed that Adam took it in stride. But she began to see that he was somewhat bothered. By the fact that he was the center of attention or the subject in what had to be the biggest urban legend in SHFD history, she couldn't tell.

"Don't mind the girls," Adam said, waving a hand as all the other guys jumped in to tell their story about him. Each one more fantastical than the last. "They love to eat, gossip, and tell tall tales. When they get in front of a pretty lady, they seem to forget their manners."

"I grew up with most of them," she said, ignoring the little thrill at him calling her a pretty lady. "I actually introduced Ryan to his wife and Luke to his girlfriend." At the mention of the ladies of the SHFD a few of them straightened up.

"That must be it," Adam said, "because I don't remember talking girls and bro-talk when they had female guests at the house. They had on their best faces."

Harper's heart rolled over when she realized he was bothered by the stories. Not that they were telling stories, but that they were telling them in front of her, and didn't that make him all the more irresistible. It also made this faux-mance seem all the more real.

She just wasn't sure who he was trying to convince—her or his crew.

"He's right, Miss Owens," McGuire said, extending a toned and drool-worthy arm her way. "Where are our manners? We always take pretty ladies on a tour of the station. We can start in the equipment room while Adam here tightens his apron."

Adam frowned something fierce. "If anyone is playing tour guide it's me." He slid the casserole in the oven. "I'll show you the engine bay."

"But I already saw the engine bay," Harper pointed out, but Adam already had her hand in his, a possessive move that seemed to surprise him more than it did the rest of the room. And that was saying a lot.

As the guys watched, Adam led her out of the kitchen and down a narrow hallway, ignoring the whistles and laughs behind them.

"I never took you for a hand-holding kind of boyfriend," she said when they were away from prying ears.

"Me neither. Then again, I never imagined I'd have a girlfriend's hand to hold. Especially at work."

She slowed down. "Is this too weird? Me being here?"

"It should be, but it's not."

Lacing their fingers, he moved them down the hall until they reached the door to the engine bay, which was as pristine as the rest of the house, but they kept walking. Until they reached a little patio on the back side of the building.

It was isolated and incredibly romantic, with little twinkle lights hidden in the shrubs and dangling from the umbrella. Harper's heels clicked on the cobblestone floor as a warm evening breeze blew past, bringing the scent of rosemary from the small chef's garden, which sat in the back corner. Right below a window into the kitchen, where she could see the guys pass by.

So if he didn't want privacy, then what?

"So pinups, huh?" she asked.

He slid her a sideways glance. "You shouldn't believe everything you hear. Those guys can make a timid brush fire out to be a bold blaze."

"So you aren't the type to run into a building and singlehandedly save someone you've never met?"

"Urban legend." Adam walked them over to a wrought iron table and pulled out a chair, but didn't sit. He also didn't let go of her hand. He just stared down at her with a cool, assessing gaze. "And legends always disappoint."

"Ah, so this is the whole *the myth is better than the man* warning?"

Harper had heard it before, but this time it felt different. She'd seen the way Adam had interacted with his men, how he took the ribbing in stride since it worked to blow off steam and bond the rest of the crew. How incredibly sweet and patient he'd been with her students. "In this case, I think the man is better than the myth."

His lips curled up slightly. "Why is that?"

"First off, regarding that whole Five-Alarm Casanova business, they're actually talking about the monthly game at Pricilla Martin's."

Harper knew this gathering well since Clovis regularly attended. Harper had even gone a few times with Clovis. It was loud, wild, and high stakes—but panty tossing? She couldn't see it.

The Pi Etas were a secret society of bakers and poker players in wine country, who loved to mix playing cards with swapping crust recipes. Sure, when things got too vanilla they'd spice it up by betting coupons or tricks of the pie trade. But strip poker? No way. It was an apron-required kind of event.

Unless, however, they'd invited the Masonic Lodge for a tasting. Then all bets were off.

His laugh, which lit up his entire face, said it was one and the same, which meant that it had been a more *pie enthusiasts* and less *pinup dolls* type experience.

"Why don't you just tell the guys the truth?" she asked. "The rumors can't be helping any with the promotion." He shrugged and Harper had a niggling feeling, similar to the one she got right before Clovis dropped a bomb—like, she needed someone to post bail or hide a body. "There's more to the story."

"A whole lot more," he admitted on a sigh. "The call turned out to be from Aunt Connie's place, where I found Selma Roux sitting at the kitchen table disoriented. The curtains were charred and she had no idea how she'd gotten there, or why she was in nothing but flour and her bloomers, holding a burned blackberry pie and a fire extinguisher."

"She snuck out of the assisted living facility to bake a pie?"

"No, this was right before she went in, and she didn't know where the pie came from. My best guess is she made it at my aunt's," Adam said. "I guess she'd wandered off before, but she'd find herself in the garden or her front yard, never a few blocks over. In the middle of the night. She was a mess, broken up about the thought of leaving her house and all the memories. And when she learned that Connie had called the fire department she started crying."

"Oh, poor Selma," Harper said, remembering how difficult that transition had been for the older woman. She'd lost her husband a few years back, and with him, her memories. It was as if her pain and sadness disguised itself as forgetfulness, and the woman who used to remember every kid's name and birthday in town could barely remember how to get home. "So you made up a story so that you wouldn't have to call Adult Protective Services?"

Adam shrugged. "I made her a deal—if she let me drive her home and promised to contact the assisted living facility the next day, my aunt would invite a few neighbors over. Selma agreed and the ladies showed up with pajamas, liquor, and an outpouring of compassion. Ended up staging what turned out to be the monthly Pi Eta strip poker party. With everyone in their skivvies, Selma didn't seem so out of place when the crew arrived."

"And you became Five-Alarm Casanova."

"The guys razzed me some, and I think it cost me my first shot at lieutenant, but it didn't matter. Selma was able to say goodbye to her home on her own terms. Not the department's."

"Saying goodbye on your own terms is important," Harper said quietly.

There were so many people she'd wanted to say goodbye to growing up, but never got the chance. It was as if as certain as the sun would rise, her world would change. Never once had her mother thought that maybe Harper didn't want to leave, didn't want to say goodbye. Wasn't ready to move on to the next chapter.

"You only get one shot. If you mess it up, you have to live with it forever," he said with so much intensity that Harper didn't think he was talking about Selma anymore either. She wanted to know more, but he asked, "What is the second reason?"

"What?"

"You said *first off*, meaning there was another reason you think the man was better than the myth. What's the second?"

"Are you fishing for compliments, Mr. July?"

"Just the truth, sunshine."

Adam stepped forward and slipped his hands around her waist, linking them low on her back, and she had a hard time thinking.

Because performing normal brain activity when this close to a melt-down was impossible. Almost as impossible as it would be to settle on just two reasons why she liked him.

Over the past week she'd compiled a complete and comprehensive list, which was why she'd almost declined when he'd asked her to stay for dinner. But the chance to spend time with him when his guard was down like it was now was too tempting to pass up. Now, here she was, adding him to her collection of people she cared for.

"You're sweet."

He laughed. "I said the truth, not fluff. If I wanted an ego stroke, I'd go back in the kitchen."

"You. Are. Sweet. Adam Baudouin," she said, putting a finger to his lips when he went to argue. "I mean it, the way you care for others and look out for them is amazing."

"I get paid to care for people. It's part of the job description."

"Nope, it's more than that. You care so much it scares you."

"Sunshine, that I'm caring is the last thing most people would say about me."

"I'm not most people, and too bad for them that they don't take the time to see that about you," she said, and meant it.

Sadly, Harper had been one of those people until recently. Now that she knew better, she couldn't believe she'd ever let herself be fooled by the cape of swagger.

"People respect you because you take the time to see them so clearly for who they are," Harper said. "Even more amazing, you call it out and recognize that." He'd seen in her things that she hadn't been brave enough to see in herself. "You find a way to celebrate traits most people overlook, just like you did today with Tommy. That's a special talent."

"It's called making friends."

"It's called making connections, and the ability to connect with others is an impressive quality. If Lowen doesn't see that, then he is missing out."

His arms tightened until she found herself pressed against his chest, looking up at his lips, which were hovering over hers. "Is it crazy that the only person I care about impressing right now is you?"

"No, you've been tricked by science," she mumbled, because his mouth was hovering mere inches above hers. "True story."

"Science, huh?"

She nodded. "Red shoes, direct eye contact, enough cleavage to make you question what I have on beneath. The perfect dress for a date with the boyfriend's coworkers. All planned, and all trickery."

"That is an amazing dress," he said. "The way it hugs your body when you move, and how it keeps flashing me little glimpses of the blue lace you've got beneath."

"I didn't think you noticed."

He grinned. "Oh, I noticed, sunshine. I've been noticing you all night, but it wasn't the dress or the shoes or even the cleavage, although all that is quite inspiring. It was just you."

"I tried hard to make it look real." It was silly that she was so thrilled by his admission. "I was thinking sexy thoughts too."

"Sexy thoughts like this?" His mouth teased her lips, nipping at each corner before slowly pulling her lower lip into his mouth, and that same unforgettable fire she felt the first night shot through her.

"Just like that, but—"

"But?"

"I thought we weren't doing this."

"Me too." He shook his head. "I just can't seem to remember why right now."

"Because we both have a lot on the line. Because you don't do complicated. And because you wanted to be friends."

"Right." His gaze locked on her mouth as he reached out and traced its seam with his thumb. "Problem is I don't know what my other friends look like naked."

This was a problem, one her nipples seemed to ignore because they popped their corks in welcome.

"I had on lace," she whispered.

"I remember."

"Do you also remember how we decided this"—she looked at his mouth, which was a breath away and descending with purpose—"would complicate things."

"Funny, the only thing I remember is what you taste like. Which makes *this* suddenly seem simple." His voice was low and gravelly and made her tremble in the best kind of way. So did the way his hands slid down her back to her silk-clad bottom, pulling her flush against him, until he couldn't even breathe without her feeling the rise and fall of his chest.

Oh my God, he was going to kiss her, right there on the patio on their first date and it was going to be amazing. The kind of caught up in the moment, waiting for the rush to take over, like you're free-falling from thirty thousand feet without a chute kind of kiss.

He smelled incredible, and she knew he'd taste even better. Like hot, sexy, turned-on man and—*be still my heart*. She had to close her eyes to be sure, but she did and it was. Adam smelled like freshly baked peanut butter cookies and sex. Her mouth watered at the thought.

She felt him shift closer, and that tingle of hers grew to a full-body hum. Then she opened her eyes and saw the kitchen window behind him, and that was when the last important realization set in.

Or maybe it was a reminder. Of what this was and exactly what this wasn't.

"Adam," she said, trying hard to keep the hurt from her voice. "If this is for show, then we don't have to do this. I don't think anyone is watching."

"Nothing about this is staged." He pressed her against the table with his body, and there was the hard proof that this was real. "As for watching, you just go on and keep your eyes open, and let me know when it gets complicated."

Sweet baby Jesus, it was already complicated. At least the rhythm her chest had taken up sounded like a college marching band, because his mouth lowered that final breath and slowly, ever so slowly, captured hers in a way that was all gentle steel. The kind that scrambled a girl's thoughts and soothed her fears until she forgot that this wasn't real. That he wasn't collectible.

So instead of taking a step back, like a smart girl would have done, Harper kept her eyes wide open and melted—into him and that promise she tasted on his lips. Because in that moment, with him holding her as if he were vowing to never let go, he felt like hers.

And, *God*, how she wanted to be his.

chapter
fifteen

A dam felt the moment Harper gave in. To the chemistry and to him.

Even though he had no right to, he let her fall. Warm and wildly sexy Harper who couldn't enter into anything without giving over her entire heart and soul. And he watched her hand it over and didn't say a damn thing.

He couldn't. It felt too good.

From the second she had walked back into the station, her little blue dress had been doing a serious number on his head. The way it shifted and danced across her body did truly amazing things from his vantage point. But it was her smile that did him in. Full, real, so damn bright it was infectious.

He'd flirted with her because of that dress, but he'd kissed her because of that smile. Now he didn't want to let go. Not when her body was shrink-wrapped around his and her hands were playing a dangerous game of hide-and-seek. And especially not when she was making those breathy little sounds that drove him crazy.

Hell, everything about her drove him crazy. From her cute freckles to the polka dots painted on her toes, Harper did something to him that he'd long ago dismissed as fiction. She was sweetness and fire, and he was addicted.

His internal alarm told him as much, warning him to proceed with caution. To step back and assess. But he'd done that and it had landed him right back here. In her arms. And if facing down some of the most dangerous wildfires had taught him anything, it was that sometimes you had to walk into the flames to gain some control.

Only karma disagreed, flipping him the bird by blasting her own warning, just in case he had any idea of continuing *this* . . . here.

"Shit," he said, resting his forehead against hers.

Harper pulled back, her lips wet and warm from his, her eyes lit with hunger and confusion as the red light above the patio strobed in sync with the ear-piercing bell.

"Time to go." And there they were, the last three words he'd ever said to Trent, seconds before the flames engulfed them both. The same three words that defined the rest of his life—and Trent's death.

Three words Harper would get real familiar with if she let this continue.

Promotion or not, Adam's career would forever send him into some of the most heated shit storms, personal and professional, without a moment's warning.

Harper wanted stable, and his life was as unpredictable as a wildfire.

Only instead of peacing out, like any normal woman would do—like Harper *should* do—she gifted him one of those smiles and said, "Be safe."

Four hours, a nasty commercial fire, and a dump truck of adrenaline later, Adam grabbed the to-go picnic he'd fashioned for his and

Harper's abandoned dinner off his passenger seat and strode up the back steps toward her apartment. He didn't need to check which door was hers. If the potted lemon tree and hanging flower garden, complete with rainbow-painted tin-can pinwheels and garden gnomes, weren't a dead giveaway, then the view he had through her front window cemented the fact.

Billowing fabrics, a patchwork of bold colors, mismatched furniture that somehow worked together. She'd transformed a sterile apartment into a magical place that was warm and welcoming.

Something that was difficult to do when renting a tiny downtown apartment. By design, apartments were temporary and generic, yet Harper had managed to put herself into every inch of the space, and she'd taken the time to turn it into a home.

"Shit." Adam nearly tossed the dinner in the garbage, turned back around, and headed toward his car.

Not a single thing in the place was staged or for show. Just like there was nothing about the tenant that was staged or for show. Harper Owens with her sunny smile and melt-your-soul eyes was one hundred percent the real deal. She wasn't a temporary kind of girl, and Adam would never be a forever kind of guy. And yet, there he was, dinner stuck under his arm, a bag of homemade cookies dangling from his hand, ringing the doorbell—wanting her to be asleep and needing her to answer the door.

The door opened, and Adam felt as if everything he'd done up until this moment had been playing it safe. An odd feeling for a guy who jumped out of planes and ran into fires headfirst for a living. But there it was.

And there she was, appearing behind the screen door like a fucking dream, and Adam felt as if he were taking the biggest jump of his life. Gone was the slinky dress and red heels from earlier. He wondered if they were in a pile with the blue lace she'd been sporting, because Harper didn't look like the kind to use hangers unless she was expecting company. And he was pretty sure she wasn't wearing a bra.

Her face was fresh and clean, her hair loose from the complicated updo she'd worn earlier and still wet from the shower she'd taken. And those curls, *holy hell*, they were wet too, hanging all the way down to the curve of her back—wild and out of control. Just like he liked them. She was dressed in a pair of pajama bottoms with lace trim and a little drawstring. Tied in a bow, which sat right beneath her bellybutton, and was the only thing keeping them on her hips. They were pink, silky, and—*thank you, Jesus*—too short to hide those legs of hers.

Her top made it a matching set. A scrap of silk held together by two thin straps that draped over her almost-naked shoulders. Also pink. Also edged with lace that followed the deep vee of her neckline until it met in the middle with another cute bow that was designed to make men think about untying it. Which, point to Harper, was all he could think about. Untying that bow. With his teeth.

Then she smiled, warm and open and just for him, and everything inside him stilled—simplified. It was as though with one smile, she could make all the crazy and all the struggle disappear, and turn him from thrill-seeking daredevil to someone who didn't have to face down death just to feel.

"You were safe," she said, opening the screen door and stepping onto the porch.

He noticed she didn't ask why he was there or ream him about it being so late. She was just happy he was safe. He also noticed she was wearing glasses. Teal, boxy frames. Not sexy by design. But on her?

Sexy art teacher came to mind.

"And you're ready for bed," he said, holding up the bag. "I just wanted to bring you that dinner I promised."

"I stopped by Emerson's food truck on the way home."

Of course she had. It was midnight on a weeknight, she had work early in the morning, and there he was on her doorstep.

"But I always have room for dessert," she said.

There was something about the way she said it, the way she was holding his gaze and turning pink in the cheeks that had him saying, "I brought cookies, if that's what you're after."

"Cookies?" Her smile faltered and she worried her lower lip—clearly unsure of what he was really offering. "What else is on the menu?"

Adam leaned in and, making himself clear as fucking day, whispered, "Anything you want."

"Anything?" Harper blinked, as if she hadn't really expected that to be an option. Neither had he until he said it.

Indecision played across her face and—whoa, wasn't that interesting? The ball was completely in her court and that was completely terrifying and exciting, because Adam knew her answer would be equally as unexpected. Everything about her was unexpected.

If he were a smart man, this was where he'd hand over the cookies, wish her a good night, and get the hell out of there before she invited him in. Because he could tell she was processing her options. Knew she was going through each and every scenario. Each and every time he'd played with her, only to walk away. But he wasn't a smart man because he wasn't walking away this time.

Not tonight.

Not unless she asked him to leave, which with every second passing he started to wonder if that was the direction she was going. Which would totally suck. So he found himself saying, "Anything."

She looked at him for what felt like an eternity, and he told himself to be patient. Told himself to give her time and that no matter what she chose he'd be happy. And okay, happy was pushing it, because although sharing cookies and time with Harper would be fun, he was really hoping she took a risk on him and went for the fun-fucking-tastic option.

He knew the minute she'd made her decision. Her lips curled up into a sinful smile that was all temptation and trouble, and unexpected didn't even begin to explain the situation.

Her arms slid around his neck, her soft curves lining up just perfectly, and her mouth, *yeah*, that mouth of hers rested right on his. Not kissing, not teasing, but applying enough pressure to blow his fucking mind.

"I choose you," she said. Then, as if that wasn't the biggest green light in the history of the fucking planet, her eyes fluttered closed and she kissed him. Right there on the front porch next to the gnome colony and beneath the flickering night-light, like they were teenagers and this was their first date. Which had Adam thinking about their second date, and the one after that—and, finally, the one where he screwed it up.

Then he stopped thinking because the only thing thinking was giving him was a headache, and kissing Harper was the biggest rush he'd ever felt. And he felt a lot—her hands in his hair, her tongue in his mouth taking the kiss deeper, their connection stronger. So strong he found himself wanting more, so he walked her backward into her apartment, kicking the door closed behind them, and wondered how he'd become such a lucky SOB.

Her hands were on the move, roaming down his chest, her fingers stopping to fiddle with that bow. Not the one on the bottoms— if he didn't open his mouth they'd get to that—but the one holding that top together, because—

Ho-ly.

Shit.

This was happening.

And why the hell not? They both wanted this, had for a while now. And she had made her choice.

Only she chose him, which surely meant something. But with her tugging on that bow he couldn't wrap his mind around what. Okay, his mind knew—it was his dick that was in denial. He didn't really think she fully understood what that choice meant, because if she had, she would have said, "I choose sex," or maybe, "I choose to get my cookies naked, up against the wall, while you make me scream out your name."

All adequate responses for a woman who knew the deal. But she'd chosen him, a guy who no sane woman would choose. And sure, Harper was a crazy cutie, but this was disaster in the making. She pretended like she knew the deal, was cool with the deal, but it was clear she didn't and she wasn't, otherwise she wouldn't have given that bow another little tug, this time with enough pressure to loosen the ribbon.

"Are you sure about this?" he asked. *About me?*

She looked up at him, so sincerely as though weighing his question with the utmost importance, as though searching past his words to the heart—his heart—and seeing him for everything he was. More importantly, everything he wasn't.

"More than sure."

"I don't do relationships," he reminded her.

"And yet you're already in one," she said. "It would be a shame not to at least explore the benefits."

"I do love exploring," he said. "Where do you think we should start?"

"How about we start with this and see where it leads?"

Without warning, Harper reached up and gave a final tug of the bow. He could hear the slide of the fabric as the bow became toe ribbons. And the ribbons became insignificant as inch by incredible inch the fabric fell to the sides, exposing more and more of that silky strip of skin beneath. Until finally, *finally*, she let go and the top fell to the floor in one swoop, leaving her in nothing but those fuzzy slippers and silk bottoms, and confirming that (a) this was going to happen, right here, right now, and (b) she wasn't wearing a bra under that silk, which led him to (c) that if he thought Harper in a lacy bra was smoking, he was about to go up in some serious flames, because Harper in nothing was about the hottest thing he'd ever seen, which finally brought him to (d) that unless she was sporting the tiniest of G-strings under those shorts, then—

Holding her gaze, he traced a fingertip down the curve of her neck, across her flat stomach, and all the way to her waist, loving how her muscles quivered in his wake. Then with purpose he slid both hands around until they were cupping her amazing ass and, *man*, two perfect handfuls.

"Are we talking a matching set, or do you have Honeysuckle under there?" he asked.

"Seeing my panties is strictly a third-date event," she said with a sinful smile. "Being that this is our first, I didn't wear any."

"Thank Christ for first dates," he said, his body tightening at the information. With a growl he lifted her up. "Wrap your legs around me, sunshine. This exploration is about to get real."

She did as she was told and he had every intention of walking them into the room, but she started kissing him and playing with his belt, and before he knew it, his pants were around his hips and she was pressed against the wall.

"Here?" he asked against her lips.

He thought she mumbled something about a cat but it was hard to hear what she was saying with her tongue down his throat. Then her legs tightened around him and so did her hand and—*sweet baby Jesus*—his eyes rolled to the back of his head and his knees started to buckle.

She was an artist all right. Fucking Picasso, with the way she used sure, smooth strokes and deliberate brushes to drive him right up to the edge, again and again, until he was certain he'd go all the way over if he didn't do something quick.

Using the wall for leverage, he slid one hand down her ass and beneath, pulling the perfectly-too-short shorts to the side and doing some creative reaching to give a stroke of his own. It wasn't Picasso, because, hell, he was limited holding her with one hand, but it was enough to have her gasping. The second stroke had her moaning his name, and the third? He added a little brush combo at the end that had her whole body tensing. So he did it again, loving how she grabbed his wrist and held him there, as if afraid he'd stop before she got her cookies.

Not his style.

"Tell me what you want, Harper. More of this?" Stroke. Brush.

Her head fell back against the wall, thrusting her breasts up and her hips forward, increasing the friction—and the heat. Always good with orders, he started pumping and stroking and the way she closed around his fingers when he sank even deeper was enough to drive a man insane.

"Yes, more of that," she moaned.

"There you go again, making this too easy. You haven't heard the other options. Like this," he said, giving her a kiss that was meant to rock her world, and by the way she clung to him, he figured he'd rocked it hard.

"Or maybe some of this?" Tilting his head down, he captured her nipple in his mouth, which was right there begging for attention. He gave a sharp bite, then soothed it with his tongue. "What will it be, sunshine?"

"All," she said on a scream.

Adam did just that. He had her groaning in one kiss, shuddering with a well-placed nibble to her swollen breasts, and exploding when he applied the right kind of stroke in the right kind of spot. Her body clamped around his hand as her orgasm took her higher and higher.

She sighed and one leg slid to the floor and that was when she looked up at him through desire-hazed eyes and said, "I want it all."

And with her hair messy from his fingers, her lips bruised from his kisses, and her voice hoarse from crying out his name, Adam decided he wanted it all too.

Things got a little frantic, him working the bow, her searching for the condom that was—*bingo*—in his back pocket. A few seconds and one hell of a rubdown later, he was wrapped, she was ready, and they met in the middle with a single thrust.

She gasped. He nearly cried. Then neither of them moved, neither one of them breathed. They stood there, her right leg on the floor, her left locked around his back, and he was finally where he wanted to be.

After he could breathe without the fear of his lungs collapsing from pleasure, he shifted his hips ever so slowly, and she landed a move that was so unexpected it was like a wrecking ball right through his chest.

She tightened her arms around his neck, then kissed his nose, his chin, and finally his lips as she moved in sync with him.

Sweet, God so fucking sweet it hurt, then she pulled him in for what had to be the most erotic and all-encompassing embrace he'd ever been given and he knew he was in trouble. There they were, half naked, fucking up against the wall, his pants around his ankles, his shirt bunched up around his waist, and Harper somehow made this moment special. Made him feel special.

And he liked it. More than he should.

"You feel so good," he said, but what he really meant was that around her he felt good. Terrified, confused, scared shitless, but good.

As if this were right.

She tightened her arms around him in a way that was all Harper, and Adam finally let go.

The free fall started, pumping through his veins and rocking his body. Harper felt it too because she started to tighten around him, and breathing turned nonexistent, as if his chest were too big for his skin, and he wanted to deploy the chute and free-fall forever all at the same time.

Then she lifted her head to meet his gaze straight on, looking at him as though he was her choice, the right choice, and—bam— he was a goner.

The pressure built, hotter and higher, and Harper must have let go too, because he felt her start to shake and then she was crying out his name. Chanting it really.

Not that he was one to talk, since he was doing some chanting of his own, and he finally gave in to the heat. Everything went black and he dropped his head to her shoulder, pressed his face to her throat, and took her in, while she melted into him, both breathing hard.

"Those were some pretty amazing cookies," she said into his neck.

Adam laughed, and when he was no longer afraid of his legs buckling, he looked up and what he saw looking back had him smiling. Man, she was gorgeous and sweet and funny—a total turn-on.

"I was thinking that the next batch could be enjoyed in bed," he said.

"That depends."

He lifted a brow. "On what?"

"How do you feel about Grumpy Cat?"

"Never met a kitty I couldn't get purring." To prove it, he threw her over his shoulder in a fireman's hold and headed down the hallway.

chapter
sixteen

It had been several days since the impromptu dinner at the station—and dessert at her place—and Harper could still feel her body tingling. No matter how many times she told herself it was just chemistry, or applied soothing body lotion, the tingling wouldn't go away.

It had started in her lips the minute she realized it wasn't a *for show* kind of smooch, spread south when she found him on her front porch, and finally reached her toes when they staged an impromptu photo shoot in her apartment Friday morning, and continued tingling straight through the weekend. It stuck with her through Monday's papier-mâché class where Tommy mistook a bowl of paste for pudding, Tuesday's nine hours of burning the midnight oil with the campaign mockup, and this morning's argument over why Spanx for men was not upping the store's swagger.

"Tell me again why we're putting the girdles at the back of the store," Clovis said, resting her cane between two display shelves, creating a makeshift rolling rack.

Jabba lifted his head from the garbage can under the counter and locked eyes on the cane.

"Maybe you need to get a hearing aid to go with that cane," Ida Beamon, one of Clovis's oldest friends, said. She was hanging a collection of nude-colored body-slimmers from the cane. "The girl already told you that girdles don't really say *youthful allure*."

"Tell me how alluring it is when all that vintage-grade cottage cheese is flapping in the wind," Clovis argued, but she picked up one end of the cane, while Ida grabbed the other. Together, they navigated their way toward the back of the store, Jabba hot on their trail. "Plus they're our biggest sellers. There's no sense in making people walk all the way to the back to get the biggest sellers."

"Actually, back-loading the store with everyday necessities that are not necessarily sexy is a perfect merchandising strategy," Harper said as she slipped a summery-style negligée over the mannequin in the front window. "It forces people to walk past the beautifully displayed babydolls and French décolletés with the matching garter-panties you just got in."

"I agree with Harper. Babydolls up front is smart merchandising," Peggy said from beside Harper, and everyone groaned.

Not that Harper didn't appreciate the support, but Peggy had been agreeing with Harper all morning. She'd walked into the shop with a bag of cookies and a smile, sporting Harper's cardigan and a necklace that looked vaguely familiar, then planted herself directly at Harper's side.

"I don't look good in babydolls," Clovis mumbled, moving the girdles to the hooks on the back wall. "They make me look top-heavy."

"You don't *look* it. You *are*," Ida said to Clovis, who repositioned her top half with pride.

Peggy grabbed a babydoll off the rack and held it up to her frame, then looked in the mirror—more specifically at her top half.

She twisted side to side a few times, watching the material flirt in the mirror on the far wall.

"Plus, National Underwear Day is Tuesday," Harper pointed out, fully aware that Peggy had turned to stare at her mouth. "We want to highlight the seductive side of the shop. Show the customers that lingerie can be fun, flirty, sensual."

"Seductive side," Peggy repeated, her voice pitched eerily close to Harper's. "Fun, flirty, sensual." She drew out each word, careful to bite her lips on each hard consonant.

Ignoring the mockingbird to her right, Harper went back to her mannequin. Which meant Peggy smoothed the mesh over her cleavage, then released a big sigh before going back to her own mannequin.

When Peggy couldn't keep her eyes off the babydoll, Harper asked, "So how did it go with the *teeth too white to be real* guy at the senior center?"

"It was going well until that floozy from the over-fifty-five community started flaunting her menopause glow around the dance floor," Peggy said, her voice much softer than her words. "The man leaves his glasses at home for the night and suddenly every AARP card–carrying woman in town notices him."

"I'm so sorry, Peggy." Harper's heart went out to the older woman. "But if he gets dazzled by something as ordinary as menopause glow, then he's"—Harper lowered her voice and repeated the best advice she'd been given as of late—"a dumbass."

"You think so?"

"I don't think, I know. Just like I know there is someone even better out there for you," Harper said confidently. If someone hadn't been brave enough to tell Harper the same thing, she'd still be waiting on a man who was dazzled by designer boobs. Instead she'd had cookies—a baker's dozen to be exact—with one of the sweetest, sexiest, and most sensitive guys in town. "And if you want that baby-doll, then get it for *you*. Not some guy with too-white teeth."

Peggy patted Harper's hand in gratitude, then blinked back a little moisture. When the blinking didn't work and the tears became real, Peggy diverted the attention off her by asking, "Is that magenta trim on the blue netting?"

"It's actually bougainvillea-colored silk trim on aqua mesh. I think it will capture a lot of foot traffic." It was vibrant, breezy, flirty—and exactly what they needed to appeal to a new variety of clientele. The same clientele Lulu Allure was targeting. "And it would go lovely with your eyes."

Even though Harper knew she'd have to rehang and reshelve everything the ladies touched, and make sure Clovis didn't put the girdles in the window display the second Harper left for work, she loved spending time with her grandma and the girls. They'd been a steady fixture in her life since she was a little girl. Her mom would shuttle Harper from theater to theater, but when a big role came along she'd drop Harper off at Clovis's.

All three of these ladies had taken her in as if she were theirs. Embraced her and all of her eccentricities. Treated her as if who she was at her core was too special to be overlooked.

Harper's phone buzzed from the pocket of her dress. She fished it out and sucked in a breath. "Oh my God. It's Chantel." She showed the caller name on the screen to Peggy. "She must have received the few photos I sent over."

Harper had wanted to make sure that what she was doing matched Chantel's expectations. But she'd only sent them that morning—it was too early to hear back. Unless she loved them.

Or didn't.

"If you mean the ones of Mr. July pulling a Magic Mike in my back room, then put it on speaker so the girls and I can hear," Clovis said, dropping the girdles and hobbling across the store.

Harper didn't bother to ask how *the girls* knew about those photos. They'd been taken in this very shop and touched up in her apartment, which her grandmother had a key to—and used at will.

"We don't have all day. Answer it before she gets impatient and we miss out on talking about those photos," Ida said.

"You think this will be one of those video chats?" Clovis asked, her voice all atwitter. "If so, she might hold up those photos so we can get a better look at them. See if he was stuffing the shorts or if it was real."

It was real all right. Everything about Adam felt real when they were together. So real that the tingling had lasted for days.

Harper took in a few calming breaths so she wouldn't sound as if she were hyperventilating, or daydreaming about her faux-mance that was turning out to be the most real romance she'd ever had, and swiped the screen. "Hey, Chantel."

"Sorry I'm calling so early. It's going to get crazy busy here later, and I didn't want to miss the chance to call."

"It's perfect timing, I'm at the shop," Harper said, and walked out the front door to gain some semblance of privacy. Not that it worked, as three frosted heads and one drooling dog pressed their faces to the window. Harper turned to face the street. "Actually, I'm working on a new window display for National Underwear Day."

"If it's anything like the images you sent over, I want to see it," Chantel said, and Harper swallowed.

She looked at the bright, whimsical, summer-loving theme and then thought about the deep masculine undertones of the photo shoots. "It really makes a statement, if that's what you mean."

"Statement?" Chantel laughed. "Those images were a visual orgasm. They were raw, erotic, captivating, a feminine take on male sexuality. I had to open a bottle of wine while looking at them. Your branding for the line is light-years ahead of what our marketing team came up with."

"It is?" Harper did her best not to giggle, but it was hard. That tingling she'd been feeling all week spread to encompass her entire body.

"Lulu Rous agrees. She said the concept was inspired."

Harper nearly passed out. Lulu Rous was the founder and artistic genius behind Lulu Allure. She was one of the most creative minds in lingerie, and *she* thought *Harper's* ideas were inspired?

"Thank you," Harper said, sure she was gushing, but she didn't care. "I had amazing designs to work with and a subject who is a natural in front of the camera."

Adam was a natural at everything, it seemed. Modeling, cooking, firefighting . . . sex. He was a real sex ninja—and the idea of sparring with him again was tempting. The thought of doing more with him was dangerous, but dangerous had never seemed so alluring.

"That might be, but your style is in every photo you sent, and the concept sets them apart. It's so refreshing to see a real man, the kind whose muscles come from hard work and not the gym. I am so tired of these metro-sexual models who know more about fashion than me."

Harper smothered a laugh, because that was exactly what Adam had said. "I wanted to capture the kind of magnetism a guy puts off after a hard day's work. Then shoot him in his element to show that swagger is earned, not bought off a rack."

"'Swagger is earned, not off the rack,'" Chantel said slowly, as if she was writing it down. "I can't wait to see the final mockups. And your window display is probably as edgy as your photos."

"I can send some pictures of the window when it's done." Which, based on Harper's mental calculations of just how long it would take to redo the entire display to match the mood of the photos while putting together the online catalog, helping out with Beat the Heat, and doing her day job, would be Friday night. That was, if she skipped all meals and learned how to sleep standing up.

"Great. If they're anything like these, Lulu will flip. I can just see the taglines you used on these images. *Real Men Work. Real Men Sweat.* My favorite is *Real Men Wear Swagger.* Brilliant." Chantel paused, and Harper could hear her thinking through the phone. "Wait. I have a better idea. What if we came to you?"

"Here?"

"Photos can be underwhelming, so this way nothing can be lost in translation. Seeing the whole concept, how the store, the new display, the campaign, and Swagger all work together to create a singular vision would be helpful."

Harper looked inside past the three bobbleheads, to the girdles on the floor, the boxes of new sleepwear still needing to be shelved, and felt the panic settle around her neck. "Ah, when were you thinking?"

"We're launching the line on National Underwear Day, so what if we came the day before? A little prerelease where I can bring Lulu and the entire team, and if it goes well we can wrap this up before the launch." Chantel's voice went serious.

"If you like what you see, then you would offer us the same territory, same exclusive terms?" Harper asked, unable to mask the excitement in her voice. This would change everything for her grandmother. It would also change things for Harper. Just a few weeks working on this project and already look how much her life had changed.

How much she had changed.

"What I experienced when I was there changed my mind about you and the Boulder Holder. I know it will change Lulu's. She's looking for a reason to say yes to you, Harper. So am I. Your grandma was one of our first retailers."

"The first. And would Lulu really want to celebrate her prelaunch here?" Harper asked, because in-person didn't seem to be her forte when it came to people between the ages of eighteen and fifty-five. The idea of negotiating with a roomful of runway-ready trendsetters and executives made her palms sweat.

"Absolutely," Chantel said with so much confidence that Harper felt her own lift. "I just got word that Lulu will be flying out for the launch and wanted a work retreat away from the office with the team to finalize things. Wine country is sexy, romantic, enticing, and the perfect place to get in the right mindset. Plus, it's the perfect timing to showcase the new, beautiful, fresh face of the Boulder Holder."

Any concerns Harper had vanished. Meeting Lulu was the next logical step, and she had no need to be worried. Making friends was what Harper did. It was how she'd survived eight different schools before the third grade. Sure, she was quirky and sometimes a bit awkward, but she was real, knew how to listen, and, most importantly, she had heart.

Lots of it.

Obviously, that was what Chantel saw in her. It was why she was giving her a shot to prove herself. And Harper wouldn't let her down. She was going to make that shop and display come to life. She was going to take her concept, which she'd dubbed *real women want real men*, to the next level, and make sure Lulu saw that same potential and determination as Chantel.

"And what a face," Chantel said, her voice going breathy. "One wink from Adam and I wouldn't be surprised if Lulu agreed on the spot. Oops, that's the other line, I have to go. Have Adam wear plum—it's Lulu's favorite color and the accent for Swagger."

Thrilled at the idea of spending more time with Adam, and terrified of pulling off their ruse for even longer, she said, "You bet. We'll see you soon."

"I don't care how big your banana is, that dipstick is not welcome anywhere near my booth or my houses," Nora Kincaid said to Ida Beamon, all piss and vinegar, jabbing her cane toward her hand-crafted mailboxes that resembled miniature Victorian houses, and nearly poking out Adam's left eye. Adam managed to dodge it and took in the remaining chaos at the registration table.

"My dipped bananas are *the* crowd favorite. Grabbing one on the way into the fair is tradition for families all around town," Ida argued, pointing to the TOWN FAVORITE star on her I TAKE MINE DOUBLE-DIPPED AND WITH NUTS shirt. "Veteran vendors get first dibs on last year's booth. Last year I had booth one, like I had it the thirty years before. And just because some bonehead didn't consult the map doesn't mean you get to run me out of my booth."

"The hell it doesn't," Nora said, raising her cane to smack-down level. "I was here early so I could get in line first, then I turned in my form. First!" She shot up a finger, then pointed a more appropriate one at McGuire. "Where that bonehead there assigned me booth one."

Adam grabbed the cane before it struck bone, and when someone lobbed a chocolate-dipped banana at the registration table, he put himself between the blustering old biddies. After a few kicks to the shin, an elbow in the ribs, and someone goosing him from the sidelines, he knew he had to change tactics—and fast.

A mob of ladies swarmed the registration table, demanding to see if they still had their promised street-facing booth.

Not just ladies—angry old biddies with a bone to pick. It was as though every quilter, crafter, and banana-on-a-stick master, from the dawn of time until the present day, had been promised a street-facing booth. Adam felt genuine fear take over.

"One more elbow flies and I will give the entire front row of booths to the Gardening and Flower Club."

A collective gasp came from the crowd, but the elbows lowered and everyone took a step back. Everyone, except Ms. Moberly, the town's librarian. She stepped forward and looked over the rim of her glasses at Adam in a move that was pure velvet and steel, and had silenced rowdy kids for over four decades.

"Well, that would make for some interesting talks at home," she said. "Since the garden club is doing a presentation on orchid pollination, they will be selling their giant white asparagus by the bunches."

"So?" Adam said, pinching the bridge of his nose, not making sense of any of it.

"This year's crop has been quite the talk. It's bigger than normal and quite impressive with its *thick stalks* and *bulbous crowns*," Ida added, the *if you know what I mean* clear in her voice.

"Oh geez," Adam said, holding his hand up.

Ms. Moberly pushed her glasses farther up her nose, and suddenly Adam felt as if he were twelve again, slipping *The Joy of Sex* in his backpack. "Putting the bananas and asparagus together would negatively influence the topics for the Build Your Own Book project I have planned."

"Like her dipped bananas and melons won't give *Dick and Jane* a whole new spin," Nora argued. "Which is why my wholesome mailboxes will be street facing."

"I'm selling my apple pie by the slice," someone else said. "It doesn't get more wholesome than apple pie."

"Well, that young man there promised me booth one," Nora said, pointing to McGuire again, as though there would be no further argument.

McGuire smiled. Ida did not. Neither did Peggy Lovett, owner of the Paws and Claws Day Spa.

"Well, the one with the tight tush promised it to me," Peggy said, looking right at Seth. "I'm teaching people about proper summer safety to keep their animals cool, and selling my Beat the Heat–inspired doggie couture. I called my supplier and ordered extra hat fans this year after I found out I was in booth one."

"Well, as I've said, I've been setting up in booth one since the first year of this event, and as a veteran vendor I have dibs!" Ida flapped her form in the air.

A wave of frenzy took over the crowd as women started pushing forward to be next in line. Seth and McGuire barricaded themselves behind the table.

Shaking his head at his first responders, Adam stepped forward. "Settle down."

When that didn't work he let out an ear-piercing whistle that had people zipping their lips. Then he thought about Harper's lips, and wished he'd made time to grab a quick kiss before starting his day. Because he knew that quick kiss would turn into more if he allowed it. And instead of playing mediator to a bunch of grandmas, he could be wrapped around Harper, playing hide the banana. "How many people were promised a street-facing booth?"

Nearly every hand went up. Which was impossible. There were ten street-facing booths and at least twenty women claiming them. "Keep your hand in the air if Seth here promised you one of the ten street-facing booths." Half of the hands remained. "Now, if it was McGuire you spoke with . . ." The other half went up.

Adam glanced back at his men, who were standing behind separate tables, with separate plot maps, and looking at the ground like two kids caught with their hands down their pants.

"I didn't know Freshman over there was giving out the same booth numbers," McGuire said, as if it were all Seth's fault.

Adam sighed, long and hard, because Ida was right. He was surrounded by boneheads. Of course, he could be a card-carrying member, considering he'd been the one to make the executive decision to place Seth and McGuire in charge of booth registration. He'd also chosen to spend that past hour watching Harper flutter around town again instead of keeping watch over his team.

First, because Harper was a hell of a lot more fun to look at. But mostly, being under someone's thumb never helped Adam any. And he didn't think it would help these two.

When he was younger, and an FNG himself, being under someone's thumb only made him squirm. It wasn't until Roman let him screw up enough to learn, but not enough to get singed, that he became the firefighter he was today.

He figured that Seth and McGuire needed some direction, maybe a little example of how to manage a situation, but he didn't think they need their fucking hands held.

"Freshman or not, he is your teammate, McGuire, and you, as the *senior* member, should have had his back," Adam said, wondering why he sounded like his old man.

"I'll remember that, sir." McGuire gave a single, tense nod. Translation: order received and understood, now go fuck yourself.

Adam opened his mouth to tell McGuire he was already doing a good enough job of it, when something hit him. What his men needed was a positive example, the guy who Harper swore she saw when she looked at him. The shit of it was, he needed that guy right then too.

Adam placed a hand on McGuire's shoulder and leaned in so only the two of them were privy to the conversation. "I know you don't want to be here, man. I don't blame you, this is a shit assignment, but it's important to the town and the department, which was why I requested you." McGuire's shoulders lifted at the praise. "You have a lot of expertise to share, expertise that I think this event and Seth can benefit from. He needs to be shown how things work, and I am counting on you to make sure there's open communication among the crew. That he fits in. Can you do that?"

McGuire's chest puffed out about four thousand feet and he smiled. "Yes, sir."

Adam clapped him on the shoulder, then turned to the crowd and plastered on that Baudouin smile women loved so much. "I apologize about the mix-up. Unfortunately, we have ten street-facing booths and twenty of you claiming them."

"Too bad, those booths are rightfully owned by ten veteran vendors," Ida hollered.

"I've been at booth seven since sixty-eight," someone in the back yelled. "And now those yahoos from the yoga studio are claiming it's theirs!"

"Sixty-eight sounds like it's time you gave someone else a shot!"

All at once, everyone began shouting. It started with locations versus sales, quickly moved to how smooth last year went, and took an ugly turn at "If I don't get my booth, I want a refund!" Which meant the event would fail. Under his direction.

No booths meant no booth fees—and no Back-to-School Packs.

Adam counted at least seven women heading for the parking lot, seven registration fees he'd have to reimburse—and seven families who might not participate in the day's events. Right then, he knew he couldn't charm his way out of this.

Time to lead then.

"Hang on," he said, picking up the Beat the Heat official binder off the table. He held it high in the air so everyone could lock their beady eyes on it. "Now, these guys here volunteered—on their own time, I'd like to add—to help make this community event a hit. For everyone. Not just a few booths."

He paused to eye the most vocal protestors in the crowd and locked on until they knew he was good and done. "Being that this is their first year not only planning Beat the Heat but attending it, I was expecting a bit more help from you ladies. More of that St. Helena neighborliness you're all so fond of bragging about."

People stopped walking and a few of them even had the decency to look ashamed.

"In the past, we have always allocated spaces based on history with the event. People get the chance to register for the same booth every year, and only when someone forfeits their space does it go to someone else. Correct?"

That got a few heads to nod.

Adam clapped his hands. "Great. Then I need you to form a single-file line in order of your booth number from last year. Ida will take the front spot, since she and her bananas have been booth one since before I was born. And if someone is not present, or their form is not already on file stating they wanted to renew their spot, then it will go to the next person in line. Understood?"

There were a few grumbles, but people started lining up.

"What about my mailboxes?" Nora asked. "Do I get stuck in no-man's land because she's been hogging the same spot for all these years? I've lived here just as long as she has, but only started selling my wares after God spoke to me in the form of a naked statue of a no-good two-timer. I helped lop off his pecker, then got busy building my business. Should I be penalized for that?"

"You're not being penalized for anything," Peggy said. "But Ida here has put her heart and soul into making those dipped bananas the Beat the Heat town tradition. It wouldn't be right to take that from her either."

"That's why it's up to Ida," Adam said, looking Ida right in the eye. "If she wants to give up her booth or switch spaces, that's up to her. That's how the rules have been for years, so as the current tenant of booth one, it's her call."

"I wouldn't mind sharing," a sweet-as-sin voice said from the back. Adam watched as Harper made her way forward. She had on a flowy sundress, sexy heels, and that smile. "I'm not street facing, but the Fashion Flower's face-painting booth will be stationed right next to the stage, which is a great location. Most of my kids' moms do yoga at Get Bent, so our customers would cross over."

"Thank you," the owner of Get Bent said. "That would be great. I always get lost in the back, and people don't find their way to my fruit smoothies until dark, and then who wants a cold treat?"

"That would take all the fun out of the event," Harper said, releasing that smile on Ida. "Don't you think?"

All eyes went to Ida, who was glaring back at Harper. Peggy had moved in too and was practically hovering over the other woman, giving her a reprimanding eye.

Not Harper. She didn't crowd, didn't badger, didn't even raise her voice. But she also didn't give the older woman an out. Just flashed some of that warm welcome and understanding she was so good at and waited, as if confident that with time and support Ida would reach deep and find her best behavior.

Ida took in a deep breath and began shaking her head vigorously, several times in fact, before letting out a disgruntled huff. "Fine." She turned to Nora. "If you'd like, you can set your mailboxes up in the grass space of my tent. I never use that area."

"I'm not asking for a handout," Nora said.

"I'm not offering one. You want to share the booth, you pay for it. Ow!" Ida jerked her head toward Peggy and rubbed her foot. Peggy just smiled on.

Nora crossed her arms, then made a big show of playing it cool. "Deal. But if I'm paying half the rental fee, then I want all the space for half the time. I'll take the second day."

"But Sunday is the bigge—" Ida whipped her head around. "That's my bunion!"

"And this is a community affair," Peggy reminded everyone. "And as the tenant of booth nine, I would love to share my space too. For both days."

"That's nice of you, Peggy," Harper said and gave Adam a wink.

The older woman waved a self-conscious hand, the impact of Harper's attention and words making her flush. Adam understood the affliction well. "I'm showing kids how to make organic dog bones at home," Peggy said, "and selling some critter couture, so I won't need all of the table."

Ida's lips went into a thin line, before offering Nora a tight smile. "Sunday at a different booth sounds lovely," Ida said, her face folding in on itself as if she'd eaten a lemon.

"Great," Adam said, his eyes locked on Harper's. "And if anyone else would like to share or swap, just let McGuire here know. He will be filing all the papers and handing out booth numbers."

Adam looked at McGuire, who stepped forward. "After you get your number, Seth here will show you where your tent is located on the map, and where you can load and unload your stuff tomorrow morning."

"Any questions?" Adam asked.

"Yeah, you going to be putting up that big ladder tomorrow?" Nora asked. "If so, I'll bring my camera so I can get a picture for the ladies in my extreme couponing club. A snap of your backside is worth three triple-points coupons."

Blaming the warm weather for the heat climbing up his neck, Adam looked back at his guys, and he knew what he had to do, finally understanding the right way to lead. "This year we're switching it up a little too. McGuire and Seth will be running the ladder demo and have the honor of picking out our little firefighters. So make sure you come by, and have your cameras ready."

He watched as his guys took control and started doling out booth numbers. It didn't take long for the one vendor he'd been waiting to talk with to make her way forward, and when she did it was as if the air suddenly turned electric. And his pulse picked up a few notches, because seeing her in that pretty summer dress with her hair piled high in some fancy knot on top of her head had him thanking God that today was his last day at the station. Come tomorrow, he'd have the next three off. Granted, he'd be working

Beat the Heat, but he'd be working it with Harper. Exploring more of those benefits they seemed to be enjoying so much.

"That was a very lieutenantly thing you just did," Harper said sweetly, handing him her registration form and one hell of a punch to the gut. Because her dress wasn't just pretty, it was incredible. Tight where it should be tight, flowy enough to have his mind wandering, and the same color as her eyes. Electric blue.

And don't even get him started on the heels. Black and high and designed to make men think about sex. The woman, though? She was designed to make men think about other things. Things that made his chest feel warm and full.

Over the past few weeks she'd somewhat muffled her quirky side to make room for her sexy and flirty one. The funny thing was, he liked both sides. Hell, he liked pretty much everything about Harper.

"Working with the kids had a big impact on me. I figure it might have the same on them," he said, wanting to kiss her. He could tell she was open to the idea because her eyes were dilated and he could see her pulse beat at the base of her neck. So he did.

Right there in front of jury and witness. And Nora Kincaid, who had her camera phone aimed on them snapping away. So he kept it PG, okay maybe PG-13 since it lingered long enough to leave a mark—and elicit a handful of hoots and catcalls.

"What was that for?" Harper breathed when he pulled back.

"For walking in like a ray of sunshine and making my day brighter," he said, and had this been any other guy with any other woman, Adam would have gagged. But this was Harper, and he meant every word of it.

"Thanks to you it's an amazing day, so I thought I'd share the excitement," she said, looking up at him with hero worship in her eyes. He tried to harden himself against the way it felt to be looked at like that by a woman like her. But one blink of those big doe eyes and a different part altogether hardened. "Chantel called yesterday."

"And?" He didn't have to ask what was said—he could see the genuine pride in her eyes, and good for her. She deserved to be recognized. She was smart, talented, and one hell of a special woman.

"And she loved the photos so much that she's bringing her boss here to see the shop on Monday. To meet me and you. And hopefully sign a contract."

"Harper"—he pulled her in for a hug—"that's great. And well deserved."

She looked up. "Then you'll come on Monday? To the shop?"

"I wouldn't miss it." In fact, if they stuck to the agreed-upon plan, it would be their last day together as a couple. Something that should have instilled relief, not more confusion. "We should celebrate tonight."

She looked at his uniform. "Aren't you working?"

Adam gripped the back of his neck and groaned. This was one of the reasons he didn't do relationships. He'd seen too many guys try to balance the job and family, missing anniversaries, first steps, all the important stuff in order to handle all the life-and-death stuff. The other reason, if he was being honest, was fear of failing.

Not himself, but others.

Adam knew that everyone experienced failure. It was a part of life. Only Adam never failed the small stuff. It was the moments that really mattered, the times someone was counting on him to pull through, the big shit that he always managed to drop the proverbial ball.

He'd done it with his family, with his team . . . with Trent. Even with every warning sign waving clear as fucking day, he'd still managed to make the wrong call.

Trent was as hotheaded and gung ho as Adam, but Adam should have used more caution. He shouldn't have said they had this fire locked down when he was in no position to make such a claim, and he shouldn't have spoken up without thinking through the consequences. The regret cut deep.

A warm hand slid into his and Harper gave him a little squeeze. "That's okay, you can buy me a chocolate-dipped banana at the festival. Tonight, I'm helping Emerson with the food for tomorrow, which means I get to stuff my face with really yummy food that I didn't have to cook. Then Shay is stopping by to help organize the decorations and help me brush up on my face-painting techniques."

"Which means they get to drink wine while you bust out the Halloween paints?"

"Pretty much."

Adam smiled. "Have I told you thank you for saving my ass?"

"Several times," she said. "But you can tell me again, Saturday at the fair. When you let me paint your face."

"Like unicorns and bunnies on my cheek?"

"Or a super manly mask. Like Robocop or the Black Flame. Anything but a zombie or skeleton, which the older boys ask for. Last year a group of them snuck into the girls' dance team tent and scared them so bad that they couldn't perform. So as the newbie running the face-painting booth, I was asked to come up with new ideas this year," she said. "If the older boys see you going superhero and not villain, they might do it too."

"First off Robocop is a cop, and that's lame. Black Flame? A super *villain*. And a girl." Harper gave a little shrug as if she knew that and was teasing him. "How do I know you're not just saying you'll paint something super manly, then paint a bunny on my cheek? Because I've only ever seen bunnies at these things."

"Because I've never done the face-painting booth. But now that I am, there's going to be some new manly designs to choose from. In fact, if you wanted, I could paint your face so that you'd look like Hephaestus, because I'm that good."

"The god of fire?" he asked, impressed he remembered. "What, did you go to face-painting school at the National Academy of Arts?"

"Better."

He looked down and found their hands swinging. The Five-Alarm Casanova was standing in the park, with his girlfriend, swinging hands—and liking it.

Wasn't that unexpected?

"I got my training in body painting"—Harper leaned in, good and close, until he could feel her dress brush his thighs, her lips skate over the ridge of his ear—"from a legend in the field. And, yes, bunnies were my specialty, but not the fuzzy kind that hop on all fours. I painted on the bodies of Hugh Hefner's Bunnies."

Adam swallowed. "You worked at the Playboy Mansion?"

"How do you think I know so much about lingerie?"

With a final squeeze to his hand that said she was dead serious, Harper took her booth number off the table and walked toward the Fashion Flower, proving with that practiced sway that she was all about the unexpected.

chapter
seventeen

That night Harper and Shay sat in Emerson's apartment, picking out face-painting masks while testing a nice selection of the following day's menu items. They had an even better selection of wine.

"How about I make you a fairy?" Harper asked, dipping her brush into the aqua glitter paint.

"Do you want dessert?" Emerson asked, snatching the tray of her famous baklava right before Harper could grab a piece. "Because if I see one fairy option then you will never get another one of these again. And never is a long-ass time."

Harper raised a paintbrush in surrender. "No fairies, got it."

Emerson's six-year-old sister, Violet, had, up until recently, believed that fairies were real, that *she* was a fairy, and, therefore, would only answer to Pixie Girl. It had taken Emerson two years to get Violet out of her wings and into normal clothes, so Harper could see how it was still a sore subject.

Harper looked back to her paints, the emerald green and gold glitter catching her eye. "How about an Egyptian princess?"

Shay thought about that for a moment, while taking a long sip of wine. Her eyes went wide. "I want to be an Egyptian *queen*," Shay clarified, her expression turning mischievous. "Cleopatra. She had cats, and Jonah would make a handsome Mark Antony." She leaned back in the chair and sighed. "I can just see him feeding me grapes in one of those loincloths. Maybe I should text him to make sure we have grapes."

Shay picked up her phone and started swiping, while Harper went about picking out the colors.

Shay's phone pinged. "Jonah says he's stopping by the store on his way to get me, so Cleopatra it is!" Her phone buzzed again. Three times. "He's leaving right now. Oh, he says he's using the sirens." Shay looked up. "We'd better hurry."

"Seriously?" Emerson set the tray on the coffee table and plopped onto the couch. "This is supposed to be girls' night. Something both of you made clear. So against my better judgment, I agreed, and even hosted it so I could kick you out if it got all emotional."

"I can tell you about how sweet Jonah was the other day when the herd of baby chinchillas I rescued got scared, so he cuddled them."

"You shouldn't tell anyone that story. Ever," Emerson said. "And the only two rules of girls' nights are no guys allowed and no one leaves until the bottles are empty. Those were your rules, Shay."

With a shrug, Shay picked up one of the bottles and drained the remaining bit. There were still two half-empty ones left.

"That's okay," Harper said. "You guys cut off hours of prep work for me tonight by helping out with the decorations. All that's left is getting everything to the park, and displaying my Sprouting Picassos' artwork, which I can finish tomorrow." She took a sip from her glass.

"If you guys help me prep the petting zoo pen early, we can set up the art show together," Shay said.

"Perfect." Harper dipped the brush into glittery emerald-green paint and lifted it to her friend's forehead. "Close your eyes."

Shay did as told, while Harper outlined the whimsical design she created in her mind. Working off a design was usually her MO, but sometimes it was fun to design while she was creating.

"What are you going to pick, Em?" Harper asked. "Make it something that will surprise Dax."

"You should be a queen too," Shay mumbled through still lips. "Then you can boss him around when he gets here."

"Nah, I already do that." Emerson picked up the binder of ideas and flipped through it. "Camo is Dax's favorite color. You got anything camo themed?"

"Oh, how about GI Jane?" Shay asked. Harper didn't hear the response. She was too lost in the creative process to pay attention. Mixing colors, enhancing people's best features, creating a portal into make-believe—she'd forgotten how much she enjoyed this.

"How about you?" Emerson asked. "Harper?"

Harper took onyx paint and followed the natural curve of Shay's eyes, making them bigger, more catlike, and exotic. "Oh, well, Adam likes bright colors, so maybe a mermaid," she said, then remembered their earlier conversation and felt her belly warm. "Or a bunny."

The room fell silent. Harper finished the last touches on Shay's other eye and looked up—to find her friends looking back. Confusion and something akin to suspicion etched their faces.

"What?"

"I was asking if you wanted more wine," Emerson said, holding up the bottle. "Seriously, a bunny? That's about as sexy as your cat sweaters."

Harper didn't bother to point out that Adam had a magic touch when it came to kitties, because talking about his sexual prowess would lead to talking about sex. With him. And she wasn't sure she wanted to talk about that with her friends. Not until she understood it herself, because there was more going on than just sex.

"Ah hell." Emerson plopped down on the couch and leaned her head back. "I should have known something was up when you started wearing your pageant hair."

Harper patted down her hair, which was silky and smooth and had taken her an hour to straighten. "What's wrong with my hair?"

"It looks like something off Miss America, or that nightly newscaster on the local evening news. No curls, no pencil holding it together, and way too sculpted to be anything good." Emerson zeroed in on Harper until she was sweating. "He charmed you."

"Adam is very charming," Harper said, busying herself with cleaning the brushes off in the water, neither confirming nor denying the accusation. "And what does my hair have to do with anything?"

Emerson sat forward, her eyes going serious. "Rodney Fletcher. Seventh grade. He asked to borrow your history notes, the next day you came to school with highlights, only they were more hydrogen-peroxide orange than platinum. Rodney didn't notice because he had a thing for Laura Fuller, who needed a history tutor."

"Laura Fuller," Harper said, smiling. "Rodney ended up running into her after college and they got married. Talk about destiny."

Emerson was not impressed by the information. "Curtis Kemp, senior year. He asked to sit next to you on the bus to Disneyland. You showed up with your ends burnt from the iron you used to straighten your hair. He *did* notice because he was gay."

"I still can't believe he played it off so well."

"He didn't. I knew, the school knew. His parents knew. Everyone knew." Emerson wasn't done. "Jessie Long. You went red, he went to Columbia the next week for college. Lance Miller liked Posh Spice so you cut your hair off, and he cut eighteen months off his sentence by returning the rats he stole to the lab."

"They were doing animal testing on them and he was sensitive to the cause," Harper defended. "And he's an animal-rights lawyer now."

Emerson rolled her eyes. "I don't even want to know how you know that."

"Because we're friends," Harper said. "Just because it didn't work out how I dreamed doesn't mean I don't want them in my life."

"You're right. If you keep picking men who are looking for a bestie or a beard, then you won't ever really lose them. It also means you never really had them," Emerson said, and Harper felt her heart thump at the statement. "If you never open yourself up to more than friendship, then you'll never have someone who is completely yours."

Harper wanted to argue the point, because Emerson was making it sound like she did it on purpose. That she invested her heart into relationships she knew had no real potential of going anywhere, which wasn't true. It couldn't be.

Because there was nothing more that Harper wanted than to have a family of her own. A husband and kids and that safe haven that she saw others find so easily.

But facts were facts and if what Emerson was saying was false, then how did Harper manage to get over Clay, the guy she'd invested nearly a year of her life in, in a matter of days?

A question she didn't want to ponder sober, much less after a few glasses of wine. Because the answer might break her heart. "Yes, Adam charmed me—he is sweet and fun and makes me feel sexy. But just because I don't want him as my ex yet doesn't mean I want to make him mine either."

Shay placed a hand on Harper's knee. "What if you did?"

"You guys are the ones who told he wasn't looking to be collected."

"That was before he invited you to dinner. At the station," Emerson said. "Then brought you dessert."

Harper closed her eyes on a sigh, partly thinking about that dessert, but mostly thinking about how they had three days left in their deal. "He only invited me because I cornered him into being my boyfriend. He had to make it look real," she admitted, feeling ridiculous and terrified about the whole situation. Ridiculous that she had to corner a guy into agreeing to be her boyfriend, and terrified that she wanted it to be true.

Shay laughed. "I may not have lived here my whole life, but in the two years I've been around I've learned a lot about those Baudouin men. First, no one can corner them, unless they are looking to be caught."

Another fact, but her lie had also put Adam in a professional corner. One that might have cost him the promotion. Harper knew he cared about her, the same way he cared about everyone in his life. His brothers, his crew, the town. Adam had a big heart, and he was offering her a small piece. But the whole thing?

"We're just having fun while it lasts," Harper said, closing up the lids on the paint jars.

"And what if it lasts longer?" Shay asked.

A scenario Harper was too scared to even hope for. Outside of her friends, no one in her life had ever lasted. Not her dad or her mom or her family on the sets. Clovis was the only real family member who had stood the test of time.

Then there were her friends. Always there, always loyal, always happy to fill up that place in her heart when she became lonely. Oh, Harper knew the secret to making friendships that lasted forever.

This thing with Adam, she feared, had already gone past friendship. Past being charmed, past a simple crush, and into something much deeper. She'd seen it happen to her friends, more times than she could count, seen the moment when they fell in love, and, even better, had that love reciprocated. But it had never happened to her.

She knew she was capable of great love, she just wasn't sure the reciprocated part would ever happen.

"I don't think he's looking past next week."

"Have you asked him?"

A knock sounded at the door, and Harper plastered a smile on her face. "Mark Antony's here to get his queen."

"I can tell him to come back," Shay said. "Emerson's right—this is girls' night."

"And this is romantic." Harper pointed to the door. "He rushed to come and get his woman, and you want to let him doubt that your urgency equals his?" Harper shook her head, then stood to walk to the door. The spring in her step was much lighter than her heart.

Harper looked through the peephole and—*sweet holy mother*—her entire body sprang to life at the sight of the best backside in wine country.

"Is it Mark Antony?"

"Right gladiator body," Harper said. "Wrong hero."

Because facing her apartment door, leaning a shoulder against the wall, was everyone's favorite firefighter—who was supposed to be on duty. But he wasn't wearing the standard-issue SHFD uniform. Nope, he wore a fitted gray T-shirt that clung to his body, proving that the back would be as impressive as his front, and a pair of battered jeans that hung way too low on his hips to be decent. But it was what he held in his hand that had her heart pounding.

She looked over her shoulder at Shay and whispered, "What's the other thing about Baudouin men? That says they want to be caught?"

Shay smiled, big and knowing. "That when there's dessert involved, they've started casting their bait."

Harper swallowed at the implications, her heart picking up at the possibility.

"And this here is double-chocolate-chunk bait."

Harper jumped at the sound of Adam's voice. It came through the wood door, but sounded as if he were right there—on her side.

She peeked through the hole.

"Crap." He was facing Emerson's door now with a big, badass smile on his face, waving the proverbial carrot—a double-chocolate-chunk proverbial carrot, which now that she put it like that almost seemed healthy.

"They're homemade," he said. And when she didn't open the door he lifted it to his mouth and took a bite. A big bite. "My step-mom's recipe. A real keeper."

Harper reached for the doorknob, but Emerson beat her to it and yanked open the door.

"Wait, you bake?" Emerson asked, face wide with shock.

He smiled. At Harper. "I can cook too."

"How is that possible? If it isn't on a grill, Dax burns it."

Adam shrugged, then took another bite of the cookie. The big jerk. "You picked a cop. They think it's all about the size of the gun. Real men, like firefighters, don't have props to rely on, so we have to be the real deal."

"Real men fight fires?" Emerson asked.

He winked at her and she rolled her eyes and went back to the couch, but not before snagging a cookie from the bag, which she sniffed and licked before tasting. And if her dreamy eyes meant anything, then those cookies were the real deal.

And Harper was beginning to think Adam was too.

"Why aren't you at work?" she asked.

"One of the guys needed some overtime, so I gave him my hours," Adam said. "I told Roman I wanted to help you get ready for tomorrow. You know, loading up the cars, lifting heavy objects, lending a hand with the face painting." He looked down at Harper and grinned. "Anything you need."

Her friends' brows perked up in question at Adam's offer, and Harper's nipples did some perking of their own.

Adam looked at Shay's face mask. "I see you already got started."

"I'm Cleopatra," Shay said, turning her face side to side, modeling it.

"I know. Mark Antony was at the station helping me organize the tents for tomorrow when you drunk-texted him."

"I'm not drunk," Shay slurred.

Adam looked at the three empty bottles and lifted a brow.

"Okay, maybe I'm a little tipsy."

"Which is why Jonah is on his way." He shifted those blue pools to Harper. "And I came here to make sure you got home safely."

"I'm still on my first glass and I live across the hall." She pointed at the door two feet behind him to prove it.

"Then I guess the cookies will still be warm when we get there." He picked up her backpack from the entry table and flung it over his back. "Oh, and sunshine, don't forget your paints."

"Take your shirt off."

"That's not how this works, sunshine. Fair is fair, so if I lose mine, you lose yours." Adam sat back on her couch, making himself comfortable. Arms behind his head, legs stretched out so that they were brushing hers, he said, "Ladies first."

"That's the problem," Harper said, picking up her paintbrush. "If I take my top off then you take off yours, it will be ladies first and I will never finish your face mask."

"Ladies first is never, ever a problem."

To prove it, he sat forward and rested his hands on her knees, slowly sliding them up her thighs—and higher until Harper's body wept to give in. And what was wrong with giving in? She'd had a particularly long day, he looked like a tall drink of exactly what she needed, and the bulge in his pants said he felt the same kind of need.

Her eyes wandered down his body and he flashed her a knowing grin, pure badass and challenge. It matched the positively naughty look in his eyes. His lips twitched higher and his hands were back on the move. She allowed this for a moment, long enough to feel her body tingle, her eyes slide closed, and—

"Stop." She gently snapped the back of his hand with the brush. "Unless you want me to get paint all over your shirt, lose it."

"I like it when you're bossy." Reaching back with a single hand, Adam lost the shirt in an innately male, testosterone-fueled move that had her imagination spiking—along with her pulse.

Sinking her teeth into the wooden tip of her paintbrush, Harper focused on his masculine jawline, shadowed stubble, and strong, full lips. The lips of a man who knew how to kiss a woman. She allowed her eyes to follow the lines of his body, across his broad shoulders, over his perfectly sculpted pecs, and down every succulent ridge of his stomach, to the happy trail leading into the promised land.

He was impressive.

The body of a fighter, the air of a leader, and the mouth of a lover. A powerful combination that was impossible to resist. And exciting to paint.

Dipping her brush into the metallic gray paint, she placed the bristles on the curve of his neck and followed the ridge of his collarbone.

"I thought you were making me into some kind of firefighting superhero," he said, and she noticed that he flexed his muscles.

"I changed my mind."

"Is this where you tell me you're making me a bunny?" His pecs bobbed up and down every time she tried to paint over them. Her body tingled.

"Stop doing that." She laughed. "And no, I'm making you more you."

He looked down as she worked. "Well, I can promise you that the real me doesn't wear glittery gray."

"It's chainmail. Is that manly enough for you?" She didn't stop to hear his response. She just let her instincts take over. "Body painting is an artistic representation of the real person inside. It's supposed to enhance all of the hidden qualities, as well as the obvious ones, to give a visual voice to the subject."

"Do you believe that?"

Harper looked up at Adam, and given the vulnerability in his eyes, he wanted her to believe, because he wanted to believe. She hesitated, because when she finally put the brush down, and he realized how she saw him, there was going to be no more hiding. Art was about expression and truth, and maybe Shay was right. Maybe it was time for Harper to put herself out there.

Allow the hope of extraordinary to outweigh the fear of rejection.

Eyes locked on his, holding his gaze for what seemed like an eternity, she whispered, "I do."

He thought about that for a long moment, watched her silently as she worked to cover his entire arm, before moving on to the rest of his body. She was lost in the work, highlighting every hard-won muscle he had and smoothing out a few to show the softness beneath the strength.

She tugged his pants lower on his hips, worked her brush in soft, sure strokes across every inch of his exposed skin. It was intimate and erotic, and she could feel his desire wrap around her and take hold.

She wasn't sure how long they stayed like that, her putting out all of the respect, reverence, and sheer adoration she'd come to feel, and him silently watching. Giving in to the moment made her exposed and vulnerable, and yet she'd never felt so much power flow through her body.

Hands tired, body sweating, muse satisfied, Harper dusted him with a light powder to set the paint, then stepped back to admire her work. To admire the man she was pretty sure she was falling in love with.

"Can I look?" he asked quietly.

Heart in her throat, Harper nodded.

She watched Adam turn to look in the mirror. Watched him inspect her work, taking his time to see the piece and all its parts. His silence grew, took on a shape, until finally his eyes met hers in the mirror—and held.

"This is how you see me?" he asked, his voice husky, stripped down and raw. "As a gladiator?"

"Not just a gladiator." She stepped up behind him and smoothed her hands down his shoulders. "Spartacus."

His face went carefully blank. "As in one of the most badass rebels in history?"

She would have laughed if he hadn't sounded so offended. "Yes, Spartacus was a badass." She reached around him from behind, sliding her hands over his armor of paint. "Strong, loyal, a great warrior. But he was first a leader, determined to lead his men to safety." Her hand came to rest on his heart. "Contrary to popular belief, and Hollywood interpretations, Spartacus never attempted to overthrow Rome. He just understood the power that came with freedom."

Adam's eyes never left hers, proving that rule number three, when combined with rule number one, equated an appeal powerful enough to win hearts and launch wars.

Without moving he said, "It's my turn, sunshine—lose the shirt."

chapter
eighteen

You want to paint me?"

"Not want to, going to." Adam turned around and picked up the brush. He dipped it in daffodil yellow and walked back over. "So unless you want that top of yours to get dirty, I suggest you lose it."

Harper didn't mind losing the top. After what they'd just shared, her body was already humming with anticipation. But painting her, seeing his true thoughts about how he saw her, that didn't sound like something she was ready for yet. She was just coming to terms with her feelings for him, and if his didn't match hers, she didn't want to know just yet.

Cold paint seeped through her top, instantly hardening her nipple. "Hey. This is my favorite dress."

"Mine too," he said, then painted the other nipple. "And if you don't move it fast, it's going to be covered in paint, because I'm feeling a little impatient at the moment."

He dipped the brush in purple, mixing the colors and—

"Okay." Harper quickly removed her dress, and the second it hit the floor she heard Adam suck in a breath. Because she was in nothing but sandals and Honeysuckle.

"That's what you had on under there all day?"

"It made me feel sexy," she admitted, then realized it was another half truth. And they deserved better than half truths. "You make me feel sexy." He looked down at her shoes and she kicked them off. "Better?"

His smile went wicked. "Almost there."

Harper froze. She started to ask what that meant, but then he glanced at her Honeysuckle.

"Keep going," he said.

"But I thought—"

"Oh, you thought right." Adam's hand went to her waist, sliding down over her panties and up to cup her through her bra. "But tonight I want to paint my own lingerie on you, and I don't want to ruin those."

Unwilling to ruin anything that this moment was offering, Harper unclasped her bra and let it fall, then slowly slid her undies to the floor. No bold clothes or lace left to hide behind, Harper straightened to face him, and the hungry way his gaze gobbled her up was heady.

Erotic.

Harper stood there, waiting for him to say more, make a move, anything to give a clue as to what he wanted her to do. For as many bodies as she'd painted and people she'd photographed, Harper had never been the subject of anyone's work. And when Adam was in work mode, she was learning, he was focused, intense, and all in. Which made her heart feel as if it were going to explode right out of her chest.

"Have you ever painted before?" she managed.

"No. But I'm a fast learner." He crooked his finger at her in that come-hither way that had her knees wobbling.

She managed the final steps, and then she was in front of him, the anticipation so consuming she could feel the coolness of the paint on her skin. Gliding over her body—all of her body.

"Do I have to paint a thing or a pattern, or can I just paint what I see?" he asked.

"And what you feel. There is no right or wrong." It wouldn't matter anyway. In the end, she would be able to tell how he really felt. Was he reeling her in for more benefits, or was Shay right, and he was hoping for more?

He dipped the brush back in the yellow and brought it up to her breast again. He did it slowly, giving himself time to think, and her time to move away if she chose. She chose to move closer instead, and lean into the brush.

The rough bristles touched her sensitive peak, the chill of the paint oddly erotic on her heated skin. He dragged the brush around her breast, and she moaned at the sensation, prickly and smooth, thoughtful yet bold. He finished with one breast and moved on to the other, painting it the same bright yellow, then connecting it with a band of orange.

The brush stopped and his forehead crinkled above his brows. "What I feel, right?"

She nodded and he smiled and dropped the brush. He squeezed different shades of orange and pink and red into a paper plate, until it looked like a brilliant swirl of colors.

"Good, because I like to feel my subject out." Flattening his palms in the paint, Harper watched it push up through his fingers. One had orange the other pink. "And I feel I am much better with my hands than a brush."

A fact she knew well.

Settling one hand low on her waist, he pulled her into him. "Do you know what I was going to paint you as?"

"No."

He met her gaze. "A summer sunrise. Bright and warm and something people wake up to catch a glimpse of."

Her breath caught, and a warm glow started in her chest and radiated out at his words. "That's how you see me?"

"That's how the world sees you, Harper. I'm just lucky enough to finally be in that world."

Without another word, not that there were any that could follow that up, Adam brought his other hand up to cup her neck, then drew her in for a kiss. It was slow at first, gentle and coaxing as if he were reeling her in. Then she sank her fingers into his shoulders, letting him know that she was holding on for the ride, and things got real hot, real quick.

Their mouths slid together. His fingers, slick with paint, traced down her spine and over her curves, leaving a trail of heat and colors as he went.

Harper lost herself in the sensation of being seen, of being exposed for the art and cherished as a woman. She lost herself in Adam.

When was the last time she'd allowed herself to get lost in a man? Fully and completely?

Never.

She'd never gotten so lost that she couldn't find footing. But with Adam holding her as if he couldn't get enough, her whole world shifted, and the last thing she was worried about losing was her footing. Her heart was right there, ready to find its home.

"Sunshine," he said against her lips. "You taste like sunshine."

She didn't know what it was about that statement, but the way he said it, the things his tone implied, stirred something inside of her. Started a chain of reactions that she was helpless to stop. Emotions and realizations that she didn't want to stop.

Adam's hands disappeared and she groaned at the lack of connection, but then they were back, with new paint and new direction. His hands came up to hold her breasts, weigh them, mixing

NEED YOU FOR MINE

the paint until it resembled the colors of a sunrise. She arched back, giving him all the room he needed to create—feel.

He followed her ribs down to her stomach, then her hips, cupping her ass as if he owned it. A jolt of electricity raced down her spine when he scooped her up and turned her around, arranging her until she was facing away, he was standing behind her, and his big body was nudging her legs apart.

His fingers danced down her arm, painting as they went, before lacing with hers. He drew her arm up and around his neck. He bit her shoulder, her neck, kissing his way to her ear. "Open your eyes, Harper."

She did and noticed that he'd arranged their bodies so that they were centered with the mirror, her arms were out of his way, and he was completely and gloriously naked. Then she caught her reflection and everything seemed to still.

Her hair was messy, wet with paint and starting to curl again. Her eyes were wide, bright, and lit with passion. Her body was a fusion of colors—vibrant and bold, soft and sensual. But there was something else, a connection that glowed from the inside and sparked between them that spoke to a sexual need so strong it was visible, tangible.

Combustible.

"See all that pink," he said, retracing his work. "That's for your sweet romantic side that makes me smile. The yellow . . ." His hands dipped lower. "That's for how you care, so easily and with abandon for your friends, your family. For me." His hand slid between her legs and held. "The orange is for your uninhibited side. The part of you that is unique and bold and desperately wants to live loud. I picked the brightest orange because most people are so in awe of your sweet and giving side, they miss the adventurous one. And what a shame that is."

Harper couldn't breathe. She'd lived most of her life with some

- 237 -

of her biggest pieces being shadowed and overlooked. Adam wasn't just looking, he was seeing her, shining a light on her for the world to notice.

"You are so fucking beautiful," he said, leaving his hand between her legs and raising the other, the one that was painted with armor, to cup her breast. "I want you to watch how beautiful you are."

His fingers didn't delve, they merely teased the outside, creating enough delicious friction that she felt her body ramp up. Tighten as he increased the pace. Unable to stand the pleasure, Harper's head fell back against his chest and her eyes slid closed.

"Open up, baby," he whispered.

She parted her legs, giving him more room.

He chuckled. "I meant your eyes, but that works too."

It worked pretty freaking amazing. Her heart was struggling to keep up with her pulse, as he explored every dip and crevice until she was pressing against his hand, moaning for release. Adam was a master of nonverbal communication, listening to her needs.

And he gave in to her every need until she was screaming out his name.

Harper felt her body tremble, her legs buckle, but Adam was there. Strong and steady, he placed her hands against the wall, on either side of the mirror, then braced her hips back against him. She could feel his need pressing into her.

"The red," she asked on a harsh breath. "What does it mean?"

He traced the only red paint on her body. It was a distinct handprint on her right breast.

"It means sexy." He kissed the side of her neck. "Seductive." The other side. "Addicting." The back. "Arousing." The hand splayed across her breast, making a perfect outline of the paint mark. "Mine."

His eyes met hers in the mirror, holding her in place, while he slid home with a single stroke.

Harper gasped as Adam didn't waste any time and pulled out,

all the way out, only to slide back in—hitting the spot that had her moaning.

"Adam—"

"Hold on," he said, clearly not stopping for anything.

Still riding the high from her last standing O, she dug her fingers into the wall, bracing herself and holding tight as they started to move together. He came forward and she pushed back and the outcome was life altering.

Ecstasy.

"Christ, Harper," he said, his body coiled as if it were ready to snap. "Open your eyes so you can see what I see."

When she didn't—couldn't—because she was dying from pleasure, he whispered, "Stay with me, baby."

The word *stay* did something to her. And when coupled with *me* there was no way she could deny him. Willing her eyes open, she watched. Right there with him. Watched as his hands gripped her hips, as his body curved around hers, moving farther between her legs. Watched as they moved with a grace that wasn't only chemistry or desire.

Harper noticed they moved as if they were connecting, listening and understanding each other, even though neither made a sound. Adam noticed too, and it was in his fierce gaze—which was all zeroed in on her. To be on the receiving end of that intensity, so much raw passion, took Harper by surprise. It also took her higher and higher, as she fell deeper and deeper.

So deep she knew there was no turning back.

Unbelievably, she felt herself tighten again, and before she knew what was happening Adam slid a hand between her legs and she exploded around him. At her sweet cry of release he buried his face in her hair and came with her.

Neither one moved, just stood there, Adam draped over her and still connected, both of them waiting to come back down. Harper wished they never would. Wished they could stay here in her apartment, sharing their worlds, their fears, and their dreams.

"That was"—life altering, mind-blowing, a glimpse of what happily ever after felt like—"incredible."

Adam nuzzled her neck, laying a few gentle kisses there, then lifted his head. His hair was standing on end and tipped with all the colors of her body. He looked incredible. And like happily ever after wrapped in a gladiator package.

"Sunshine, that was"—he kissed one cheek, then the other—" extraordinary."

It was. And so was the fact that Harper was truly, madly, irrevocably in love. And there wasn't an expiration on that kind of feeling.

It was dark when Harper opened her eyes. It took her a moment to realize she was in her bed, nestled in a warm cocoon that was all biceps, sinew, and sleepy man.

Sexy sleeping man.

After cleaning up the front room, they'd come in to make a mess of the bedroom. Which they'd done a spectacular job of. There were blankets on the floor, sheets smeared with paint, and crumbs on the nightstand.

It wasn't the thought of the last two double-chocolate-chunk cookies that had pulled her from the best sleep she'd ever had. It was something that Adam had said, a word really that kept rolling around in her head, pulling her from her sex-induced slumber.

Mine.

There was no reason for him to say that unless he meant it. Sure, they were in the heat of the moment, and things had gotten intense, but at that point she was a sure thing, leaving him no reason to make such a statement. Unless it was true.

When he'd said it, it had felt true. Possessive even. And Harper wanted it to be true. She wanted to belong to someone.

She wanted to belong to Adam.

His arms flexed around her, snuggling her close. Their bodies were plastered together, her face pressed into his chest, while he nuzzled her hair. "I know what you're thinking about."

She froze. "You do?"

"Uh-huh." His hands slid down her back to palm her butt. "Cookies."

She felt herself relax.

He lifted his head and laughed. "I'm right. It's three in the morning and you want cookies."

She offered a small smile. "Yup."

"Don't move." He kissed her nose and climbed out of bed. Not concerned in the slightest that he was traipsing through her house butt-ass naked and painted like a gladiator.

Bed still warm, he slid back in, sure to lift the covers all the way and get a good view of her. With a groan, he hauled her up against him and offered a bite of cookie.

"God, those are good," she moaned.

"How good are we talking?"

"Scale of one to ten, a nine-point-nine."

"A nine-point-nine, huh?" He took a bite and frowned as though not sure how he missed that tenth of a point.

She tilted her head up to look into his eyes, and smiled sweetly. "The kind of cookies I was looking for are measured on the *Oh* scale."

"I know," he said, taking a bite of the cookie. "I was just preheating the oven. Because this next batch will blow your mind."

And then he spent the rest of the night proving that when it came to cookies, Adam was her man.

chapter
nineteen

It's not even seven and already I'm sweating," Shay said, fanning herself with a stack of paintings.

As always, Harper's friends had come through. It was Saturday morning, the main day of the festival, and they'd shown up at the crack of dawn to help display the kids' artwork at the park, even though they all still had a ton to do for their own booths.

Not that they seemed to be feeling the time crunch. Nope, they were both sitting on the stage, legs swigging off the edge, sharing a bag of kettle corn that the hunting club was providing, and staring out toward Main Street.

"Yup," Emerson said, reaching into the bag. "Hot."

Harper hung the painting in her hand, a sweet rendering of a firefighter holding a cat with an apple tree behind them, then sat down between her friends and—*whoa!*

Across the park, behind the first row of booths and headed their way, were three beautiful men in work pants and BEAT THE HEAT ball caps pulled low, working in tandem to carry a wood table. And there was sweat. Lots of glistening, sweaty muscles.

Jonah was at the back of the table guiding them forward, while Dax stood in the middle, muscling a good portion of the weight. Which left Adam, with his ripped abs, cut arms, and tight backside, negotiating the monstrosity of a table through the crowd—backward.

"What are they doing?" she asked.

"Hauling out all of the chairs and tables from the town's storage shed," Emerson said around bits of popcorn.

Harper reached into the bag and grabbed a handful. "Don't they know the high school football team is coming at eight to set up the eating areas?"

"Maybe someone should tell them," Shay said. But no one bothered to move—except to pass the popcorn.

"And ruin everyone's fun?" Emerson jerked her chin to the senior ladies' water aerobics team, who had left the community pool in their swim caps and suits to watch the show. Eyes big, camera phones rolling, they lined the upper railing of the senior center.

The guys set the table gently on the ground, their muscles straining until Harper heard a few breathy *Oh mys* flutter over from across the way. And okay, she might have groaned in appreciation too, but who could blame her? It was like watching three gladiators prepare for battle.

Harper smiled at the reference, then felt her body heat rise thinking about last night. It was a hot enough image to have her searing, and she wasn't lifting anything heavier than popcorn.

After a round of high fives, the guys dusted off their hands and headed back for the storage shed at the far corner of the park. Only Adam stopped to stretch out his arms, lifting them up and over his head, which caused the waistband of his pants to slide down and over the two cute dimples he sported.

Shay turned to Harper. "Is that glitter on Adam?"

Harper tore her eyes off Adam and stifled a giggle. "It's paint. I practiced some, uh, face masks on him last night."

Shay snorted. "Then why is it on his lower back?"

Harper looked closer and smiled. *So it was.*

It looked like he'd missed that spot when showering this morning. Granted, she'd been doing her best to distract him with the soap—and other things. She'd distracted him into a frenzy, then he'd distracted her three times, before dragging her back to bed.

"Huh, I guess it is." She stood. "Maybe I should go tell him."

Emerson grabbed her hand and yanked her back down. "That smile says you're going to do a lot more than tell him. So do all those curls." Which were held together by a paintbrush and sheer stubbornness. "What happened last night?"

"I guess he likes curls," she said, still fighting the ridiculous urge to giggle. "He likes it straight, and up, and down." She shrugged. "He just likes it."

And he likes me!

"Of course he liked it, you were probably naked," Frankie said, rushing up to the stage. Her hair was wild, her eyes a little crazed, and she was sweaty—in her normal black-on-black with steel-toed accents. But she looked ready to cry.

Or punch someone.

Not equipped to deal with either outcome, Harper asked, "What's wrong?"

"I'll explain everything, but first I need water and I need you to open your shop," Frankie said. Blanket was trailing behind, his sides heaving as if they'd arrived on foot, from twenty miles away. In a full sprint.

"Emerson, can you get a bottle of water?" Harper asked. Then to Frankie, "I'm not working today. I'm helping out at Beat the Heat."

"Shit." Frankie looked around at the crowd. It was still pretty sparse because of the early hour, but the crowd was growing. "I need to buy something. Now." She looked at Shay, who was her sister-in-law, then handed her the leash. "You watch him. And you," she said, looking at Harper, "come with me." She grabbed Harper by the arm and dragged her away from everyone. "I need to buy a test for the . . ." She mouthed *baby.*

"Oh my God!" Harper took the woman's hand in her own. "You're . . ." *Pregnant?*

Frankie looked at their linked hands and back to Harper, obviously not comfortable with physical contact, or maybe it was public displays of affection, or neither. Harper released her hand and played it cool. "So the weekend getaway worked then?"

"I don't know. I feel the same, but Blanket's been acting weird, nuzzling my belly, giving it little love bites. Then last night he started dropping his teething rings on my belly. Two blue rings, right on my belly. It's a sign, right?"

Harper stood there, mouth open, looking like a fish gasping her last breath. "Uh, I'm not sure alpacas have the gift of fertility detection." When Frankie looked as if she disagreed, Harper asked, "Have you taken a test?"

"That's why I'm here. I need you to open your shop so I can take one."

"We don't sell, uh, those at the Fashion Flower. Or the Boulder Holder." In case that was her next question.

"You sell stuff on how to get . . ."—Frankie's expression told her to fill in the word *pregnant*—"and stuff for when you're . . ." *pregnant* . . . "but nothing to actually see if you are" . . . *pregnant?*

"Why don't you go to Bottles and Bottles?" Harper said. "I know the pharmacy will have some. And why are we still not saying the word?"

"I don't want to jinx it, and do you think I would be *here* if I could go *there?*"

"No?"

Frankie glanced around and, clearly not satisfied with their current level of seclusion, dragged Harper even deeper behind the big oak tree. "Look, Mrs. Peters plays poker with Aunt Luce, and she is cousins with Nate's grandma. And ChiChi has the biggest mouth in town. If either one of them hears I bought a test, then I'll arrive home to a baby shower. And then what if I'm not and everyone thinks I am?"

Harper saw the problem. If Frankie wasn't pregnant or if something went wrong, she'd have to explain to the whole town what happened. That would be as humiliating as it was heartbreaking.

"Do you want me to take you to the doctor?" Harper asked.

"No, I want you to go buy me a test."

Harper froze, stock-still. "Same problem applies here. I walk in there and ask for a test and the rumor mill will start sending out smoke signals about me before I get back to you."

"Mrs. Peters won't suspect a thing if you walk in there all smiles and goodwill," Frankie said, a little desperate now.

"What if we ask Shay? She's married. No reason for gossip."

"Are you crazy?" Harper wanted to point out that no, she was not the crazy one in this party, but Frankie wasn't done. "If Shay finds out, Jonah finds out. And since all my brothers gossip like a bunch of little girls when they get together"—Frankie shook her head—"it would be safer to take out an ad in the paper."

Frankie took a deep breath, as if to center herself, and Harper could see actual tears forming in her eyes. "I don't even know if I'd be a good mom. When people see me, maternal usually isn't something they think. But Nate swears I'll be the best mom, just like his, and when he talks like that I believe him."

The confidence and love she heard in Frankie's voice when speaking of her husband, and their bond, was moving. Inspiring. It made Harper want to find that for herself—with Adam.

Taking a deep breath, Harper said, "This is a bad idea."

"No it's not." Frankie took her by the shoulders. "We'll just make up some story."

"You do remember I'm the worst liar on the planet, right?"

"I know, but you've got two blocks to work on your craft."

With a twenty in her pocket and a smack to the butt, Harper was sent on her way. Five minutes and a creative story about running out of paint stirrers later, Mrs. Peters handed over a super pack of pregnancy tests with a suspicious grin, and Harper found herself standing outside a porta-potty, sharing a Pop-Tart with Blanket.

"What's taking so long?" Harper asked. "The directions said two minutes. It's been like ten. People are starting to notice something is up."

"Two per test," Frankie said through the plastic door. "I'm taking all three, which is why I needed the water. I still have one left."

"What did the first two say?"

The door opened and Frankie peeked her head out. Then she held up the sticks and Harper felt a rush of joy push through her system. Because she was witness to the first-ever pregnancy confirmation by alpaca—and Adam was going to be an uncle.

Harper was magical. That was all there was to it.

St. Helena's community park looked like a scene from *Pollyanna*. The night sky twinkled with lights, every oak tree and booth post on the property had glowing mason jars hanging from it. The picnic tables were covered with red-checkered tablecloths and baskets of various wildflowers, and they were overflowing with families and residents.

McGuire and Seth had handled the ladder raise like pros, Harper's casino tables were a huge hit with the over-sixty crowd, and there wasn't a single kid without some kind of face art and honorary firefighter's hat running round. They'd already raised enough money to pay for Back-to-School Packs for every kid on their list, and the barbeque dinner, which had been smoking all day and sending off some serious mouthwatering scents, had yet to be served.

And dinner was the biggest moneymaker of the night.

This event was, by far, the best Beat the Heat Adam had ever been to. People had been telling him as much all day. Based on the way Chief Lowen was grinning in Adam's direction, people had been telling him too.

"The chief was telling me that an opening came up for an incident command position in a special operations wildland firefighting team in Colorado Springs. He wants to send someone from our unit so they can come back and train our firefighters here," Roman said. "It would be a six-month post, minimum."

"Six months with those guys would be invaluable," Adam said, thinking about the lucky SOB who'd get to go balls to the wall with some of the most elite firefighters in the country. He wanted to be that SOB so bad he could taste it.

"It would also mean getting six months closer to lieutenant, which is why I want to recommend you."

And there it was. That addictive buzz that preceded a major rush. It started in his chest, pinching and gaining volume, then moved up and out until his entire body was intoxicated at the idea. "Thank you, Cap."

"You did the hard work. I just want to acknowledge it," Roman said. "Your experience as a smokejumper has given you the ability to evaluate the big picture in a matter of seconds, but the way you handled McGuire and Seth and getting everyone involved in helping with the event cemented that you're a real leader."

"I learned from the best."

Roman gave a short, tight nod, then cleared his throat before he spoke. "I've known that you were a great firefighter, but now when you talk, the guys get in order and go."

"I work with a great crew. They're like my brothers."

"This isn't the time to be humble," Roman said with a laugh. "They follow you—not just because they like you, but because they respect you. You've earned that respect. Including mine."

Adam wasn't sure what to say. For the first time in forever he was at a loss for words—an overflow of emotions could do that. So could being conflicted.

Did Adam want to be the IC on that special ops team? Hell yeah. He was willing to do just about anything to make sure he was the top candidate on that list. Anything except put Roman in a tight situation.

It was no secret that Lowen and Adam weren't BFFs. Just like it was no secret that Lowen would rather promote McGuire than see Adam rise in the ranks.

"What about the chief?" Adam asked, suddenly regretting every prank and play-it-loose relationship he'd had.

Roman smiled. "With everyone telling him what a great job you did managing this event, and how you pulled everyone together to get it accomplished, if I back you, you're in."

Adam was beyond humbled that a man like Roman, decorated and admired, saw enough in Adam to put his name on the line. But he also knew there was someone else who was behind Beat the Heat's success. "Harper really came through for this event." She'd also come through for him, in a big way. Because of her unwavering support, he'd been given the chance to prove himself. "If you can make sure some of that praise you're doling out makes it her way, it would be appreciated."

Roman's smile faded and he went serious. Too serious to be anything good. "Actually, Harper is the reason I haven't brought you up to Lowen yet," Roman said in a low voice. "I wanted to talk to you about the position first. Make sure it worked with you."

"No need to talk, everything about this works for me," Adam said, his shoulders relaxing a bit. "Being so specialized will put me in a management position when I get back, not to mention on the fast track to lieutenant."

Roman lifted a brow, as if waiting for Adam to see the catch. But there was no catch—this was a golden opportunity.

"It will also put you an airplane ride away from your girlfriend."

Adam's chest pinched at the thought of not seeing Harper every day. He wasn't sure what was going to happen come Monday when that clock expired, but he liked the idea of seeing where things led. Harper was sweet and funny and sexy, and she got him. Got him so completely that he didn't have to pretend to be anybody but himself.

And he didn't want to lose that.

Harper would tell him he could have both. That he'd be an idiot to pass it up. And she'd be right.

Adam smiled. "Harper knows how much this job means. She would be behind it all the way."

Roman lifted a brow. "But how much does she mean to you?"

A question that should have been a breeze to answer. A question that a few weeks ago wouldn't have sent his mind racing and his heart thumping. Harper was so many things to him: a lover, a confidant, an unwavering support, and, most importantly, a friend.

Adam found himself smiling at that last one. Harper would punch him if she heard him say that, but he didn't care. As far as he was concerned, that was her most amazing quality. That and her smile.

"She's special." And after this talk he was going to find her and buy her that chocolate-dipped banana, then hold her hand and walk around the festival. Maybe even try to win her a teddy bear. Nah, a bunny, she'd like that better.

"The thing about special people is that if you make them wait around, you risk missing out on everything that's special," Roman said, all cryptic.

"You go to the Golden Noodle and clean them out of fortune cookies again?"

NEED YOU FOR MINE

"All I'm saying is that six months is a long time."

"It's six months. I've been gone for longer during bad fire years," Adam said, wondering what was going on. Roman was acting like Adam being gone would be a problem. "Unless you think it will affect my position here."

"No. The opposite." Roman opened his mouth to say more, then wiped a hand across his brow and sighed.

Something was up. That was for sure. Roman was blunt by nature, always said it like it was and didn't waste time on making it frilly. It was why he was such a good captain. But right then, Roman was acting like he was navigating a minefield, and Adam didn't want anything to detonate.

"The only person who hates BS as much as I do is you," Adam said. "So what's going on?"

Roman nodded, a sliver of respect in his eyes. "I need to know before you go all-in and I take this to Lowen that you and Harper have talked and agreed that this is what you want."

"Oh," Adam said, then laughed. Because, *shit*, Roman had him confused. But now he got it. More often than not, when a guy with strings was offered a promotion that required relocation, they'd always check first with their other half. Who would undoubtedly take issue with their spouse leaving for so long. Since Adam had neither strings nor a spouse, he had no problem saying, "I'm good. I mean, Harper is sweet and special and we've been having a fun time, but it's not like that."

By *that* Adam meant that while Harper might have been his other half while planning the event, had even been the perfect pretend girlfriend in a really hot affair, they weren't officially at the check-in stage. In fact, come Monday they wouldn't be official anythings. Except partners in a sexy game of pretend.

Roman didn't need to know all the details, those were between Adam and Harper, but he needed to understand that his job came first. So even though Roman's eyes were darting over Adam's shoulder, clearly telling him they had company—probably Lowen—Adam added, "What's real is this opportunity and the chance to become a better firefighter. A better leader for this department. Harper and I, she's great, but it's not that serious."

A weird heaviness pressed down on Adam's chest the second he said the words. Taking in a deep breath, he tried to ease the tension, but it was as if there was a misfire between his brain and his body. It was too connected to his heart—which was telling him that this was more serious than he was allowing himself to admit.

Roman stared at him for a long moment, his expression uncharacteristically closed. "I heard different."

"You heard wrong." There went another misfire. This one bigger, stronger, impossible to ignore.

"Actually, he probably heard the rumor that I bought a pregnancy test," a very familiar female voice said from behind.

Adam wasn't sure what caused his lungs to freeze up more—the fact that Harper was standing directly behind him or that'd she said *pregnancy test*. He closed his eyes, playing over exactly what he'd said, praying she hadn't overheard, then slowly turned around.

Yup, she'd overheard all right. Enough to have that permanent smile of hers so dimmed he could barely make it out. The hurt in her eyes, that was as clear as fucking day. The second she looked up at him, *bam*, the hurt and disappointment swimming there knocked the wind right out from under him.

"Harper," he said, then trailed off. Because what the hell could he say to come back from that?

Adam had been here before, in this very situation, and he knew the aftermath of speaking first and thinking too late. There was no coming back. Just ask the best candidate to come out of the Cal Fire academy, who Adam managed to take out with a few simple, thoughtless words. They were spoken from inexperience, naiveté, and an ego that was too big to question. But it wasn't until Trent died that Adam realized he'd said them out of fear.

"Man, rumors travel as fast as secrets in this town," Harper said with a self-conscious shrug. She stood there in that pretty dress that had been calling out to him all day, holding on to two frozen bananas and enough hurt to make him a thousand kinds of bastard. There were other things there in her eyes, things he didn't want to acknowledge. "It's just a rumor."

"So you didn't buy a pregnancy test at the pharmacy?" Roman asked skeptically, as if his checkout-counter intel was solid. The problem was, in St. Helena it usually was.

"I bought three."

Shit. Adam felt everything bottom out. He was free-falling— out of control, with no parachute, and too many strings wrapped around him to breathe.

"No need to panic, they weren't for me. They were for, uh, a friend," she said, maintaining eye contact. One of the things he'd seen on her cute little Allure List. Only right now she didn't look cute. She looked crushed, and he was the cause.

"How much did you hear?" Adam asked.

"Enough."

Right. He already knew that. The look of utter humiliation on her face said she'd heard everything she needed to.

But instead of crying or ripping him a new one, like any other woman would have done, she plastered a sweet smile on her face that made everything he'd said, every bonehead decision he'd made, that much more real. And painful. Because even when Harper received a direct shot to the chest, she still managed to look after everyone around her.

"Enough to know that whatever position you give Adam he will rise to," she said to Roman. "He's a great firefighter and an even better guy. He deserves this."

She looked at him for a long, tense moment, the same fake smile in place that was breaking his fucking heart, and Adam wondered what Harper deserved. Certainly not this. Not for it to be publicly announced that what they'd shared hadn't been important or special. Because, *Jesus*, that made it sound as if she weren't important or special.

When she so was.

"Enough to say that I am so excited for you," she said, and he could hear the sincerity in her voice. It was right under the hurt and disillusionment. "I guess all that's left to say is congrats."

Eyes on Harper, Adam asked Roman, "Could you give us a minute?"

"That's okay," Harper said, the panic tightening around her neck.

She didn't want to be alone with Adam. Because in one minute she would be doing the only thing that could possibly top her most humiliating moment. Bawling her eyes out over discovering her pretend relationship had been pretend.

But Roman was already nodding and walking away, which meant she needed to dig deep and tap into all of those acting skills her mother had tried to instill in her.

"I really am happy for you." He went to speak, so she shoved the banana in his hand. "Hurry before it melts. Gotta go."

"Harper." His voice willed her to stay, but the pity she knew was on his face had her legs moving. She made it three steps when she felt a warm hand gently lock around her wrist, halting her escape.

"What you heard . . ." he began, and to his credit he did seem genuinely upset that he'd hurt her. "It came out wrong. You are special and—"

"Don't." Harper spun around, the anger from a lifetime of rejection building up inside of her. "You have never lied to me, so let's not start now."

His face fell at her harsh tone. "I'm not lying. You are special and sweet."

"And your friend?"

"Yes." He said it as if it weren't shattering her heart. Erasing everything that had happened in the past few weeks.

"Then we could have left it at that," she said, her voice cracking. "I was fine with friends. Fine with naked friends. You were the one who made me believe it was more."

"It is more." Adam reached out to touch her face, but she backed away before he could. She would crumple otherwise. She could feel it. Her stomach was already chilled and a sharp stabbing sensation was forming behind her ribs.

"How much more?" She needed to know, because she wasn't going to let him put this on her inability to read signals. "Because you said you'd wake up just to catch a glimpse of me, that I was your sunrise."

She stopped and felt a hysterical laugh build up. "Oh my God, they were lines. That's what you say to someone at a bar, and I thought it was charming." She placed a hand on her mouth to keep the sob from escaping. It didn't help. "I thought your pickup lines were charming. How stupid is that?"

"They weren't lines, Harper." But she wasn't listening.

"You charmed me. Made me feel sexy and beautiful and like I was special."

"You are. God, you are."

"I don't feel very special right now. I feel stupid." Just like she had when she'd discovered Rodney liked her friend, and Curtis didn't listen to Ricky Martin for his music, and Clay wanted to date a Mom-bot.

Only this was worse. This wasn't humiliation—it was devastation. Something she hadn't felt since she'd learned her mom had been only two towns over and hadn't come to visit. Something she'd gone out of her way to avoid ever feeling again.

And she'd done a damn fine job until Adam charmed his way in, and now he'd blown a hole through her chest to get out.

"You told me you weren't a sure bet, that you didn't do long-term, and I listened," she said, and that was when the first tear broke. "But then you said *mine*, and I believed that too. Believed it so much that I stopped believing all of the rest, stopped listening to that voice inside of me telling me that this was too good, that you didn't mean it, that you couldn't love curls. I believed you to the point that I let myself become yours. Heart and soul, Adam."

He stared at her, horrified, as if her declaration had stunned him. Stepping close, he reached out to tuck her curls behind her ears. "I do love your curls."

"But do you love me?"

Adam opened his mouth and nothing came out, just a rush of air, and Harper's chest caved in on itself. She might not be great at nonverbal communication, but he'd just made himself crystal clear.

"I guess the problem was I didn't take the time to think it through." But in that millisecond she thought everything through, realized that this wasn't just an isolated event, and finally, *finally*, understood what had started with her father when she was three, repeated itself with her mother, then repeated over and over until she was ready to listen.

She wasn't ready now, wasn't sure she'd ever be ready, because once she accepted it, her life would never be the same. It wasn't about sensuality or allure. It was sadly about love.

Closing her eyes, Harper went up on her toes and placed a gentle goodbye kiss on his cheek. She let her lips linger, taking in his smell, putting to memory the way his skin tasted.

With a final brush of the lips she whispered, "No matter how much I love someone, it doesn't mean they'll ever be mine."

chapter
twenty

"I always said Dax was the biggest asshole of the family." Frankie leaned back on the front porch steps, sipping on some lemonade and passing judgment on Adam as he lathered up Blanket.

Judgment that was more than accurate.

"I was wrong." She said it as if the words were painful. "I hate being wrong."

"I know you do, sweet cheeks," Frankie's husband, Nate DeLuca, said, walking out onto the porch to sit behind his wife. He rested his hands on her shoulders and started rubbing.

"He had us all fooled. I mean, Dax is pretty hard to top," Jonah said, grabbing some lemonade off the tray and emptying it in one swallow. He was sitting between Frankie and Dax, who had the nerve to agree.

"You think he's got the girly squirrelies?" Dax held his stomach in sympathy. "That was the worst part. Just out of nowhere I'd feel like I was going to lose my lunch."

It was like a big family reunion, right there in the middle of Adam's screwed-up life.

"I'm standing right here." Adam waved the sponge he was holding in their direction, brown, soapy water running down his arm. "And I can hear you."

Nate just smiled, and Adam fisted his hands. Even though he was married to his sister, and was normally a standup guy, he was still a DeLuca—and pissing Adam off—which meant a swift kick to the ass wouldn't be frowned upon.

Only he was pretty sure he'd get one shot in, then his brothers would step up and get his back. *Nate's* back, not Adam's. Not that he blamed them. The only person who deserved an ass kicking was Adam.

It had been two days since the main Beat the Heat events, and Adam hadn't caught a single glimpse of Harper. Not around town, not at the Sweet and Savory, not even at her grandma's shop. The last part had him deeply concerned, since tomorrow was National Underwear Day and the front display was only half-finished.

Adam had tried calling, even stopped by her place to talk, but either she hadn't been home or didn't come to the door. The only communication he'd had was a text late last night, explaining that she no longer needed him at the Swagger prelaunch. Not that he could blame her. Hell, he wouldn't blame her if she never spoke to him again.

A sharp pain lanced his chest at the thought, taking away any pleasure he'd felt from Lowen offering him the IC position. What should have been the biggest moment of his career thus far had fallen flat. It felt hollow because he couldn't share the moment with Harper.

"See that," Frankie said. "That constipated look he has going on? He knows he's an asshole."

"Been there," Nate said, pulling Frankie back against him. "It's rough, man."

Adam dropped the sponge in the bucket, water sloshing over the side. "Seriously, I'm out here, washing your damn alpacas with this"— he smelled his hands—"flowery soap and you're giving me shit?"

As if that weren't bad enough, Mittens chose that moment to drop pellets. Then he shook, which had Blanket doing as his daddy did, and in two seconds Adam was drenched and smelling like wet fur.

"It's oatmeal lavender. It soothes their skin and protects them from sunburn," Frankie said, walking down the steps to lay a hand on Blanket's newly naked rump. The smaller alpaca started humming. "Which wouldn't have happened if you hadn't flaked on babysitting. I had to call in Aunt Luce on her poker night. Which means these guys ate nothing but bar food and mai tais. Then Luce lost big to Pricilla Martin and had to sell their fleece. Pricilla's knitting her granddaughters sweaters out of it." Frankie snapped her fingers. "Maybe Adam could knit Harper a sweater. With a cat on it."

Dax grimaced, then weighed in. "It would have to have a card with it that says *this asshole loves you* if it were to work."

"I thought you two would be all over my ass to back off," Adam said. "You're married to her best friend," he said to Jonah, "you're marrying her other one," he said to Dax, "and as you said, Harper is sweet and I'm . . . me."

"That's just it. You aren't acting like you," Dax pointed out.

"How the hell would you know? You've been back in town, what, six months?"

"He's getting all pissy," Dax said to Jonah and Nate.

"I know. It's the first sign," Jonah said, as if Adam weren't standing right fucking there.

Adam wanted to ask him what sign had them smiling as if the entire world was in on some big joke, except Adam. Only, he wasn't sure he wanted to know, so he took the sponge and went to work on Blanket's legs.

Dax laughed and clapped Jonah on the back. "He's pretending he doesn't have a woman problem, second sign."

"I have never had a problem with women," Adam scoffed.

"Yeah, neither did I," Jonah said, flashing his gold band around like it was a Super Bowl ring. "Now I'm wearing one of these."

Dax did the same. Nate didn't flash his wedding ring, though. He circled his wife's belly instead and the glow on Frankie's face said it all.

"Are you guys pregnant?" Adam asked.

The happy couple looked at each other, and no confirmation was needed. It was in the way Nate held her close, tenderly rubbing their child. It was also in the way Frankie looked up at Nate, with total and complete faith. In her husband and in their love.

"Blanket thinks it's twins," Frankie said, then burst into tears, and all three brothers gave her a wide berth. Frankie didn't do tears, just like she didn't do witnesses to her tears. But to Adam's surprise, she didn't reach for her bat. She smiled.

Big and watery and proud.

Like she was happy to be crying. Or maybe she was crying because she was happy. Hell, it could just be the hormones. Either way, it took the male members of the family a few seconds too long to react.

"And I expect hugs," she sniffed. "Not that bro-pack high five crap you usually do."

That's when it settled that there was going to be a new baby in the family. A round of hugs and congratulations went around, as Adam took in the moment.

And that's when he saw it. After years of disappointments, mis-connections, and struggling to find common ground, they were finally a family with spouses and kids and enough pets to fill Noah's ark. And while Adam pulled back from the group hug, something empty and raw settled in his chest.

Every single one of his siblings had done it. Somehow, despite being raised by a guy who ruled his home with impossible expectations and tough love, they'd managed to find their peace. A happiness so real it was visible and humbling.

Adam was pretty sure he'd found his too. With Harper. Only he'd looked right into the eyes of forever and went for the quick high, proving he was more like his old man than he'd ever like to admit.

Worse, his shortsightedness and insecurities had hurt Harper. Badly. She had finally allowed herself to be seen, to open herself up to the idea of more, and he'd passed her over at the first sign of something flashy.

And Adam knew exactly how that felt.

"What if long-term isn't for me?" he heard himself say, and everyone went quiet. But all he could think about was Harper being his, and what that meant. Because if this was what disappointment felt like after a few weeks, he couldn't imagine what it would feel like in a few years when he made a mistake, after the *I do*s and kids and making a home. And he would make a mistake. It seemed to be in his blood. "This thing with Harper was different than you and Shay."

Jonah grabbed an extra glass of lemonade and walked it over to Adam. With an arm on his shoulder, he said, "Remember when you told me that if you ever had a woman look at you the way Shay looks at me, then you'd do anything to keep her?" Adam nodded and Jonah looked him in the eyes. "This is your girl, bro."

Mine.

He rubbed his hand over his chest, trying to ease the raw ache that was growing. It didn't help. Nothing he did seemed to help. It just got worse.

Deeper.

"She gave me everything I could have ever wanted and I freaked . . . *Jesus*." He thought about how Harper must feel, putting herself out there only to be smacked back down. By the one guy who had told her to stop hiding. "I don't want to be another guy who lets her down."

"Then don't," Dax said. "Be the guy who makes her world. That's what love is."

"I don't know if I could give that kind of love," Adam admitted.

"Yeah you do. You already have. Only love could make you pose in your skivvies," Jonah said quietly, and Adam felt a small flutter warm his chest at the thought of loving Harper.

Which was ridiculous.

He told himself the other night to let her go. That it was better this way, to walk before they became too invested, even though he knew he was already committed.

Harper said he'd made her believe, but she'd done the same for him. He believed in his skills, his character, and his ability to be the kind of man he could be proud of. The kind who found happiness and held tight.

"Fuck." He leaned against Mittens, or maybe he swayed. He wasn't sure, but suddenly the weight of what he'd had and then lost was too staggering to remain upright.

"That's the last sign, bro. The realization that knocks you off your feet." Jonah clapped him on the back. "Now you need to figure out how to win her back."

"And it better be good or Emi won't let me in the house," Dax added.

Jonah snapped his fingers and looked at Adam. "How about a kitten? We just rescued these Siamese littermates with the most amazing markings."

"Not every woman swoons for a freaking cat," Dax interrupted. "Whatever Adam does, it has to be as unique as the woman."

"The woman wears them on her sweaters," Jonah defended.

She also has them on her sheets, Adam thought.

"Plus, cats are unique. They all have different personalities, and if you match the right fur baby with the right girl . . . it's powerful, man."

But it wasn't Harper. Harper was warm and giving and so damn sweet in her cat sweaters she melted his heart. But she was also sexy and a little crazy and deserved to be recognized as the extraordinary woman she was—in a way that was as unique as the woman. Nope, flowers, chocolates, and cats weren't enough.

Harper deserved to be loved with the same fierceness she gave to others. She'd spent her entire life collecting people and making them feel as if they belonged. And he knew just how to become part of her collection.

And maybe, if he was lucky, she'd let him collect her.

chapter
twenty-one

News that Hadam was officially over spread through town like wildfire. Harper couldn't go outside of her apartment without seeing the pitying looks. More humiliating were the condolences and sympathies she received as if someone had died.

That would explain why Harper felt as if she were in mourning. No matter how many times she tried to smile her way through, the numbness remained. It was as if all of the brightness in her world had disappeared and she was left in the shadows.

It had taken every ounce of creativity she had to finish the mock-ups for the calendar. And every ounce of willpower she had not to burst into tears as she stared at image after image of Adam, looking for the perfect shots for the Swagger campaign. So Clovis and the girls had stepped in and offered to tackle the front window display, and in a moment of heartache-fueled desperation, Harper had agreed.

"Just tell me that they didn't use girdles in the display," Harper said to Emerson as they walked down the back stairs of their building.

"No girdles, but I did see them arguing over what color man-hammock was the most manly," Emerson said.

"Oh God, this is going to be a disaster."

Chantel and Lulu were due to arrive in an hour, which gave Harper fifty-nine minutes to make magic. A hard task when dealt nothing but hammocks and body-shapers. Not to mention she wasn't feeling all that magical right then. And without a game-changing display or the face of her campaign, they were pretty much sunk.

Harper stopped at the bottom of the steps. "Maybe I should just go back to bed."

When Harper turned to do just that, Emerson grabbed her by the arm. "It won't be a disaster." Harper slid her friend a look. "And if it is, I have three dozen cookies from the Sweet and Savory ready to go, just in case."

"Confetti cake batter cookies?"

"Yup."

That confirmed it: today was going to suck. Otherwise, Emerson would have never *bought* cookies from another baker. She would have made them herself, but she knew that when things got rough, confetti cake batter cookies were the only thing that could pull Harper back from the ledge.

"You could go grab the cookies and meet me on the couch. We can watch *Sharknado* in our PJs." Because explaining away the condition of the store and Adam being a no-show were two things Harper didn't think she could deal with.

Emerson shook her head, then went serious. "Before we round the corner, I want you to know that I love you."

Harper's throat tightened, because Emerson didn't use works like that often. Harper knew her friend loved her, but had difficulty voicing it. She'd gotten better since finding forever in Dax, but outward emotions were still rare.

"I love you too," Harper said, pulling Emerson in for a hug, and Emerson hugged her back. Warm and safe, Harper let herself lean on her friend and release some of the pain for a few moments so she could breathe without feeling as if she were going to die from the ache. "Thank you. I needed that."

"I was going to say the same thing."

Allowing herself exactly one minute, she wiped back the tears and straightened. "What are you thanking me for?"

"For being the best friend ever." Emerson scratched the back of her hand as if having an allergic reaction to the outpouring of girly emotions. "Without you I never would have opened my food truck, or gotten Violet out of her fairy wings. And I never would have opened myself up to the possibility of more with Dax."

"Dax is a great guy."

"But only you saw that, because you see the best in everyone. It's what makes you Harper. You're a romantic, and when it comes to love, Harper, you're the real deal. So don't forget that when you walk into the shop."

Harper nodded, knowing that someday she would believe it. Today just wasn't that day. But she had people to impress and a display to fix. Then she could go home and hibernate until fall. Lord knew her heart needed it.

They rounded the corner and Harper froze. The Boulder Holder was packed, with a line wrapping through downtown, past the St. Helena Hotel. And it wasn't just the girdle-buying crowd, although they had come out in force. It was made up of young, hip movers and shakers, all holding VIP cards and waiting for their turn to go inside.

"What is this?" Harper asked.

"Romance, Harp."

Emerson took Harper's hand and led her through the crowd of familiar faces. Some had their cameras out, others were just smiling, but everyone was watching her, waiting to see her reaction.

Then she got to the front of the line and saw what all of the squeals were about. At the door, standing in a pair of Swagger Tough boxers and a matching man-robe was Dax. He handed Harper a flyer and said, "This gets you fifteen percent off at the counter, and anything from the online store. Today only."

"What are you doing?" Harper asked, trying to keep her eyes on Dax's face. Impossible since the man was built like a DC-10 and could break steel bars over his very naked abs.

"He's part of the live display," Emerson said, then glared at the women drooling over her fiancé. "And there will be no touching of the display!"

Harper felt Emerson's hands on her, guiding her closer to the doorway, past Jonah posing in Swagger Original, and that's when she caught a glimpse of the window display. Deep fabrics and Scotch-colored accents highlighted the masculine undertones of the display. Everything was bold, smooth, edgy, and so perfect she could cry.

Then she spotted the leather reading chair in the center of the display and nearly died.

Not only was the display perfect, but the face of Swagger—and the man who had crushed her heart—occupied it. Sprawled out in yesterday's scruff, plum-colored boxers, and nothing else, he was posed beneath a giant flat screen, which looked to have been borrowed from the local sports bar and displayed a giant promo poster that had been made from one of her campaign designs. Someone had added the words REAL MEN LOVE.

She didn't know what his presence meant, or the message, but she was too afraid to hope. But then she saw the vulnerability in Adam's eyes and realized he was afraid too. And somehow that allowed her to give in to the hope.

"I told you I didn't need you," she said, in case this was a friendly gesture.

He tapped his ear, then pointed to the glass. Harper looked at the few hundred women, who were all looking back, riveted on what was transpiring. Cheeks pink, she raised her voice. "I said, thanks, but you didn't have to do this!"

Again with the ear pointing, then he gave a come-hither wiggle of the finger.

"The girl said she doesn't need you!" Peggy yelled so loudly it could've been heard from space.

"Thank you," Harper said a little sharply to the older woman, "but I've got this."

"Oh, honey, I don't think you do," Peggy said, and the bobble-heads around her nodded in unison. "Otherwise you'd be in there showing him a little thigh and getting somewhere."

Great, now she was getting dating advice from Peggy. With a sigh Harper turned back to the window, only to find the seat was empty. She looked around and watched Adam stride through the crowd.

When he was close enough to touch her, he put his hands on her hips. "But I need you."

A collective sigh filled Main Street, but she ignored it. "Do you need me or my friendship?"

"Both," he said. "I want both."

Her chest ached at his statement. "I want everything. Not just fun and fancy-free." She poked him in the chest and her finger bounced back. "I want passion and adventure and love. I want extraordinary."

"I want to give you extraordinary and passion. I want to give you everything. Hell, sunshine, I want you," he said. "Every single part of you. The yellow parts and the orange parts, even the pink parts."

"Real men wear pink," someone hollered from the back, but Adam kept his eyes on Harper.

"What about the red parts?" Harper asked, her stomach a jumble of knots, because everyone liked those parts of her. It was the rest that always went unnoticed.

"God, baby, the red ones are my favorite." To prove it, he ran his hands up her sides and back down, her body tingling at his touch. "They're all my favorite. Do you know I remember every kiss we've ever had, every word we ever shared, every outfit you've ever worn, including the bright yellow dress you wore that first night, right here."

Harper thought back to that night, the way they'd run into each other, the way he'd made her feel so special and seen, and she shook her head. "That wasn't real."

"That's what I thought too, but I was wrong. God, I have been so wrong about everything," he said. "It's all real. Every look, every kiss, every lame line. The way I feel about you, the man I am because of you—it just took me losing you to realize it."

"And what did you realize?" she asked quietly.

"That you are the most real person I know. There is no way I couldn't fall in love with you. I think I loved you when you threw your dress at me."

"She Hadam at hello," Clovis said in a dreamy voice.

"You did." Adam cupped Harper's face. "You've charmed me, Harper Owens. Heart and soul."

He dropped to his knee and the crowd gasped. So did Harper.

"Oh my God." She looked around at the swelling crowd, who had formed a circle around them, then back to the man she loved who was down on one knee, baring it all to win her back. "What are you doing?"

"Asking you to be mine. Completely and forever mine," he said, and she felt all that hope start to blossom, so full her chest expanded. "And I hope you're still willing to let me be yours. To let me be your friend, your lover, your everything. I need you, sunshine, and if you choose me, give me a second chance, I promise to spend the rest of my life making your world as extraordinary as you are."

He took her hand and placed a kiss right in the center of her palm. "I love you, Harper."

She wasn't sure if the sidewalk was tilting or if she was shaking—either way her world was spinning at his words. His sweet words that made her breath catch and her heart sing.

"I chose you weeks ago, remember?" she said and saw the moment it registered. "And I would choose you again and again, because I love you too."

A small hint of a smile started in his eyes, then spread. By the time it hit his mouth she was in his arms and he was kissing her. Kissing her as if he were saying, *Mine.*

"Do you think this was for show or did they really just get engaged?" a pocket-sized woman in bifocals and a sheath dress said from the sidelines. "I didn't see a ring."

Harper looked over and found Lulu Rous with her entire team. They'd watched the whole moment and looked as swept up as Harper.

"Oh, it's real all right," Adam said. "As for the ring, you might want to add a little pocket inside the boxers for occasions like this. Because if your customer is a real man, then love happens."

"Are you taking notes?" Lulu asked Chantel, who was scribbling frantically, and Harper knew by the excitement in the woman's eyes that she liked what she saw. "Real men love. Brilliant."

"When you meet a woman like Harper, it becomes the truth." Adam wiggled his pinky finger, and that was when Harper saw her grandmother's ring. It had seen her grandparents through a lifetime of love and belonging and family. That Adam knew she'd want to wear Clovis's ring proved how clearly he saw her.

"Marry me, Harper," he said. "Marry me and be mine. Because I want to wake up to catch a glimpse of you every morning for the rest of my life."

"Only if you promise to be mine."

Adam's mouth covered hers in a kiss that tasted like the beginning of forever, and she felt herself fall, felt the rush take over. Only this time she knew she wasn't falling alone. Just like she knew that wherever they ended up, they'd be there to catch each other.

chapter
epilogue

Eight Months Later . . .

"How about this? Is this any better?"
Harper opened her eyes as wide as they could go and gave her brightest smile.

Adam took his time to study her thoroughly, his gaze taking in every inch of her dress, her bare legs—and everything in between. "Perfect."

"I was talking about my eyes." She batted them. "Do they look misty?"

Adam grinned. "Like you're about to burst into tears. Maybe we should just tell everyone the truth today."

"What? No. Today is about Frankie and Nate." It was a day to celebrate their growing family with friends and loved ones. Which was why Harper and Adam had made the long trek from Colorado Springs a week early. "Do you know how hard it is to carry around twins? The woman deserves a baby shower twice this size."

Harper glanced across the vineyard, through the acres of grape-vines, sagging with spring blossoms, to the gathering of friends and family at the far side, and she felt her heart pick up. Round tables adorned with yellow roses and violets lined the patio, while cream-and-blue bootie decorations hung from every oak tree and fence post on the Baudouin winery. It was like a scene from a Norman Rockwell painting, only no one was playing a part. This was real life.

Harper's real life.

"It's not too late to go back to the house and hide out." He pressed his mouth to her ear, and Harper closed her eyes. "Maybe in bed."

"We just left bed." Moments before they'd arrived, in fact. And when she was with Adam there was no such thing as hiding. He loved and cherished every part of her equally. "I still have bed-rumpled hair and your handprints on my dress."

"That's what newlyweds do." His hands gripped her hips, and he walked her backward under an oak tree. "We might as well take advantage of it."

"Nobody knows we're married." Harper's eyes fluttered closed as his mouth worked magic. "Plus, we're already late."

"You don't look like you care all that much that we're late."

"I look like this all the time," she whispered. "It's the look I get when I remember that this is real." When she remembered that two weeks ago Adam had officially finished his IC command and was coming back to St. Helena with a lieutenant promotion under his belt, and that she'd opened a branding and marketing company that had already signed five huge accounts—including Lulu Allure.

Best of all, it was the look she gave when she remembered that they'd officially started their lives together.

"It's real, sunshine. This was real from the moment I kissed you." Her breath caught at the look of fierce adoration and love in his eyes as her husband of three days leaned down and kissed her in a way that had her heart melting and her toes curling. "And it gets more real every second I'm with you. Every second you're mine." Adam wiggled a brow. "Plus, I read in that magazine of yours that there is no better place to practice having a baby than at a baby shower."

With a final kiss that held so much promise, Adam took Harper's hand and led her through the vineyard and toward their families—and the best kind of extraordinary that Harper could have dreamed.

acknowledgments

Thanks to my agent, Jill Marsal, for your advice, dedication, and unwavering friendship. And to my editors, Maria Gomez and Lindsay Guzzardo, for taking the time to push me to grow as a writer and dig deeper with each story I tell. To the rest of the Author Team at Montlake, thank you for making every book special, and for welcoming me into the amazing Montlake family.

As always, a special thanks to my husband, who is not only a real-life hero, but *my* real-life hero. I love you.

Read on for a sneak peek of Marina Adair's
next heartwarming romance from her
Sequoia Lake series

it started with a kiss

Available early 2017 on Amazon.com

chapter one

If life was an adventure, then Avery Morgan needed to fire her travel agent and demand a refund.

She wasn't a demanding person by nature, but that's what happened when the universe issued an early expiration date on living, it gave you cojones. So Avery issued herself a new passport on life, and was ready to put some stamps in each and every column.

Her first destination required crisp mountain air, fireside s'more-tinis, and a real get-back-to-nature kind of adventure—one that would hopefully give her the skills needed to live out loud.

Avery looked through the windows of the local Moose Lodge at the imposing Sierras, a rugged mountain range that cut through Northern California and towered over her quaint hometown of Sequoia Lake.

"Before you begin your climb, you want to make sure you give the chest harness a final tug to ensure it's secure," she said as if she were the foremost expert on extreme adventures. As if her entire world—up until a year ago—hadn't consisted of managing retirement portfolios at her family's bank and listening to couples talk about their senior cruise to Alaska.

She bent over slightly to click the last carabiner into place, securing the leg straps to the chest harness.

There was something so poignant about that sound, about how with one click the device restricted her freedom and pressed down on her scar, a reminder that she was strapped in and fully committed to the climb.

"I'll tug it," Mr. Fitz offered, his bony fingers already reaching out to help. Or grope. Avery couldn't be sure, so she stepped back out of range.

Mr. Fitz was three thousand years old, with teeth too white to be real, and, even though he looked like a harmless old-timer in his TOO BIG TO THROW BACK fishing hat, his eyes were laser pointed at Avery's chest—which was prominently on display because of how the harness fit her body.

"I'm fine." Avery swatted his hands away right before they made contact. "But thank you for the offer."

Mr. Fitz backed off, taking his seat, but looked awfully disappointed.

Senior X-Tream Team, the town's invitation-only fly fisherman's club, had asked Sequoia Lodge to their monthly meeting, since the first topic on their agenda was to finalize their big summer excursion. And since Avery was Sequoia Lodge's newly appointed adventure coordinator, it was her job to go out into the community and solicit new customers. If she secured all twelve members for this excursion, then she'd meet her entire quota for September in one fell swoop.

She straightened her shoulders—an impossible task due to the climbing harness—and held out a clipboard to the crowd. "Now, if that answers all the questions, let me tell you about the amazing views from—"

Mr. Fitz's hand went up.

"Mr. Fitz?" she said thinly since this was his ninth question.

"If I fall on this climb, will you be there to catch me?" he asked, and a dozen gray heads bobbed in support.

"Your harness is secured to a safety line and a main line," Avery said, reiterating verbatim the lodge's safety manual of the precautions taken in any excursion that included chest harnesses. But to ease the concerned looks, she added, "Plus your adventure guide is with you every step of the way to make sure your trip is exciting and safe."

Another hand flew up. The captain, as he preferred to be called, was the president of Senior X-Tream and seemed to be the ladies' man of the group. With his silver-streaked hair, captain's hat, and deck shoes, the man looked as though he'd just stepped off his boat and was ready to impress. He was also trying his hardest not to look at Avery's chest. "If you fall, can I catch you?"

"I don't go on excursions. I just coordinate them," she said, leaving out the part that with every party confirmed, she got a bonus adventure for herself.

A series of disappointed mumbles filled the room, and she dropped the clipboard to the table, silencing the room with a bang. "Now, can all of those in favor of Senior X-Tream starting off their fall season with the River Rock climb please raise their hands?" she asked in a tone that usually had her customers signing on the dotted line.

Not a single hand went up. Which was odd since she'd come here to pitch the Fern Falls fly-fishing day trip and the group had specifically asked her to explain the River Rock climb, even going as far as having her demonstrate how the harness worked. And since that trek had a special place in her *Living for Love* passport, she'd suited up.

Only now, she was afraid she'd secured the carabiner incorrectly. Even though she'd followed the directions exactly, she couldn't seem to loosen the harness or get the carabiner to open. Not that she'd let them know that.

"Mr. Fitz, how about you?"

Mr. Fitz shook his head. "My wife would have my head if she knew I was even thinking about climbing River Rock. That's a young man's trail, and I had a new hip put in last spring—no way could I take the pressure of that harness."

Avery had made it through a surgery of her own last year, and could tell him, without a doubt, that healing bodies and harnesses were a tricky combination. But that the pressure would be worth the thrill he'd feel when he got to the top and looked out over Sierra Nevada.

"Then why did you ask about the trip in the first place?"

Mr. Fitz looked at the floor, his ears going pink. In fact, most of the men were avoiding eye contact. A clear sign that Avery had been played. "You weren't planning on booking any trips today, were you?"

"We've been going on the Fern Falls fly-fishing excursion for nearly twenty years," Prudence Tuttman said from the back row, not sounding all that excited about going for number twenty-one. She was the only female in the group, outweighed the heaviest member by twenty pounds, and held the county record for gutting the most fish in under a minute. "Nelson has taken us out on the last five trips and said he was sending you down to handle all of the paperwork."

"Said he had some big trek today and didn't have time for paperwork," the captain said, and Avery wanted to point out that no one had time for paperwork. It was the nature of paperwork. But refrained because a trek wasn't why Nelson had sent her.

Nelson Donovan used to be the top-rated adventure guide at Sequoia Lake Lodge, fitting since he'd owned the lodge for over forty years. He'd survived a helicopter crash, three avalanches, and the loss of one of his sons ten years ago. Nelson was the kind of man stories are made of. Only lately, his memory had been slipping, and on bad days he struggled to remember his own story—which was why his wife hired Avery. When she wasn't booking his trips, she was managing the schedule and rechecking any and all safety equipment he touched—stealthily.

Pride was a tricky thing, and Avery was careful not to take that from him, too.

"What if I were to tell you that as Sequoia Lake Lodge's official adventure coordinator, I have the ability to customize your trip," Avery said. "Give you exactly what you're looking for."

"We've been pitched custom excursions before, but our group isn't large enough to absorb the cost," Prudence explained. "We asked Nelson, but he couldn't seem to come up with one that would fit within our budget."

It was true that customized trips were always on the higher end in pricing and usually reserved for cooperate retreats and large group events, but with all of the fall specials and their senior discount, finding something new and exciting within their means shouldn't be that difficult.

"No sense in signing up for a journey that you've already taken." Avery pulled her calculator and the excursion price guide out of her travel pack, setting them on the poker table that the Moose Lodge provided as workspace. "If you guys are bold enough to chase a new view, I *know* I can plan the perfect customized trip for your group and come in close to budget."

Well, if that didn't get their attention. The excitement in the room rose until it crackled, but it was Mr. Fitz who spoke up. "I guess the Fern Falls fly-fishing trip has become old hat for us."

A few amens sounded from the group. The captain even took off his hat and leaned in closer as Avery started scribbling down some rough numbers.

"At least with Fern Falls we know what we're getting into," Prudence cautioned the group. "This bean counter doesn't even know how to unlock that carabiner. How is she going to come up with a trip we'll like?"

Bean Counter held up the Sequoia Lake Lodge guide. "Because I am a master planner and know this book inside and out." When they didn't look convinced, she added, "What's the fun in knowing exactly what you're going to get?"

"Knowing it won't suck," Prudence said.

"Adventure is about trying new things, straying off the known path." No one spoke. "And if you book today, I will take ten percent off the total."

She wouldn't get her bonus trip, but she'd get the credit for bringing in her first custom trek, which would go far with her boss. If there was one thing that Nelson admired, it was assertiveness.

And if there was one thing seniors loved, it was a deal.

Twenty minutes later, Avery walked down the front steps of the local Moose Lodge and onto Poppy Street, painfully aware that the safety harness was jammed and not coming off anytime soon. The sun was setting behind the lush peaks of the Sierra Nevada, streaking the sky a brilliant orange. A cool evening breeze blew through the thick canopy of ponderosas and crape myrtle trees that lined the main drag of town.

Avery shifted her bag, which housed the signed, customized excursion contract for the Senior X-Tream Team, farther up on her shoulder and waited for the thrill of landing a big client to come.

It didn't. Odd, since once upon a time, say just a few months ago, coming out on top would have had her flushed with excitement, and okay, for a small moment in there, when all twelve sets of eyes had been riveted on her, the adrenaline of a job well done had made a brief appearance. Fooling her into actually believing she was one step closer to her own adventure.

But that was just it. Avery had been Sequoia Lake Lodge's acting senior adventure coordinator for most of the summer, yet the closest she'd come to a real adventure was waking up to a band of raccoons partying in her cabin. They'd torn through the screen door and made off with a box of Oreos, peanut butter, and two pairs of her favorite underwear—which told her they were male raccoons.

Avery hoped her job would entail more than senior center visits, working the farmers' markets booth, and helping lost guests at the lodge find the restroom. So far, she spent more time talking about all the different trails the Sequoia National Park offered than actually taking one. In fact, adventure coordinating wasn't all that different from managing retirement funds, except her desk was outside and travel insurance covered more than lost suitcases.

Even the bright sun and gentle breeze couldn't distract from the feeling that she was once again sitting idle, waiting for life to find her. Instead of waiting for the net to appear, she was going to leap.

Determined to talk to Irene and Nelson about running this trek on her own, she headed toward the yellow Victorian with violet trim at the end of the street that had HOOT & HAMMER and an owl painted on its leaded windows. It wasn't a hardware store, but she'd seen enough sawdust and heavy woodworking machinery to bet the owner possessed a screwdriver and set of hands strong enough to pry open the carabiner. Convincing Nelson she was ready to take clients into the great outdoors while she was stuck in a harness wouldn't make the kind of impression she was going for.

Only, before she reached the shop, she noticed the Closed sign hanging in the window. She also noticed a big, shiny, black ego-trip with mud tires, a lift kit, and a mountain bike secured to its top.

The truck was parked directly under the town's flapping banner—which read COME FOR THE ADVENTURE, STAY FOR THE PEOPLE—and practically on top of her Mazda's bumper. Not only did it have a toolbox in it's bed, the box appeared to be unlocked—and it's owner nowhere in sight.

A private person by nature, Avery would normally ask for permission to rifle through someone's personal affects, but since no one was around to grant nor deny her access, Avery reminded herself that living loud required no permission. So she pulled her journal from her purse. It was made of a buttery leather and had a vintage map of the world burnt into the cover.

Avery lightly traced a finger over the branded message on the bottom edge.

"Don't go where life leads, lead your life in the direction you want to go," she whispered, her voice thickening with emotion.

"Life's an adventure so live it," she whispered, her voice thickening with emotion.

Brie Hart, a friend from Living for Love, a local bereavement group Avery belonged to, had given it to her the day Avery started dialysis. She was still in shock over the news that at twenty-six she needed a new kidney when she'd met Brie, a two-time transplant survivor, and the two became immediate friends.

Brie had given Avery the courage to hope and the strength to fight, even when Avery felt as if she were losing every battle. More importantly, Brie had given her something to fight for and someone to fight with.

When times got rough, and treatments got longer, they scoured travel magazines at the hospital together, clipping out pictures of all of the places they'd go and the things they'd do when treatment was over. It had all started with an article on an amazing island in the Pacific that had endless beaches, bottomless daiquiris, and a surplus of suntanned men, but as time went on the clippings grew, and little mottos for life and affirmations about enjoying the journey were added to the pile, until Brie had pasted them all in the journal.

Avery carefully thumbed through the pages, her eyes burning as she flipped past the map of Disneyland showing all of the hidden Mickey ears in the park, the island off New Zealand where Tasmanian devils lived, skipping over the article about the jellybean factory in California that gave out free samples, and stopping when she found what she was looking for. Brie's favorite saying.

LIVE LOUD, WITHOUT FEAR AND WITHOUT APOLOGY

Brie was the strongest person Avery had ever met, yet in the end she'd somehow lost the war—and Avery had lost her biggest alley and her closest friend. So after the funeral, she'd taken that journal and made a list of things she'd do if she weren't afraid. Some were hers, some Brie's, and others were in honor of the women she'd met at Living for Love, who would never get the chance.

Yet there she was, just cresting the one-year mark, and there were more blank boxes than check marks in the column.

Avery scanned the street for again for passersby. With the streets empty, she suppressed the urge to jump up and down because that kind of motion in the harness would end badly, and instead reached over the side to play with the latch and—

"Look at that?"

With one toggle the latch came undone, two and Avery had the lid propped open and was staring at handy dandy screwdriver sitting on the top, as if waiting for a stranger in need to happen by.

She was a stranger, and she was in need, and when she happened by no one was there, which meant no one would know she borrowed the tool for a second or two.

Palms sweating and heart racing, Avery did one last quick scan of the area, then snatched the screwdriver and quickly stuck the flat edge between the opening of the carabiner. With a calculated twist she wedged open the two metal clasps and—

"Shit. Shitshitshit!"

The tip of the screwdriver launched itself up into the air only to come down and land near the storm drain. Avery scrambled to catch it before it rolled out of sight, but her short legs combined with the restrictive harness made retrieval without diving head first into the greater Sierra sewage system impossible, leaving her stuck in a harness and holding a stolen tool.

She couldn't leave without coming clean and a promise to at least replace his screwdriver, but she couldn't stay too long either because Nelson headed for home around sunset. And if she didn't catch him tonight, her adventure would have to wait until Monday.

And Avery was tired of waiting, so with the first hints of orange peeking over the mountains, she pulled out her brightest lipstick— stiletto red with a gloss luminous enough to be seen from space that she'd bought when she'd decided to start living bold. Propping her knee on the hood of the car, she gripped the windshield wiper for leverage and pulled herself up.

Perched on top of his hood on all fours, she took a bold breath and ever so carefully scrawled across the front windshield: I OWE YOU A SCREW—

Damn it! Her lipstick, warm from the day's heat, broke and rolled down below the wipers and out of sight. She leaned forward and slipped her fingers inside the crevice to get it, thunking her forehead against the windshield when she realized it was just out of reach.

"Either you were going to write in your ex's phone number or this is my lucky day."

Avery slowly turned her head, and what she saw sent her heart to her toes. Leaning against a lamppost, looking relaxed and incredibly dangerous in a pair of battered hiking boots, low-slung cargo pants with a million and one pockets holding a million and one surprises, and enough stubble to tell her it was five o'clock, stood a mountain of hard muscles and pure testosterone—wearing a Sequoia Lake Lodge ball cap.

She reread what she'd written and felt her face flush.

"This isn't what it looks like," she said, because it was so much worse. Two seconds into living loud and she was caught defacing the truck of a man who, although she had never seen him before, she could tell by the well-worn but well-kept Gore-Tex mountaineering boots, wasn't a weekend warrior.

But a Sequoia Lodge member—and a serious climber. That he found amusement in her situation told her he knew she wasn't.

"I figure you're either testing out a new lip color or making a declaration, in which case you might as well save us both some time and just give me your number."

"My mother warned me about giving my number to handsome strangers. She said they either call or they don't, but either way you're in for a world of hurt."

"Handsome stranger, huh?" He pushed off the lamppost and approached the truck, his hand extended. She ignored it under the pretense of looking for her lipstick. "Easy fix. Name's Ty."

Just that. *Ty.* With a shrug. As though Mountain Man was too badass for anything more than a couple letters thrown together— and big enough to get away with it.

In her experience, big, badass men who pretended to be bulletproof were the first to take cover the second that whole *through sickness and in health* part came into play. Unfortunately, big, badass men who dropped five hundred bucks on a pair of hiking boots also tended to drop serious cash on adrenaline-pumping excursions, which meant she needed to appear somewhat neighborly.

And normal.

Eyes making direct and unwavering contact, she said, "I'm Avery. Avery Morgan."

"Well, Avery Morgan, if you aren't making an offer, then my guess is you mistook the hood of my truck for a mountain." He chuckled, and she found herself smiling back.

He had a great laugh, warm, deep, and a little tired. Living loud might not require permission, but in this case is did require an apology.

"It's not an offer, just an apology," she clarified, giving her most apologetic look, which was completely wasted on him since he was too busy staring at her ass to notice.

"And just what does one need to do to receive that kind of apology?" When she went back to looking for the lipstick, he added, "You know, so I can be prepared."

"Underestimate me," she said, then smiled over her shoulder. "Or keep staring at my ass."

Mountain Man grinned. Slow and sexy and completely annoying. "I was staring at your harness. It's really wedged up there. Looks painful."

Avery was well aware that she was sporting the biggest wedgie known to man, and yes it was not a comfortable experience, but she'd rather die than admit that to him. The man looked smug, capable, and like the kind of guy who could spot weakness a mountain away. And this wasn't her finest moment. "I'm fine."

"You sure?" He stepped even closer, turning his ball cap around to get a closer look and—*sweet baby Jesus*—Mountain Man was seriously sexy. Rugged sexy with a strong jaw, piercing lake-blue eyes, which were currently sparking in her direction, and a confidence that said he was prepared and ready.

For anything.

And why that made her stomach flutter she had no idea. Avery was on a flutter-free solo adventure, damn it. No fluttering allowed, sexy stranger or not.

"Yes, just part of my job."

"As what? A window washer?"

Shrugging off the little voice reminding her she was on the hood of a truck in a pair of strappy sandals, pressed capris, and a safety harness, she said, "As an adventure coordinator."

She had to give him credit, he didn't laugh. But he wanted to, she could tell. Why was it so hard for people to understand that she was perfect for this job?

Sure, she might have been hesitant at first too, but after settling in she realized that she had all of the skills required to be awesome at her job. She just needed time to gain her bearings, then she would be proficient. And, as Avery had learned over the years, with proficiency came respect. And confidence.

Something she needed a shot of right then. Fully embracing her new mantra, *live like you aren't afraid*, she said, "So as you can imagine, this is nothing I can't handle."

She lay flat on her belly and held on to the windshield wiper, annoyed that she was going to have to scoot to the end, since her legs were too short to reach the ground. Something he seemed to notice because before she'd even reached the grille, one big hand closed around her waist, the other on the back of the harness, and suddenly she was airborne.

"Put me down," she ordered, her legs flailing as she tried to spin herself to face him. It didn't work. "What part of *I got this* did you not understand?"

"The part where you got it." He placed her on the ground, and she spun to look at him and felt her heart stutter. The man was bigger than she'd originally thought, so tall in fact that she had to take a step back just to glare up at him. He was grinning, the big jerk.

"Yes, well, I would have had it." At least she hoped that she would have, but she wasn't entirely sure. That little flight had her a bit off-kilter.

That he was staring at her made it even worse, so she channeled her inner awesomeness, the same way Brie had taught her to do when facing down unexpected outcomes, and stared back, not noticing how well he filled out his fitted tee or how her belly quivered when he smiled. Hard to do when her body revved every time he so much as breathed.

"Interesting," he finally said. "Your eyes are dilated and you're breathing hard. Admit it, you like me."

"Not possible." Only it was. Go figure that the first time she had a reaction to a man in three years, and it had to a lodge guest. Which meant that it was time for her to leave.

"Then you're apologize again. Even better. Does this mean I'm on your IOU list?"

She rolled her eyes, not amused.

"No?" He studied her for a long minute, then leaned in and whispered, "How about now?"

Both of those big hands, strong enough to break granite, wrapped around the front of her safety harness—bringing his fingers right within grazing range of her nipples, and they noticed—then tugged her close. So close she could feel the afternoon's heat roll off his skin. He smelled like fresh mountain air, pine trees, and sex—not the kind of sex that could be penciled in between meetings, but the kind that lasted for days on end with only body heat for sustenance.

And if *that* thought wasn't enough to get her moving, then the reminder that she'd lost her best shot at happily ever after when Carson decided his love only covered the "in health" part of the deal.

He'd not only hesitated when she'd explained her kidney was slowly dying, but he'd walked out when she'd needed him most.

Turned out the only dead weight Avery lost in the surgery was Carson, and even though it had been a rough time in her life, she was a stronger person for it. Now she was a pain free, Carson free, and ready to move forward.

In theory, she was making progress. Her feet were moving in the forward direction. Only Ty's hands were still on her harness and—*oh my God*—he was staring at her lips. Like a wild bear settling on his prey, and she was pretty sure he was either going to throw her over his shoulder and take her back to his cave or kiss her. Either way she couldn't seem to get traction. Unless she counted shuffling closer.

Page six in her memory book flashed in her mind and her belly heated. She hadn't kissed anyone since Carson, and she'd never kissed a stranger—and this stranger looked as if he were about to kiss her.

His grin went full watt and her breath caught as he closed the last shred of distance and whispered, "You're welcome, *Avery Morgan.*"

Avery felt the pressure in her chest release on one big whoosh as the harness slid down her legs, the straps clanking against the concrete. She was free. "How did you do that?"

"Extremely talented fingers."

about the author

Photo © Tosh Tanaka

Marina Adair is a #1 national bestselling author of romance novels and holds a master of fine arts in creative writing. Along with the St. Helena Vineyard series, she is also the author of the Sugar, Georgia series. She lives with her husband, daughter, and two neurotic cats in Northern California. She loves to hear from readers and likes to keep in touch, so be sure to sign up for her newsletter at marinaadair.com/newsletter.